Northwest Vista College
Learning Resource Center
3535 North Ellison Drive
San Antonio, Texas 78251

S0-CLV-471

AXEMAN'S JAZZ

OTHER BOOKS BY TRACY DAUGHERTY

What Falls Away
Desire Provoked
The Woman in the Oil Field
The Boy Orator
It Takes a Worried Man
Five Shades of Shadow

AXEMAN'S JAZZ

A NOVEL BY TRACY DAUGHERTY

Southern Methodist University Press
Dallas

What follows is a work of the imagination. Without exception, every character and event is fictitious. The causes, incidents, and aftermath surrounding the 1917 Houston race riot have been slightly altered. Even when actual place names or geographical locations have been used, no resemblance to real institutions or locales is intended or should be inferred.

Requests for permission to reproduce material from this work should be sent to:
Rights and Permissions
    Southern Methodist University Press
    PO Box 750415
    Dallas, Texas 75275-0415

Cover art: "Preservation Hall" by Emily Sandor

Jacket and text design by David Timmons

Library of Congress Cataloging-in-Publication Data

Daugherty, Tracy.
    Axeman's jazz : a novel / by Tracy Daugherty.— 1st ed.
      p. cm.
    ISBN 0-87074-481-X (alk. paper)
      1. Racially mixed people—Fiction. 2. African American neighborhoods—Fiction.
    3. Identity (Psychology)—Fiction. 4. Houston (Tex.)—Fiction. 5. Inner cities—Fiction.
    6. Young women—Fiction. I. Title.

PS3554.A85A97 2003
813'.54—dc22

        2003057337

Printed in the United States of America on acid-free paper

10   9   8   7   6   5   4   3   2   1

For Margie,
who went there with me,
all the way

ACKNOWLEDGMENTS

NOVELS GROW from many sources—memories, suggestions, challenges, prohibitions—and with the help of many companions. I am indebted to all my teachers and friends, living and dead, from my Houston days. In particular, I wish to thank Glenn Blake, Michelle Boisseau, Rosellen Brown, Tom Cobb, Carl Lindahl, Martha Low, John McNamara, and Lois Zamora. For their part in helping me shape this work, I thank Ehud Havazelet and Kathryn Lang. For their support during the writing, I thank Marjorie Sandor, Hannah Crum, Gene and JoAnne Daugherty, and my colleagues at Oregon State University, especially Keith Scribner and Jen Richter. Finally, for their long-term encouragement and friendship, thanks to Molly Brown, Jerry and Joyce Bryan, Betty Campbell, Kris and Rich Daniels, Ted Leeson, Debra and Creighton Lindsey, George Manner, Jeff and Pam Mull, Marshall Terry, and the indefatigable souls at SMU Press, Kathie, Keith Gregory, and George Ann Goodwin.

Either I'm a nation or I'm nothing.

—DEREK WALCOTT

EACH TIME I imagined the execution I saw it from a different perspective. First as a simple observer, then as a catalyst in the tragedy. Female then male. Once I was an officer. Next time a common foot soldier.

The sky was always lime, as just before a storm. Pine trees lined the meadow where the gallows stood. A commander—sometimes he was me—called, "Halt!" The prisoners, thirteen of them, all but two cleanly shaved, stopped in the dewy clearing, the chains around their ankles and wrists murmuring in disturbed unison, like a flock of startled birds. Their military uniforms were well-pressed and pleasing to see. A pair of them had soiled their britches; shit and fear tinged the air, along with the mulch of rotting cotton nearby. Several armed cavalrymen, following the commander's orders, led the condemned men to two rows of folding chairs in the field's center. The chairs were set back to back, six on one side, seven on the other.

From the perspective of a simple observer, a young woman much like myself—someone on the fringes, that is—I see the gallows' fresh timber, flesh-colored against the green and cloudy predawn sky. (Women, of course, were officially barred from the field that day as the army dispatched its duties.)

And to be clear, when I say "flesh," I mean my own light skin, not the boggy darkness of the men about to be hanged. In its coloration, the terrible contraption looked like *me,* not them.

A bonfire licked the sky's first gold streaks. By an earlier fire's sparks, the night before, the Army Corps of Engineers had erected the death-rig on hasty, top-secret orders. This I know from my perspective as an officer, just as I know the prisoners requested, at their trial, death by firing squad, a more dignified military exit than hanging. As I stand here swatting mosquitoes, I understand the significance of refusing the prisoners' request, the example of lynching more than a dozen black men.

Am I uneasy with my knowledge? Is the sweat on my upper lip caused by more than humidity, stifling here in deep East Texas, even in fall, even in the hour before sunrise?

Might I be a better witness, come to a fuller understanding of these events, as an infantryman? *You must know everything,* a teacher once told me. So, mentally, I switch identities again, like pouring water from one cup into another. Now, standing among mesquite trees at a rough pace of twenty yards from my comrades, I see, just below a straw-covered hill, two rows of unpainted pine coffins next to thirteen open graves.

The six Mexican laborers hired by the army last night near the little river in San Antonio stand beside the crude boxes, wringing their hands. They will be asked, shortly, to untie the hangman's knots and to bury the corpses, each with a soda water bottle in his pocket holding a paper ribbon typed with the prisoners' names and ranks and the statement "Died September 11, 1917, at Fort Sam Houston." As a foot soldier, just following orders myself, I suspect the Mexicans cannot read these statements and do not know where Fort Sam Houston is; but if they *could* decipher the words, I doubt even they would be fooled into thinking this slovenly, hidden field is anything resembling a fort.

As the prisoners sit, remarkably calm, in the folding chairs, surrounded by Sheriff John Tobin of Bexar County, seven deputies, 125 cavalrymen, two white army chaplains, and a black civilian minister, the hangman adjusts his knots. The men have refused blindfolds. They stare at the two waist-high wooden triggers, manned by twelve soldiers, where the ropes converge on the platform. Softly, one of the bound fellows drones a hymn, "I'm coming home, I'm coming home." The others take it up with him, one by one, low and even.

Finally, the commander calls—*I* call—"Attention!" then I summon them, coldly (distantly, to protect myself, hunched and dyspeptic with my burdensome knowledge), to the scaffolding.

In my many varied draftings of this scene, I have never once viewed it from the prisoners' perspective. Which of the doomed would I choose to be? I've recovered a name—Cletus, Cletus Hayes—from the bottom of a cardboard box in my mama's chest of drawers. But which one is he? All accounts of that morning's events, admittedly highly subjective, possibly wildly inaccurate, agree that only two of the men were unshaven.

One of *them*, then: with distinguishing whiskers. To isolate him one more step, I could say he is one who shat his pants. But do I want this figure, with possible family ties to me, already disgraced by history, to be marred further by cowardly grime?

He steps forward with the others over a series of trap doors in the scaffolding, and I lose him again. It is too difficult to see, much less *be*, Cletus Hayes in my mind, so, as the men burst a last time into song—"Coming home, Lord, coming home!"—and the white guards from the Nineteenth Infantry yell to them, with grave sincerity, "Good-bye, Boys of Company C!" I become, again, a young, light-skinned woman—no: a *white* woman—standing on the fringes, watching in horror.

I am not supposed to be here, but because I may have suffered a trauma at the hands of one of the prisoners, the army, at my family's request, has perhaps allowed a special dispensation (no orders exist confirming this), hoping the sight of punishment will restore me to myself. But as I witness the triggers' swift arcs, the beams' awful shudders, I want to shout, "Cletus!" both to save him and to cast him into Hell. I will never again know clearly what I want out of life, and therefore, I will never again know clearly who I am. My curse is a variety of perspectives, and I will pass it on.

The army seems as paralyzed as I am, torn between the desire to comport its duties with dignity and the need to hide its shame. As soon as the bodies are hustled down the straw-covered hill, into the steaming, unmarked graves, the Mexicans are ordered to dismantle the gallows and burn the lumber. By noon, the clearing looks as if no one had ever set foot in it, and the grassy fringe where the frightened white woman may or may not have trembled now begins to expand—not just by distance, but by years. Years of silence, uncertainty, sorrow, and lies.

———

This morning, I awoke from a dream of the lynching and, naked in hot sunlight, twisted in clammy sheets, wondered for a minute where I lay. Not home in my apartment in Dallas, where I would have heard my aquarium bubbling, my parrots chattering, demanding the day's first affection. Instead, I was aware of close, rough walls, the difficulty of breathing—the *scorch* of each intake—and remembered: Houston. The leafy, humid sump, the Cajun-Southern-niggery mess of the neighborhood known as Freedmen's Town.

Yesterday evening, late, when I showed up with my suitcase on

Bitter's porch, he glanced up at me, indifferently at first, then with recognition. We stood yards apart, both aware of my daylight skin next to his night-color, and said nothing for a while. He looked me over—my short, boyish hair, my slender hips—and slowly shook his head, as if sorry for my confusing physical geometry: a creature who can't fully settle on what she really is.

Finally, I set my suitcase down on his cracked plank porch, where old honeysuckle vines, crushed and heavy and rancidly sweet, grew up between the boards, and said, "Hello."

He rattled the ice in a Smucker's jar of weak red tea, swatted a horse-fly, and watched me wipe the sweat from my face. My very pink palm. I half expected him to pitch a story, some silly yarn out of nowhere. *I'm nothing but a old mose,* he used to tell me, *spinning hot air and hoo-raws.* The old-school patter, the uncle-jive: who he'd always been, or pretended to be. Instead, he only grinned and, with a twist of his pear-shaped head, led me around back to what he called his mud-dauber shack, an old wooden tool shed, empty now except for a mattress and sheets. The shed was clustered around, he said, with "*couronnes de chene,*" and I remembered, like a lantern flaring on in the middle of the night, this lovely Creole name from my childhood visits here. "Mistletoe," I said.

He tossed melting ice from his jar into the high yellow grass. "That's right, Seamstress. So. Some of the Bayou City *did* rub off on you."

"More than you think."

"This here's my guest-house now, since I got need no more of my tools," he said. "May smell like gin. Mostly buddies of mine sleeping off weekday drunks in here. You welcome to it for now. Back door of the house'll be open when you need a john."

"Thank you."

"Pretty low-rent for a mayor's girl."

"It's just fine. It's more than I expected on such little notice."

"Well. It's late now. I'll let you get settled. Back door's open, too, when you ready to chat. That letter you sent, girl. It was *short.*"

"I know. I'm sorry. I knew you didn't have a phone—"

"Don't turn this around on me."

"I'm not. Thank you. Tomorrow? Tomorrow we'll talk?"

"Sure, we'll tow out the cotton whenever you ready. Don't see nothing, don't say nothing." That was the way he used to tell me good-night when I was little, and I smiled.

He left me then in the dusty mud-dauber shack with only a flashlight to steer by. In the corners, sprawling, elaborate spiderwebs. Dirty-towel curtains. He *wanted* me to breathe "low-rent" again, to take old sharecropper dirt into my lungs. Punishment. Nostalgia. He wasn't about to give me any of that poor-mulatta-bullshit you saw in the corny old stories or fall back praising my credentials.

As I unlatched my suitcase I remembered the word *gris-gris* and an afternoon when I was eight or nine, here in the yard, and Uncle Bitter instructed me in bayou lore. "Never pull down curtains from windows and doors to wash in the month of August. Sure as you hang a clean curtain back up in August, you gonna be hanging a shroud on your door 'fore the month is done. Never kill no spiders, neither, girl. *Never.* That's bad luck for a *long* time."

So, since we're only midway through August, the spiders and towels will stay, I thought, turning back the sheets.

And that's how I woke this morning, fresh from a hanging, surrounded by the pure good luck of crawlies and filth.

I folded yesterday's clothes and buttoned on a new cotton blouse. A piece of red flannel was nailed to the wall above the mattress, and I wondered if this was another bit of gris-gris: some happy charm for helpless drunks, or a spell to chastise long-lost kin. I remembered more of Uncle Bitter's magic from years ago. Dried frogs on a doorstep bring tragedy to a home. If an alligator crawls beneath your porch, it's a sure sign of death. If a gal cheats on her man just before baking, her bread won't rise. Bitter swore an innocent neighbor of his was beaten to death by her husband when her muffins kept failing.

"Gumbo ya-ya," my mama used to snap whenever she'd pass through a room to find my cousin Ariyeh and me sitting in Bitter's lap, listening to his tales. It meant, she told me once, someone who blabbed all the time.

"What you *Yankee* niggers know 'bout the bayou?" he'd toss back at her.

Her light cheeks turned the color of raspberries.

It's a measure of how place-bound my family has been that my Houston kin have always regarded Dallas, both suspiciously and with awe, as "the North." Mama, tight-lipped, snatched me up and took me north one day, in 1974, when I was three years old. We made four or five visits back to Freedmen's Town, all before I was ten, then never returned.

As a teenager I missed my uncle's stories, his sweet affection for my cousin and me. He called me Seamstress—Small Woman, in his parlance—and Ariyeh, Junebug, because she was chubby and round as a child. When I slipped into my twenties, went to college, then got a job with the Dallas mayor's office, I lost sight of "Down South," like my childhood had all been a fever dream. A heat rash in steamy swampgrass. I got one scribble from Uncle Bitter, on my twenty-second birthday, telling me how much it pained him that I hadn't been to see him in so many years. It didn't open "Dear Seamstress." "To the mayor's girl," it began, and ended, "You and your mama too fine for us folk?" By then, I believed that was true; I threw the letter away. Three years passed before I finally answered him, earlier this week, saying, "I need to come down. If you can make room for me somewhere, I promise not to be a bother."

Thinking back to last night, I count it as a good sign that he greeted me, finally, as "Seamstress." I suspect, too, he knows why I'm really here . . . maybe better than *I* do. I'm traveling on impulse, the way Mama used to do, and—no. No. Mama never acted impulsively in her life, and neither have I. If I could *believe* she left here impulsively I might be more at peace with her ghost, more at ease with myself. Truth is, I think, she fled deliberately because she was determined I'd become someone else, not the girl who'd grow up here.

I pluck a toothbrush and a comb from my case, walk across the yard, tap on the back door, painted blue but peeling. No answer. "Hello?" The door creaks like a rope pulled taut as I push it open, gently. I recognize nothing in the house. The furniture I've always remembered as gaudy, big, but these old chairs are faded, green, and small. Rugs cross the floor, fraying, the color of exhausted dirt. The place smells of onions. On a cutting board next to the kitchen sink I find a handwritten note: "Seam—Gone to do my Sunday business. You on your own til tonite. Some of us gather round ten at Etta's Place over on Scott Street," and he gives me an address. "See you there if you so incline."

His Sunday business, I recall Mama saying sadly long ago, was dominoes and bust-head in some raggedy-ass ice house somewhere. She used to fret about his drinking; he had what he called "high bloods."

This kitchen. I remember afternoons here, the bready smell of catfish frying on the stove, a saxophone signifying from the phonograph in the living room, and Mama running a hot-comb through Ariyeh's abundant hair. A dry, singed, old-cloth odor. I wailed, wanting the hot comb too. "Honey, you don't need it," Mama said. "You got that *pretty* hair, thin and wavy."

"But I want to look like Ariyeh!"

Even then, I was tugging against her conception of me.

On my way to the bathroom, I pass the old Crosley and stop to inspect the records. Louis Armstrong. Leadbelly's "Pigmeat." I laugh, remembering how fine the blues made me feel as a girl—all tingly, and happy/sad—despite Mama's disapproval of the music. My uncle's real name is Ledbetter, tagged after Huddie Ledbetter, Leadbelly's given name. I couldn't say the word as a child. It came out "Bitter" and stuck to him.

Down the hall, in the corner bedroom I shared with Ariyeh, Uncle's Needle Men stories whisper in my memory. The Needle Men were medical students from the Charity Hospital who roamed the streets in summer looking for bodies to practice on, "since stiffs get scarce that time of year." Uncle explained, "All they got to do is brush by you, and *bingo,* you been pricked. Some kinda sleeping poison. They whisk you away to a room 'neath the earth where they can cut on you."

I sit on the old bed, now, recalling hot breezes through the window screens filling drapes while Ariyeh and I tried to sleep. Each sound out-side—boys hurling stones at streetlamps, dogs pawing through wet newspapers, winos stumbling through weeds—became an abduction or a murder in our minds. We imagined crouched figures in green medical smocks, needles gleaming in moonlight, approaching our house. West of us, about a mile, the Southern Pacific made its midnight run; its metallic clanging was a lonely man curling his sour-egg breath through a clarinet. All over the neighborhood, children were vanishing, pricked with poison or sliced by the soft precision of a blade: in alleys and behind the markets, beside the barbershop and fireworks stands, which only opened on New Year's, Juneteenth, and July Fourth, and so were more sacred than church. Ariyeh's damp palm clung to mine; my nose, next to her popcorn-curly hair, opened wide with the pleasure of her sage and peppermint smell.

Nights, I remember, Mama quilted in her room down the hall: just a pencil line of lamplight beneath her bedroom door, a scrap of tune, a hiss of thread. Since she was so distant, I depended on Ariyeh to protect me, though I knew she was just as scared as I was. We stared at our open

window. Later, when the air had gotten cold in the room, she sometimes jarred me awake, tussling with dreams. If her hand had slipped
out of mine, I'd find it again and squeeze until she calmed, sighing back
into the mattress.

Now Uncle uses this bedroom for storage. Boxes clutter the floor
and the bed, some of them mildewed and webby. I rise slowly, hearing
the box springs' catlike creak. Ariyeh and I used to giggle about it in the
mornings.

I freshen up now, brush my teeth. The bathroom mirror is old, cop-
pery, and streaked; it dusts my face darker than it really is, makes me
feel *squirmier* here than I already did. An imposter. A mistake.

So: I have the day to myself, to see how well I recall the old neighborhood, to see what I can find of Cletus Hayes, to see how much trouble I can get into asking questions about secrets Mama told me never to
unearth.

―――――

My Taurus still smells of tacos, bought in Huntsville yesterday on
my way down from Dallas. I kick the empty food bag under the seat
and roll down my window. The streets here are narrow, old, faded bricks
knuckling through cracks in the asphalt. More weed lots than I'd
remembered: houses gone, rotted, bulldozed, scraped away for progress.
I imagine the land here has doubled or tripled its value over the years—
like a bully, downtown Houston has crept a few miles closer, gobbling
up space, since I scoured these alleys as a girl looking for horned toads.
Tall, glassy, air-conditioned bank buildings, mortgage firms, investment
companies cast fat shadows over dilapidated row houses worth nothing
compared with the rich red dirt they're cluttering up, over heaps of
wheezing washers, busted plumbing, sundered families worth even less
on paper than the materials their rickety homes are rigged with.

I glimpsed Tomorrow in the news this morning, the Business sec-
tion, open by chance, stained with egg yolk and orange juice, on Bitter's
kitchen table: *If we could clear out two dozen houses on lots along West
Gray Street, within a year we could open a strip mall that, guaranteed,
would turn a healthy profit by its second biennium.*

I'm amazed, then, it's not already snowing eviction notices here,
onto all the broken-glass-and-gravel lawns.

A Chicano boy bangs a stick against a mossy fire hydrant. A dog in a
dirt yard licks a little girl and she licks him right back. Five or six

teenage boys, like a cluster of heat-addled flies, lounge around a rusty, wheelless Cadillac, propped on cinder blocks, sharing joints and big blue cans of malt liquor. Now I *am* nostalgic for my childhood.

Shit man you got that you fucking got that, they say. They say, *That's all-reet 'bout that ol' shit man.* Slapping hands. *Yeah you got that slick I reckon you got that shit stone cold.*

They stop and watch me in my new purple car, and I imagine them thinking: White bitch. What *her* fucking business here?

Look again, I want to shout.

Instead, I give it the gas.

————

Of course, it wasn't in Freedmen's Town—"Niggertown," even *we* used to call it—where Cletus Hayes sealed his fate. I check a city map. Reinerman Street, Washington Road. Lillian. Rose. San Felipe. The heart of the riot. All west of here.

In the summer of 1917, Reinerman Street was in a nice white part of town by Camp Logan, a U.S. Army base. The camp had just made room for the Twenty-fourth Infantry, Third Battalion, an all-black unit exhausted from chasing, in vain, Pancho Villa through northern Mexico. The black soldiers were posted on a woody lot, surrounded by a barbed wire fence, about three miles from Logan and the white soldiers there. They were charged with protecting army property. A drainage ditch separated the regiment from Reinerman Street; a Southern Pacific Railroad track isolated it from even more expensive neighborhoods.

Few history books dwell on the movements of black military units, most of which were formed just after the Civil War; from monographs I first studied in school, I've learned that the army preferred to station black troops away from heavy population centers, stateside—far from white folks in the cities. But the Twenty-fourth, despite its failure with Villa, had shown uncommon valor and courage in the field. Prior to their Mexican engagement, the troops had fought bravely in the Philippines. Posted to San Francisco in 1915, the forces' provost guards so impressed the police chief, he tried to hire several of them. These were "good boys," so no one expected trouble when they arrived in Houston, an unusually courteous place as Southern communities went.

That summer in the Bayou City, as elsewhere, scores of white families were anguished at seeing their sons conscripted into the service and shipped to the widening war in Europe. The sight of *any* soldier must have rattled them. Local politics were rawer than usual then—patriotic fervor stirred the soup on every level—while the days lengthened, grew steamier, more humid, lifting indolence and anger closer to the surface of everyone's life.

Now, I park my car near a bike path winding into a neat, managed oak grove. Nearly eighty years after the events I've returned here hoping to plumb, this part of town is still nice and white. Paved. Well-trimmed. The streets have been swept and a sweet smell of late-season honeysuckle *zizzles* the air. Couples picnic in the grass. A toddler chases a pigeon. I push through brambles, deeper into shade.

No traces remain of Camp Logan. Following the First World War, the base served as a convalescent center, then it was dismantled. In the twenties, a wealthy, English-born music teacher gave millions to the city to turn the vacant land into a memorial for soldiers who'd paid the ultimate price. She had lived for a time near the base, rented rooms to soldiers' wives, played golf with them on the camp course, and had come to love the woodlands there (I imagine her as the type of person my mama always wanted to be, refined, respected, dignified, and quietly remote).

Eventually, bridle trails crossed Memorial Park; a polo club opened; no doughboy or doughboy's wife could afford to go near it. In my duties for the Dallas mayor's office, I've learned a lot about Houston. The two cities often compare themselves, competing in sports, finance, real estate. Several (white) lawyers jog in Memorial Park. Wealthy singles convene here, plumed in spandex, hoping to find True Love, or at least a love that will support them in the manner to which they're accustomed.

The ghosts of the old Twenty-fourth remain, now, only in the wind huffing through all the soft magnolia leaves.

Across the street, wood-trimmed brick homes murmur with TV baseball. Lawn mowers buzz, barbecue sauce spices the breeze . . . what didn't Mama like here?

I used to wonder why the city would place an army base so near a residential neighborhood. But the military was universally respected in those days (I'm what my stepdaddy calls a "cynical, post-'Nam babe"). Houston looked at World War I and saw a rainbow; it was the country's largest cotton port and stood to reap a bundle from the feds.

Texas's Anti-Saloon League recognized that young recruits might get rowdy from time to time and convinced lawmakers to establish a five-mile zone around all military installations, banning bars and bawdy houses. Citizens referred to these areas as white zones, long before the Twenty-fourth arrived.

Initially, the battalion settled peacefully into Houston. The city's "colored population," as it called itself then, hailed them as heroes. Businessmen welcomed the army's money. From court records following the riot, I have testimony from a well-to-do widow who lived by the base. "I didn't want those niggers tromping through my yard on their way into town, scattering all my chickens," she said, "so I decided to make friends with them right away. Baked bread for some of the boys, let them use my kitchen phone now and then. I didn't much like them—didn't like the way they *smelled*—but I figured cordiality was the best policy." So, through cordial, gritted teeth—the Southern way—the camp's immediate neighbors accepted the "dark guard," at first.

Most of the soldiers had never served in the South, had never been so intimate with Jim Crow, even on his best behavior. Right away, they resented the city's streetcar conductors, who expected them to stand at the back of the cars. They resented the stares they got from white workmen at Camp Logan. They resented water coolers in their own camp, roped off and labeled WHITE for construction workers, GUARD for the troops. Cops on the beat, noting the newcomers' attitude, began to mutter, "I never . . . ," started to whisper, "Uppity."

By most accounts, on the night of the riot, August 23, fifteen black soldiers, ignoring their white commanders' pleas, armed with Springfield rifles and ammunition pilfered from the post's storage lockers, marched down Washington Road toward the streetcar loop. They opened fire on a jitney, killing the driver, severely wounding a passenger.

Over a hundred other troops, led by a previously exemplary sergeant named Vida Henry, avoided Washington Road's bright lights, sticking instead to the smaller streets, Lillian and Rose, crossing Buffalo Bayou into the San Felipe district. They shot randomly into the dark in these usually quiet white neighborhoods. Two hours later, when the mutiny petered out, twenty people lay dead or dying in the streets.

Apparently, the whole thing had flared around the rumor that a pair of Houston cops had killed a Corporal Charles Baltimore of the Third Battalion. Later, he turned up in camp, beaten and bloody, but alive. More to the point, several weeks of "uppity" anger had broken free at last.

Court records show that Cletus Hayes, a young private, was captured neither on Washington Road nor the other rioters' paths. He wound up near dawn, by himself, on Reinerman Street.

I walk there now. This block is not so well-appointed as its neighbors. A failed flower shop, dry and cracked, drops light orange paint flakes onto the grass next to Brock's Combo Burger #2 and a row of modest homes. As a former history major, I can't help but imagine the births and deaths, the tilled soil, the spilled blood on this spot, all so Brock can make a profit, now, off his fatty foods. The march of progress. Onions in the air.

Slack wire frames a vegetable garden by a sagging wooden home. The house is painted yellow. Corn wilts in the hard soil. I recall the court transcripts, following the riot: "Defendant accosted the young lady, Sarah Morgan, in her mother's garden." But over five hundred pages detailing this single incident fail to explain the woman's presence among the cabbage at four o'clock in the morning.

That particular garden is gone; this yellow house, like those around it, dates from the thirties, no earlier. An accurate picture of the neighborhood as it appeared in the summer of '17 is impossible now.

But this might as well be the place. The Morgan home had to be near here. If Private Hayes had been hiding that night near the bayou, as MPs later claimed, then he would have approached this block from the southeast, up Oak Street or Pine, past the spot where a pimpled high school kid flips burgers now in Brock's cockroachy kitchen.

Sergeant Vida Henry, the riot's leader, shot himself by the bayou at around 2:05 A.M., several hours after the uprising ended. Private Hayes never denied accompanying him, though he claimed at the trial he'd never raised his weapon. Realistically speaking—if nothing else, peer pressure would have been irresistible—he'd probably shot out a window or two, shattered some white woman's crystal lamp as she crocheted in her den.

If only I could see wholly from his perspective, slip past the surface details I've gathered and melt into the man . . . his strategies, hopes, rages—at whites? Women? *White women?*

Standing at the garden's edge, I concentrate so hard my head hurts in the swirling afternoon heat. I try to lose myself, pour my ego from one container into another . . .

If I were Cletus Hayes that night, what would I do? I'd chuck my rifle, my cap, even my coat, so in the dark, in the swift sweep of head-lights, I might not be recognized as a gunner. I'd stick to alleys and narrow paths between homes. I'd want to return to camp as soon as possible—to claim, perhaps, I'd never left my bunk. I wouldn't dawdle—why would I dawdle?—in a wide-open vegetable garden in an all-white neighborhood.

Am I dumb? Impulsive? Arrogant? Who the hell am I?

Car horns blare by the burger joint. I open my eyes. Why do I care? Why go to all this trouble to snatch a ghost? Because, for some time now, I've suspected my origins are linked with his . . . but that's an abstraction, no realer than believing the Founding Fathers had me in mind when they formed this nation. No realer than the Needle Men.

But maybe Cletus is my hoo-raw: a spirit dragging life and death behind him, like a wedding car's clattery tin cans; a breath from the past who could fill my present if only I can inspirit him, *inhabit* him . . . so I shut my eyes . . . take up his uniform . . .

. . . and slink like a scarecrow down Reinerman Street, shivering, rank with dirty bayou water. I hear sirens south of here where several white-owned businesses—the Ruby Café, Claude's Coffee Shop, Jack's Fine Shoes—flatten in flames. Gunshots echo in the dark. No lights illuminate the homes. I pick my way past small magnolia trees, Fords big as buffaloes parked in narrow drives, wooden porches large as gallows, until I come to a neat, clear patch staked out in Bermuda grass. There—waiting for me?—among cabbages, tomato vines, and yellow-tipped cucumbers, a young lady in a blue cotton dress.

Then I lose him again. My perspective shifts to this other family ghost. Sarah Morgan, whose father has fallen on hard times. He's lost his cotton farm—hard to manage in this glorious war boom—and moved with his wife and child to the city. Sarah stands there among the scorched, growing things, watching the young colored man, wary, exhausted, approach.

She is my great-grandmother, and I know as little about her as I do about him. I know her family was reckless with money ("Foreclosed, First City National Bank, 8/21/16"). I know her father, like his old man, mourned the loss of slavery ("The darkies were *happier* then—just ask them": signed editorial, *Houston Post,* 5/8/15). But Sarah? I know, from the transcripts, she wore a blue dress in the early morning hours of August 24, 1917, shivering in her mother's garden. She was twenty-five years old, living at home with her parents. Unmarried. Plain? Ugly? I have no photographs, no detailed description. I *do* have a handwritten letter, signed C, addressed to Sarah, found among my mama's things the week she died. C thought Sarah "exquisite, like mist in a cornfield early in the morning."

Private Hayes denied accosting the young lady. There were no witnesses, only the emotional testimonies of Sarah Morgan's folks, with references to a ripped dress and the rhetorical question, "What else could have happened?" In over five hundred pages, the young lady herself remains mysteriously silent: a special dispensation from the court, perhaps. (Repeatedly, others describe her as nervous.)

So I am left with the moment itself. The early-morning garden, trembling with the breath of innocence and the possibility of a fall. The nervous young woman, dressed as if for church. And the army private, dark as the neighborhood soil, grimed with Houston's muck. They meet to the distant sound of gunfire, a city coming apart.

The court finds him guilty and sentences him to be hanged by the neck until he is dead, along with twelve other mutinous souls. But more and more in my mind—since Mama's death and my discoveries in her lint-filled chest of drawers—he merely reaches out to touch her sleeve, to stroke the wrist he has stroked so many times before.

Does she pull back? Does she welcome his gesture? Does she know, even now, this meeting will lead to an unhappy dawn, a hidden grassy fringe, her confused shout as the gallows' triggers roar back and ropes tighten like cramping muscles?

An old woman shoves her screen door open, now, and stands, wearing a floured apron, on the yellow house's porch. She squints at me, crouching in her garden. "Hello? Can I help you, young lady?"

I rise, brushing my pants. Brock's Combo Burger burps harsh, sizzling sounds through its window screens. Jukebox guitars: lost love, country-style. Pickles and mustard. Something sour.

"No, thank you," I call across the yard. "I was just admiring your peppers."

She frowns.

I leave, knowing what Cletus Hayes must have felt many times. Harried. Undesired. But wearing my privileged skin, I can pass through town in ways he never could. I return to my car, moving with the confidence of someone secure behind a mask. I pull into the nice wide streets and vanish into the anonymous safety of white drivers going shopping or hauling their kids out to play in the parks.

————

On Allen Parkway, heading back to Freedmen's Town, I pass row after charred row of neglected public housing. Neglect is the easiest form of eviction. Eventually, folks will move out on their own, worried for their children's health (here, it appears to be mostly single black mothers and Vietnamese refugees). Then the land can be developed. It's a little trick I've seen often since going to work for the mayor.

Kids' bikes rust in glass-toothed parking lots, dogs nose through mounds of shoes, abandoned baby clothes, Burger King bags. Empty gas cans, stuffed with rags, rust among sticker burrs, as if arson were as natural as shooting hoops. A way to pass the day.

Around the block, a SWAT team, stealthy as an army, busts up a confab on a pitted volleyball court. Right out in the open, eight or nine teens, cuffed and forced to their knees. Down the street, nine- or ten-year-olds, signifying, mill around a liquor store. *Shit man your nappy haid done been hit by a hurrican'. Like a ol' rubber in the gutter, man, like your mama's funky ol' Milk Dud drawers. Facts is facts, they hard as rocks, your mama's got a pussy like a Cracker Jacks box.* I speed on by, then exit the parkway.

The part of Freedmen's Town I knew best as a girl curls around a cemetery dating back to slavery times, the Magnolia Blossom, on South Ruthven Street. Uncle Bitter's house sits across the alley from it, with the AME Church just down the block. Bitter used to tell me his grave was already waiting for him, roomy and fresh, but I didn't believe him. Visiting, I'd sit against the warm old stones on summer days, reading, coloring, or playing with my dolls.

I park my car now in front of the house, grab my bag, and head for the boneyard. Afternoon services are just beginning at the church. Voices rise to the sky. Hallelujahs and praised-bes. I settle by a tomb so ancient and worn, the only legible date is "18—." Baby's breath blooms, early, in the grass nearby: a soft, white smell. Through tree shade I see what remains, across the road, of some of the first homes built by ex-slaves here after the Civil War. Two-by-fours weak as cardboard, pressed by years of wind and rain into the ground; shingles like marked cards, forgotten by a tarred-and-feathered gambler. Sunlight warms my shoulders. A bit of a tan wouldn't hurt, I think and laugh a quiet, rueful laugh.

Three weeks ago I found in Mama's things, along with C's letter to Sarah Morgan, a yellowed copy of the *Crisis,* the official publication of the NAACP, dated July 25, 1917—about a month before the Houston riot. I pull it from my bag now. What better place than a field of ghosts to read the words of the dead?

On the journal's second page, circled in pencil, a letter appears from Private Cletus Hayes, Twenty-fourth Infantry, Third Battalion, praising the *Crisis* editor, W. E. B. Du Bois, for his "noble fight for manhood rights for our people." He closes with a promise that the "entire enlisted command of the Twenty-fourth Infantry is ready to aid you in any way."

The phrase "manhood rights" also occurs in the personal letter: "We troops are asked to defend the United States' interests abroad, when very often we are denied our manhood rights here at home. But oh my dear Sarah, when I think of your vitality, your loveliness, and your understanding, I know what I am fighting for."

Standard wartime sentiments. But the near-certainty that C was the Cletus Hayes praising Du Bois in the *Crisis,* the same man later hanged for mutiny, rioting, and rape, makes his gesture toward Sarah Morgan anything *but* common.

Why did Mama keep these things if she wasn't going to talk to me about them? And she *wouldn't* orate, ever, on anything significant. Once, when I asked her why we'd left Houston, she looked at me, said, "Sometimes you come to a crossroads," and refused to say any more.

Am I obsessed with Cletus Hayes because she was so mum about him? Sometimes, I see my search for him as defiance, but also, since her death, as a way of snuggling closer to her. Wearing her perspective as if it were a hand-me-down.

I fold the *Crisis* back into my bag. It's not an Alex Haley thing, this scrabbling after roots, though I *am* hoping Bitter can fill me in on Daddy as well as Cletus Hayes.

It's more like this story I read in college. A man fasts to astonish paying crowds. Abstinence is not a skill so much as the curse of his life. As he's dying, he admits, "If I could have found food I liked, I would gladly have eaten." Somehow, I felt the truth of that line *in my skin.* Nothing I was *supposed* to like was giving me any nourishment. And so—what? I find myself back in Houston, looking for palatable old recipes? Well, but it's not that simple.

In Dante's Hell—another outlook I ran across in college—damnation is a constant lapsing backward, repeating one's sins. Swimming against the current, never getting things right: I understood that too. But my family's original sin, the *start* of the cycle: Cletus, Daddy, Mama. It had to do with them.

Else, why would Mama have fled?

I need to know it, nail it—whatever it is—so I can shut the fucker down. "Everybody has a buried story," my teacher told me, the one who assigned Dante and Kafka. The one who told me, *You must know everything.* "And everyone's purpose in life, no matter how foolhardy their attempts may be, is to be heard."

Down the street, the church is humming now with the preacher's calls to witness. *I been sanctified, Lord, and offer up a joyful noise in Your name, amen! Sometime I get to 'membering the slothful sinner I surely usta could be, and FALL on my knees, Lord, humble before Thee, handing up my soul, amen! Touch me with your flame, amen! Take my tongue and teach your grace through me. Enlist me in your mighty army, Lord, amen!*

In the testimonies, I hear blues rhythms, the pacing of Uncle Bitter's hoo-raws, the gumbo-okra lilt of the Deep South, Louisiana, Africa, and the Caribbean, our misty ancestral sources. *I'm a rampaging, devil-dousing soldier for Christ, amen!* I hear the music of my childhood— music that, like the blues, Mama worked to drum from my head. I was sixteen the last time I set foot in a church—-the day Mama married a Dallas lawyer. By then, we were living in a perfect, all-white world, and I was, on the surface, a perfect, all-white girl. My skin was twice as pale as Mama's. I could waltz into any public place, in any part of town. My mop had thickened by then—I no longer had that "pretty hair"—and so, for both of us, to maintain the mask, Mama kept the bathroom stocked with Frizz-Away: "Deluxe Hair-Straightener—No Lye, No Muss, No Fuss!"

I'm a salesman for my Lord, stepping door to door with a surefire sin-cleaner. Its name ain't Hoover. Its name ain't General 'Lectric. No sir. It's Jesus Christ, amen! He'll leave you sparkle-plenty!

Last month, when the breast cancer finally carried Mama home, I refused her Methodist church, her lawyer-husband ("You're her *daughter,* you should *be* here!"), everything but the parched north Dallas graveyard once she'd been laid to rest. I visited late one evening, alone, carrying a sorry, paper-wrapped rose from a nearby Safeway. Her stone was simple, just her name, fitting a taciturn woman. But her last words to me rapped like a faulty pipe in my mind: "I've *tried* to be a good woman, Telisha. God spare me! God spare me from Hell!"

What was it *she* was afraid to repeat? And why? And how did her trap become my own? For surely that's part of my story, too.

She left for me her perfect world, darkened only by the whispered admission, years ago, that my great-grandmother, Sarah Morgan, was once attacked by a black man and never recovered. All the rest I've stumbled over, as through neighborhood debris, on my own.

Still no witness to my daddy. Nothing to tell me, directly, who I am. So I keep spinning from one perspective to the next.

One day I'll be coming on home, Lord, coming on home—

I left the rose on Mama's grave and determined to return to Freedmen's Town. Or at least, her passing is *one* of my reasons—my most conscious excuse—for coming back. Now, I zip my bag up tight. No matter what I find here, probably my life won't change. Even if I alter my thinking, I won't be any more, or less, welcomed anywhere I go.

So why the hell am I here?

My legs tingle, nearly asleep. I shake them out, stroll the alley behind my uncle's house, where Ariyeh and I used to prowl with empty shoe boxes, hoping to catch lizards and horned toads for Bitter to use in his spells. He'd slip the boxes from us, bend to hear the creatures' scratchings, mumble some gris-gris, then tell us to set our prisoners free. He didn't need their bodies, he said. "I drawed their spirits clean out of their skins, see. Now I hold the power in my fingers!"

The alley smells of gin, spaghetti sauce, and urine, the way it always did, and I long to see Ariyeh again, to laugh with her, run with her through drippy bayou heat, past vacant lots where the first freedmen here sharecropped and sang. I wonder if she'll be at Etta's tonight with Bitter and his pals? What will Etta's look like? I've never been inside an ice house.

Someone in the church takes up a mouth harp, wheezes a plea to God. I remember my confusion, as a child, listening to the spirituals—*Lawd, Lawd, oh yes my Lawd*—then walking home from Sunday school with Ariyeh, past the railroad tracks, hearing the winos whistle and yell at us, "Oh Lawd! Oh yeah! Gonna be *fine* someday!" What was the difference between the sacred and the old men's wolf calls? Is this what Bitter meant when he said, "The world sure does love a nigger joke. Always playing tricks on us."

The church melody evokes for me lonely soldiers in a field, squatting around a campfire, stuffing their backpacks with gris-gris—frog legs, dried scorpion claws—to give them luck in battle. For a moment, as I stand dazed in a mosquito swarm in the alley, I can almost walk up to Cletus Hayes, in my mind. I can almost see his face. Then: the mad red welt around his neck.

The church thunders with voices, mouth harp, tambourine, sharp guitar. Laughing and clapping. I wipe the sweat from my face. My very pink palm. *There's a train acoming, Lord, and I'm gointer be on it!* I know these people. Yet I don't. *I'm hoboing my way to Heb'n!* They are making a joyful noise, and keeping Death at bay.

2

THE FAINT-HEARTED won't find Etta's Place. No signs, no lights, no outside paint—just weathered wood and an illegible address on the door in orange Marks-A-Lot. I spun my tires for half an hour, up and down Scott Street, trying to ferret out the club. Now my car is the only one in the lot. The neighborhood, nearly treeless, exposed, looks as scoured and salty as a coastal town. Everything's the dingy gray-white of seagulls.

The Flower Man's house sits on a corner down the street. I remember sneaking around it when Ariyeh and I were kids. We never knew what the Flower Man did, never even saw him. But he'd covered his house with giant plastic roses, TV trays, Barbie dolls, seashells, clay birds—all nailed or glued to the walls so you couldn't see the wood anymore. A bottle tree hides his front porch: bare cedar limbs holding empty colored bottles, which, according to bayou lore, will trap evil haints. The bottles *ting* like out-of-tune piano keys. Aspirin containers, vitamin jars, sodas. Green, purple, blue. The house is like a gulf-side beach, a flotsam-catcher whenever the tide comes in. Like everything else I remember here, the place looks worn now but still glorious in its trashy get-up.

I lock the car. Opening Etta's door, I get a splinter in my thumb. I'm the only one here. Ten-thirty. Coors crates block the back wall. Microphones huddle near a Pearl drum set in a dusty corner. Termites appear to have colonized the bottom third of the bar. A gray-haired woman stands there, thin as a diving board, quivering like someone's just jumped off her. She croaks, "Take a load off, dear. Make yourself at home."

"I was supposed to meet somebody here—"

"They'll be along d'rectly. Music'll be starting up."

No sign of a band. I set my purse on a gimpy wooden chair.

The woman—Etta?—says, "Beer?"

"Yes, please. Just a—" Something ratlike skitters among the crates. "—Coors."

She attacks a bottle with difficulty, using a small hand-opener. I wonder if I should go over and help her, but she seems determined. I don't want to embarrass her in her own place. Her hands shake like water sprinklers. Finally the cap spins off, and she heads my way. "Enjoy, dear."

"I appreciate it." A sulfurous, ruined-eggs smell wafts from the kitchen, behind an open curtain near the bar. It's not really a curtain but a Star Wars bedsheet. Princess Whatcha-macallit, faded. I settle at a wobbly, ash-browned table.

Fifteen minutes or so later, two men with guitars show up, one thin and stiff as a two-by-four, the other in a James Brown outfit, purple suit, black leather shoes. His hair is oily and straight. He must weigh three hundred pounds. "Etta, you gorgeous, chicken-legged mama, you! How you been, girl?" He gives the old woman a hug. She shivers, her face buried in the wedge between his breasts.

A bass player and a drummer, both sullen, arrive, start tuning, tightening, adjusting. Still no crowd. I order a second beer, watch in agony as Etta struggles with the opener. I pick at the splinter in my thumb.

Finally, just as the band seems ready to start—as if a secret signal has sounded somewhere—Uncle Bitter walks in the door, followed by dozens of other men and women, all in their fifties and sixties, I'd guess. It's 11:20. "Bitter!" Etta croaks. "Hanging good, my man?"

"Feel like a million dollars that's done been spent. How *you* coming, *mon 'te chou?*"

"*Poly,* thank God."

While Uncle greets the band and orders beers for his friends (pointedly ignoring me, so far), three big women sit at a table next to mine. They're dressed in Sunday-go-to-meeting clothes, black crinoline and lace, red stockings. With great solemnity, they set heavy paper bags on the tabletop, then settle back in their chairs, surveying the room like teachers on the first day of class not entirely happy with their prospects. The monster in the purple suit—his name is Earl, I overhear—bows to them, saying, "Ladies." They ignore him, but not really; their turning-away is practiced, almost choreographed, for Earl's benefit. He knows this and smiles. I have the feeling I'm watching a long-familiar ritual, and I'm glad I got here first. I'd hate to walk in on this scene, interrupting it, drawing direct stares instead of the furtive ones I'm getting now.

White bitch: there it is again, in the ladies' cutting eyes. They're as disdainful of me as the sorority girls in college were when I finally told them I wasn't really one of them and not to be fooled by my skin. I sit up in my chair, sip my beer, try not to look as discomfited as I feel. After years of this, you'd think I'd have perfected a smooth disdain of my own, but I don't seem able to just let things ride. *I'll bet I know what kind of straightener you slap in your sorry-ass hair,* I'm thinking, but I keep it to myself.

Earl palms a mike and the band eases into some blues. Leadbelly. I know it right away. All about the National Dee-fense and a woman who don't have no sense.

At the bar, Bitter mimics Earl's hippy movements and calls to him, "*Un wawaron!*"—another Creole lilt I recall from long ago: Bullfrog. Its sound warms my ears. We used to sit outside and listen to the critters late at night, Bitter, Ariyeh, and me. Earl laughs, wags a playful finger at my uncle.

Very slowly, now, the women next to me remove from their paper bags elegant glass decanters of E & J brandy, along with lime juice in plastic squeeze bottles. They order Sprites, glasses with straws, and a bucket of ice. Etta brings all this on a tray, avoiding a disaster despite her shakes. The women mix their drinks with great dignity—priests preparing Communion—their long red nails keeping time on the table to the tune.

An old man who looks to be eighty, a former professional scarecrow, dances by himself next to the beer crates, sipping from a flask of MD 20/20. Uncle Bitter finally turns my way, bearing a big, sweating can of Colt 45 malt liquor. Three fellows follow him.

"This here *Seam,*" he says to his friends, waving at me. They grab chairs. Old Spice and gin, tobacco, and sweat. "Telisha," I say. "Telisha Washington. Hello."

"This your *niece?*" one asks.

Uncle Bitter just smiles; the drummer raps a rim-shot, like signaling a punch line; and I realize what I should have known, of course, a long time ago. No. I'm *not* his niece. Not really.

My skin goes clammy and my mouth dries up. I sit unmoving, hot with shame (or exposed pride, refusing to admit to myself what was obvious all these years). Bitter ignores me again. He and his cronies toast each other, chatter, snicker when the band screws up a bar.

"Hear they shutting down the Astrodome."

"Who?"

"City."

"Shit. Where the Astros gon' play?"

"Some fancy-ass new fa-cili-*tee* they building downtown, call Enron Field."

"*En*ron? Kinda name is that?"

"Name of the gas company what shuts off your heat every winter. They be owning half the town now."

"Own the hot and the winter's cold."

"Bought the balls, the bats, the *pro*tective cups."

Bitter leans back in his chair, arms stretched on the table: a fatcat senator making deals. "I saw the first game ever played at the Dome, back in '65. Exhibition with the Yankees. They let colored folks in cheap that night 'counta we passed the last bond referee-*end*um they needed to build the thing. It was gonna fail 'cause they running way over budget, see, but Judge Hofheinz—*he* owned the city back then—he lobbied us, hard, in Freedmen's Town, said we'd be welcome at all the events, and we could even work there and shit. We's the ones closed the deal, finally." He grins. "That first night, LBJ was in the crowd, and Mickey Mantle, he slammed him a homer. Real beauty, almost smacked the roof."

"'Member, Bitter, the Dome's groundsmen in them days, decked out in spacesuits, raking the infield like they's sweeping the moon?"

"Shoot, Houston booming then. Thought the moon just one of its 'burbs."

"Moon in better *shape* than Freedmen's Town. I'd move there tomorrow, could I afford it."

Their laughter evaporates when the talk turns to Texas City, and they reminisce about working oil rigs or cargo boats down in the gulf, the day half the coast blew up. 1947. I remember overhearing Bitter once, when I was a child, mention "terrible flames," and I questioned Mama about it. She told me he was there that day and barely survived the explosion. "What caused it?" one of his buddies asks him now. "Oil leak? I cain't recall."

"Fertilizer," Bitter says. "Ammonium nitrate, stored on a Liberty boat. Some asshole tossed a butt in the hold, and that was all she wrote. Fire spread to the refineries and Welcome to Hell."

"'Member Bill Southey?"

"Shit yes, and Max Low."

They trade more names of the dead, order more liquor, grow sadder, drunker. Earl has shucked his coat. He's standing in a puddle of his own perspiration. Regally, the ladies sip their brandy, shun him with intricate head twists—which only entice him closer to their table. He croons to them, "Had me a Volkswagen love, now I'm looking for a Rolls / Roll on over, Mama, let me pop your pretty hood." Etta vibrates like a tuning fork behind the bar. The skinny old man still dances by himself, grinning as if an invisible angel is tonguing his ear.

I worry the splinter, worry what I know—what I've *always* known, if I'm honest with myself. Why it slips out now, like ice spilled from the ladies' bucket, I'm not sure, but Uncle Bitter has something to do with it: leaving me on my own all day, asking me here, then pretending my chair is empty. I suspect he's not punishing me so much as making me *see,* forcing me to sit here, quietly, uncomfortably, and take it all in. Not just the place, but him. Me. Our history. Our lost years.

But the *place.* Of course it signifies for me, powerfully. I asked him once where my daddy had got to. We were alone in his yard. I was maybe seven. "Your daddy been down to the crossroads," he said. "Learned him that hoodoo guitar."

"So where is he, then?"

"Wherever the music take him."

Instead of filling in the holes after that, he distracted me with more of his spells. Mama wouldn't ever talk about it (I remember asking her one night what a juke joint was. She frowned and turned away).

Even now, I think, how can I ever know *anything*—much less everything—with so many layers to peel, starting with Bitter himself. Uncle Bitter. Uncle Remus. Uncle Tom. My God. Ever since I can remember, he's accepted the ready-made role—did the family force it on him?—bouncing Ariyeh and me on his knees, erecting wild stories for us full of magic, acting the clown. How much of all this was part of a mask at first—now frozen in place—fashioned to protect himself? *The happy-go-lucky nigger.* I may never know.

Listening to him and his buddies—

"Mistah Bogue! What up?"

"Shih. Cain't kill nothing and won't nothing die."

"Sho you right."

"Shut the noise."

"Yeah, it's like that, I got it like that."

—I'm stunned at how neatly these duffers fit my image of old black men. But where is that image born? My actual memories of elders? Television? Movies? All of it. These fellows have embraced the stereotypes. Accepted their assignment from the world. As *I've* learned, acceptance is the easiest way to negotiate things. But it's a complex transaction. Those radicals from the sixties who blew up buildings, then spent the next thirty years hiding in the open, changing their names, working respectable jobs, marrying, raising kids . . . were they *disguised* as pleasant middle-class people, masking their true violent natures, their repugnance for the systems around them, or were they, after all, what they appeared to be? Was their "radical" side the aberration? Or were they an honest, paradoxical mix? Bank robber–wealthy mom: will the real Patty Hearst step up?

Looking around now—

"Ace kool! What up, Doe?"

"Just trying to make a dollar outta fifteen cent."

—it's clear to me the choices have narrowed here. Back in the early seventies, I swear the neighborhood didn't look this poor, didn't resemble the *image* of a black enclave. The middle-class families hadn't yet caught the gravy train; those "bettered" by the Movement hadn't fled their brothers and sisters, the way Mama did. In those days, it was still possible to see black prosperity here. I remember handsome young men in African fabrics, collarless suits like Julius Nyerere wore. Tanzania's president. He was a model of dignity and success pulling us up, out of ourselves. Or *toward* ourselves. Black nationalism. Pride. Afros and musk oil.

Now, the whole place reeks of defeat: not so much alcohol and hash, but a smell of familiarity, predictability, of settling for what the world tells you to be.

Something I know a thing or two about.

Bitter winks at me across the table. "You like the music, Seam?"

I nod, swallow some beer.

"Axeman's Jazz."

"Axeman?"

"You don't recall me spinning this when you's a kid?"

"No sir."

In his voice is a pinched reproach, a cricket's rasp. He's scolding me: 'Course, I ain't *seen* you since you's a kid, have I now, Seamstress? You and your mama too fine for us folk?

"Several year ago, here in Freedmen's Quarter, there's a series of axe murders," he says in his smooth story-tone, and I *do* remember, some. "Always on Sunday nights. No one knew why. Someone mad at God? A grocer and his wife was found sliced into patties, like meat you'd feed a dog. A bartender. A streetwalker. Couple of the Axeman's intendeds survived, all whittled-on, but they couldn't agree what he looked like. One said he's a midget. Another, a monster. Cops was kerflooied.

"Finally one day a letter come to the *Informer*, our neighborhood rag. From the very sharp dude hisself. 'Reason y'all fools cain't catch me,' he says, 'is 'cause I's Puredee Spirit, a running-buddy of the Angel of Death Hisself. What y'all wastrels wallow in every day, your so-called worldly pleasures, they make me want to spit, 'cept'—he hastens to unveil this, out of the blue—'very fond I am of jazz music.' (The preachers, of course, always used to tell us jazz was Lucifer's tunes.) 'So I swear by all the devils in the netherworld, them that's swinging in their rooms Sunday nights'll be spared. But them that ain't jazzing, beware!'"

Bitter swirls his malt liquor can. "Wellsir, that Sunday eve, everybody made damn sure they had 'em some hot stuff on the phonograph. Those that didn't have no stacks of wax stole 'em. And no one croaked that night. After a few more shaky Sabbaths like this, the Axeman, he up and vanished. Shuffled on back to Hell where he belonged, folks said, toting his blade and a fiery clarinet, which you can still hear sometimes late at night, like a faraway train: a warning you been spared for now, but next time and tomorrow, who knows?

"Ever' since, it's kind of a saying 'round here. You know: you looking for peace of mind, we say you chasing the Axeman's Jazz."

"Yes sir, that's what I'm here for," I say. "You got it." He laughs. "You got it." After a minute I venture, "Mama asked for you at the end."

He looks at his hands. "Shoulda ask for me long time ago. So you ain't got a job now, or what? How come you can abandon the mayor and just hang here awhile?"

"I'm on sabbatical."

"That like church?"

"No. It's earned leave. A friend of mine is watching my fish and my birds—"

"Oh, so you a zookeeper now, too? Lot I don't know 'bout you, Seam. Like I say, your letter was short."

"There's a lot I don't know, too, Uncle Bitter."

"Might be you ready to ask?"

"Might be."

"I don't know all the answers."

"But you know *some* of them?"

He shrugs, rises stiffly, and orders another round of drinks at the bar. His buddies watch me closely, nodding and smiling. One says, "Telisha. That like *dee*-lish?" I excuse myself.

The ladies' room smells of vomit and lilac perfume. The Tampax machine lies broken on the floor. I open a stall door. Just then one of the brandy women barrels in, heading for the stall next to mine. She gives me a hooded look—something she does with her brows—like, *What* your *snowflake ass doing in here?*

She grunts and groans, and I hold back a little so as not to make much noise. So many ways to nearly disappear. I've tried them all, over the years. Dressing like everyone else. Hugging corners. Staying home. I remember sitting for an hour at a time in a bathroom stall in junior high school, because that was the only place I could escape the teasing. I'd made the mistake once, in seventh grade, of bringing home a friend; the next day, it was all over school: "You won't believe it! Her mama's *black!* She *looks* white, sort of, but she's a Negro, all right, you can tell up close. Fat lips, flat nose." In ninth grade, Troy Jones, my first crush, somehow hadn't heard the talk. We hung out together at lunch, eating sandwiches and apples under an oak tree just outside the cafeteria. He was a merit scholar and an athlete, tall and muscular, a honeyed, varnished color. His father was the first black banker I'd met. Troy told me up front he didn't want to date me because I looked too much like a boy—thin, no hips, no breasts to speak of (that hasn't changed). But he liked me "as a friend."

One day I told him what I knew about my family, hoping he *might* date me if he thought I was more like him. He stood, bread crumbs spilling from his pants, pulled me up beside him, and walked around me slowly, rubbing his chin, saying, "Mmm-hmmm. Mmm-hmmm." He ran a finger down my arm, my back, across the flat cotton bra beneath my blouse. Finally, he stepped back. "Girl, you telling me you're a *nigger?*"

When I didn't answer and began to cry, he dropped the jive act. He hugged me. "You must really be confused." No one had said this to me before—no one had *understood* it—and I cried even harder. Later that day, after classes, he caught me in the hallway. "Here," he said. "I have something for you." He handed me a paperback copy of Claude Brown's *Manchild in the Promised Land,* with a picture of Harlem on the cover. "This will tell you who you are."

"What is it?"

"Brother tells it straight, growing up black in white America. This is your heritage, girl."

For the next week I tried to read the book, but I didn't see myself in it anywhere. Claude Brown was writing about the North. The East. Most of all, he was writing about being a man. In one passage, he talked about going away to college and partying for the first time with white women. "I never would have thought that white girls could be so nice," he said. "Cats could look all up under their dresses and everything, and all they did was laugh."

One day I told Troy I didn't understand this bit about the kitties. He laughed so hard he nearly choked on his sandwich. "*Cats.* You know, guys. Fellas. Dudes."

"They go to college so they can look up white girls' dresses?"

"The girls don't mind, see. That's the point."

"I don't believe it."

"No no no. See, since slavery times, the black man has been lynched and shit for even *looking* at white girls funny. Claude's saying this is the white man's insecurity, 'cause the girls themselves, they get a kick from it."

"I'm sorry, I don't believe that."

"You're not reading *ideologically,* Telisha. Smartly. Maybe I should have started you with Frantz Fanon. He's all about the mind-set, see, how the mind-set of the perennially oppressed—"

"I don't like it when somebody looks up *my* dress."

"Telisha—"

"Well, I don't!"

Exasperated, he grabbed his lunch sack. "That's 'cause you've been raised a proper white bitch. Grow up."

I wanted to tell him he'd just proven the falsity of Claude Brown's passage, but he'd already stalked away.

In high school, I tried consciously to embrace my blackness. This was difficult in Dale Licht's house ("You married him for his *home* and his *money!*" I used to scream at Mama, and we'd both collapse in tears). Each Wednesday night he'd take us to his country club for steaks and baked potatoes. He'd chat with his weekend golfing buddies, Mama would make several trips to the bathroom—to see if she could still pass for white, I accused her—and I watched the black waiters bring us our food, yes sir-ing, yes ma'am-ing to and from the kitchen.

Among the lawyer set in Dallas, the moneyed folks, mixed-race marriages were less rare than I would have thought, and I could almost believe that color was less and less a problem all the time. But then, on any given day in the hallways at school, I'd hear light-skinned blacks taunt their darker friends until the friendships blew apart in rage and recrimination, and I realized it was a mistake to relax too much.

On some Wednesdays I'd bring a book of poetry with me to the country club, Maya Angelou, Nikki Giovanni, Ntozake Shange, but Dale would always say, "Put that away, Tish. Sit up, now, and eat your dinner."

"My name is Telisha. Don't whiten it."

"Hush now. Put your napkin in your lap. Use your fork on those peas, not your knife."

So I'd read the books at school, hiding in a bathroom stall. I loved the poems but still didn't find myself in any words I saw. My blood may have been black, but my skin didn't let on, and Mama had whisked me, early, from the only black community I'd ever known. I was living now in an all-white Dallas suburb. Shange didn't have *nothing* to say 'bout *that*. I ached for Ariyeh, then. She had been dark as the back of a closet, as a kid. She could teach me something about myself, I thought. But Mama had made it clear we were to have nothing more to do with our Houston kin.

Maybe if I learn black women's history, I reasoned, I'll discover a tradition I can respond to. But even the driest books in our school library crumbled into stereotypes: "Mammy reflected two traditions perceived as positive by Southerners—that of the idealized slave and that of the idealized woman."

And this, from an essay entitled "The Life Cycle of the Female Slave," sillier than Claude Brown—the lines so astonished me, I committed them to memory, word for word: "Most slave girls grew up believing that boys and girls were equal. Had they been white and free, they would have learned that women were the maidservants of men."

Thank *God* we didn't grow up white and free, or we'd have thought men were better than we were? After reading the lines a dozen times, I tore the essay up and flushed it, piece by piece, down the john.

Water gurgles through pipes. Wet, wheezing sighs. The brandy woman paws a roll of toilet paper, pulls up her stockings, flushes. I can feel her chill through the metal stall partition. Water splashes in the sink, a compact clicks, lips smack; the door eases shut. For several minutes, I linger until I'm sure she's gone.

———

Earl and his mates have given the floor to a new guitarist, "Bayou Slim," who has just walked in the door "hauling a scuttery-looking old Gibson and a tiny Fender amp," Bitter says. The man is ravaged, wraithlike, wearing a straw cowboy hat and sharecropper clothes: blue denim shirt and faded overalls. Drunk or doped, he prances about in small, spasmodic jerks, a Stepin Fetchit caricature. He assaults his guitar, making it snap and clatter. Voice like a wall falling down. The chords pierce my ears, as painful as the splinter in my thumb.

"Poor old soul," Bitter says. Earl and the others sit, patiently, while Slim gyrates and wails. The crowd ignores him, mostly, though quietly and politely. I wiggle the splinter and finally pull it out just as Slim reaches a shrieking climax. He drops to his knees, shaking and sweating, then tugs off his hat, offers it like an alms bowl around the room, dragging his guitar behind him. People fill the hat with coins.

"Every Sunday," Bitter tells me, "Etta lets him into the gut bucket here to do one tune. Act of mercy. Man *used* to be great. Claimed his old axe was made of wood from the last slave ship ever docked in America. Man, he *knew* them field-holler blues." He offers Slim a dollar; I follow suit. A solemn dignity attends the crowd's charity, and for the first time tonight, I sense a warm, admirable community, a fellowship whose embrace I'd happily welcome.

Slim transfers his earnings to his pockets, gathers his equipment, and shambles out the door, letting in a gust of heat and several gray moths. Earl screams into his mike, "Come on *over,* baby!" and the band lurches into a stumbling rockabilly gallop.

It's past one now. Bitter looks tired. He rubs his chest and breathes like a running man. The ladies sip their brandy, sneaking glances my way. People are dancing now, all over the room. Watching them, I realize there are no young men here. Besides me, a few other women, the drummer and the bass player (who look like they'd rather be elsewhere), everyone is well past fifty. Where are the boys? The next generation? The future? I remember the SWAT team this afternoon, rounding up kids on the volleyball court.

Someone mad at God?

The old man dancing solo careens against the crates. A fellow helps him to a chair, gently takes his flask, then orders him coffee. A woman who's been smoking in a corner hacks and gasps. Bitter's buddies are nodding off, catching themselves, shaking their heads. Bitter smiles at me. "Welcome home, Seam." It sounds like a challenge.

I push aside my empty beer bottles, lean across the table, ask him, "How's Ariyeh? When can I see her?"

"She a schoolteacher now. You knew that, right?"

I didn't.

"Have to give her a call. Or you can drop by her school tomorrow. They in summer session. She usually take lunch 'round twelve-thirty or so. How the mud-dauber shack working out?"

"It's fine."

"Not too hot?"

"Not too hot." I want him to know I'm up to his challenge. "Thanks for bringing me here. To this place."

He glances away: the same *I-don't-give-a-shit* the women have affected all night to flirt with Earl. Bitter yells loudly, "Hey man! Give us some of that 'Gallis Pole'!" His breath comes hard and he winces.

Earl turns to his mates, whispers instructions, then the band eases into another old Leadbelly tune. I remember it from Uncle's records, back when I was a girl. When I was someone else entirely. Earl chants breathlessly about needing some silver, needing some gold, anything to keep him from the gallows pole.

A chill slants down my spine. Bitter won't look at me, his way of telling me *I know what you're here for. This is for you.* Earl's voice lunges from beat to beat like the shuffling of shackled feet, and I hear in his mournful rasp all the low-down, dirty fears of a Southern-cursed man. *Dead frogs on a doorstep, 'gators under the house . . . hup, two, three, four . . . Private, that's a white woman there . . . look away, look away, look away . . .*

Keep me from the gallows pole.

I leave several bills on the table for my beer. Bitter half turns when I rise. "Maybe tomorrow we tackle some of them questions you might be ready to ask?"

"Yes," I say, swaying, tipsier than I'd realized.

"Find your way home all right?"

"I think so."

"Don't see nothing, don't say nothing."

His buddies wish me good-night; I push by the old scarecrow, who's sipping oily coffee now. Etta carries a new crate of Coors behind the bar, her back a bent scythe. In the parking lot, my car is hemmed in by two big vans. I try to maneuver between them. A man smoking in the dim-bulbed doorway calls, "You ain't gonna make it, sugar."

I stick my head out the window. "Do you know who owns these?"

"Sure. I go find 'em for you." He slips inside the bar, returns with two drunks. They grumble but move their vans for me. The smoker approaches my door. "You wouldn't have seventy-five cents, would you, so I can get me a new pack of weeds?"

I search my purse. "This is the smallest I have," I say, and hand him a five-dollar bill. "Thanks for your help."

"Damn!" he says, stuffing the five in his jeans. "You have a good night, now." Grateful. Hostile. The white princess in her fine new carriage, treating everyone like property. The good Samaritan who becomes, the instant money changes hands, just another black man begging on the street. *Damn* is right.

I pull away, past the Flower Man's house. Under sodium streetlights, its roses glow like coral. The bottle tree shivers, releasing a low, bluesy moan in the breeze.

———

I wake in the dark, in the mud-dauber shack, sweating and sore-boned. The mattress is sodden. Spiders dabble in the corner. I'd dreamed of the gallows again. Standing on the meadow's fringes, tugging nervously on my gloves, I believed I heard my name from the shackled huddle. "Sarah! Sarah!" I strained to see past the armed guards blocking the folding chairs. A hawk called in the sky. Sun broke through the clouds.

The next thing I knew, the men were shivering on the scaffolding; creaking, the nooses were lowered. A black minister strolled among the prisoners, gently touching their shoulders, asking them if they had any final wishes. No one spoke. Then, at the clergyman's urging, the men said, in unison, "Father, into Thy hands I commend my spirit. Lord Jesus receive my soul."

The dream shifted then. Ariyeh and I were little girls in peppermint nightgowns, sharing a bed. Cletus Hayes stood at the window with a broken, bloody neck. "Niece?" he gurgled. I clutched Ariyeh's hand, whispered, "If I die before I wake / I pray the Lord my soul will take . . ."

AT THREE, I'm awakened again by the heat. I sit up, still a little swirly from the beer. Flitting and buzzing, near the ceiling. I reach for the flashlight: a hoedown of roaches and moths. Groaning, I stand, then nearly trip on my bag. The *Crisis* pokes from its mouth— bold letters heading a lengthy article: "Prize Babies." I pull it out. In the piece, W. E. B. Du Bois urges black families to breed and train a "new, pedigreed Negro": "If we strive earnestly to make our children Puritan in morals . . ." The flashlight flickers; I give it a shake. ". . . there will be no baffling Negro problem a generation hence."

I laugh loudly, sending bugs scurrying toward the corners. Well now, W. E. B., if you'd come with me to the gut bucket tonight, you'd have seen that "breeding" has a lot more to do with lubricant and a good blues groove than love of the race. Look at me. I'm no "Prize Baby." A mix of God knows what, who sure as hell didn't show up with any *pedigree.*

I need to pee. Uncle Bitter said he'd leave the back door open, but I picture myself stumbling over newspapers, records, and chairs, frightening him awake like a visit from the Axeman. So I pull on my clothes, then go squat in the yard behind the mud-dauber shack. Willow limbs whisper above me. Sleek, dark creatures slice the air. Bats? It must be past their bedtime. I wipe myself with a Kleenex, then zip my jeans. Behind Bitter's yard, the alley smells of wet cardboard. I toss the Kleenex over the fence: a ragged line of rotting pine boards. I step through one of the gaps, into the alley, then out to the street. Childhood terror swarms my chest, freezing me. I remember the fascination of the street when I was small. Mama said it was a hazardous place. The passing cars startled me, of course, but thrilled me too with their sharp, metallic colors, their glorious speed. Terror had such power to arouse, and it was so available: look how easily alleys, sidewalks, grassy yards gave way to dangerous lanes. Did this mean that safe and not-safe were really just the same?

My legs tingled, as they do now, whenever Mama took my hand and walked me across hot asphalt on our way to the store. I remember her scolding Ariyeh and me not to "show out" in public whenever we acted up in the market. Other black moms were also strict, *tsk*-ing at Chicano and white kids who "ran wild." This, too, was a pleasurable terror: the core of anger in our usually quiet mothers. Later, in Dallas, Mama remained unshakably strict, a holdover of our "down low" days before she remade us both.

When I went to work for the mayor, I was surprised to learn that remaking wasn't just a black thing—it was as All-American as baseball and flag waving, two activities the mayor wore out during his reelection campaign, my first year on his staff. First pitches. Hitches on star-spangled parade floats. Mama loved these PR displays and appreciated my small part in them. But behind the scenes, the patriotic fanfare gave way to cynical maneuvering, just as smoothly as an alley slopes into a street.

Occasionally the mayor visited the city's "oldest neighborhoods," which offered the "most affordable housing." Everyone on staff understood that when he mentioned old neighborhoods, he meant the black parts of town; "affordable housing" meant project homes. In courting the black vote, he remade himself into a civil rights champion (despite his abysmal record there). His hypocrisy disturbed many of his supporters, but he'd finally come 'round to broadening his constituency, and we figured that was a good thing—even if he was spurred by polls that showed him trailing his opponent among minority voters.

I was stunned one morning when one of his aides ordered me to join the motorcade. My first limo! "Why me?" I asked. "The mayor thinks you might be useful at one or two stops he's scheduled to make." "My specialty is city planning," I protested. "I don't know the first thing about campaigning." "Well, here's your chance to learn."

I wasn't useful at all. For hours, I stood with other staffers as the mayor ate barbecued chicken and watermelon for carefully planned photo ops in an especially picturesque "old neighborhood." He coddled several prize babies. Later, an inner-circle flunky confessed to me the mayor wanted me there after someone had pointed out to him I'd checked "African American" on my job application. "Hell, she doesn't look like one," he reportedly said. "But if she knows the lingo, maybe she can bail me out if I step into a load of crap."

So the paper trail had caught up with me. The rest of the campaign, I had a seat in a limo, three cars behind the mayor, whenever he made a run into "old" Dallas. I never did a thing—what he *thought* I could do, I don't know. He was adroit, deft, and charming, a natural vote-hound. Only once did he speak to me. One afternoon, in a ribs joint on the banks of the Trinity River, he wiped barbecue sauce from his hands so he could dandle a few squealing babies, then leaned close and whispered, "That old cook in the corner, he's seventy-five years old, you believe that? That's what he told me." He nodded at a tall, stooped man smoking a hand-rolled cigarette just inside the kitchen. "He don't look a day over fifty. I swear, blacks wear their age better than white folks do. Me, I look a full ten years older'n I am—no no, don't flatter me, darling, I know it's true." He pulled a squirming girl to his chest. "Hell, this hustling life grinding me down."

I thought of the old adage *Black don't crack*. I'd heard it in high school—football jocks sizing up a buddy's sexy mom—and wondered if I'd inherited a smooth, lingering youth despite my skin color. I also thought of Cletus Hayes, slumped at the end of a rope. He'd be young *forever*. An eternal "Negro problem."

In cuteness and charm, the babies the mayor kissed were all award winners, but you couldn't say their folks were pedigreed. As with the ribs cook, their youthful faces were offset by harsh surroundings, faded clothes, callused hands. Aimlessness. Hopelessness. The mayor wanted their votes, but it was clear he didn't have any solutions to "baffling Negro problems"—chronic poverty, drug use in some of the neighborhoods, the way the black middle class had abandoned its brothers and sisters—and he didn't plan to look for answers. Often, after a day in the projects, he'd attend gala fundraisers and promise his white donors he'd pursue a "Broken Windows" policy in the city's poorest areas, cracking down on vandalism and petty mischief to deter larger crimes.

His cynicism and the smugness of his staff, who regarded the public as lazy kids to be "educated," numbed me. The mayor's girl, I wasn't. Every day I thought of walking off my job. But I also liked belonging to a team, even a corrupt team; I'd been a loner so long. Besides, the campaign season was short. My real job was helping city planners: honest, absorbing work.

One day, a week before the election, the mayor led us to a wasteland in south Dallas, a shambles of crack houses, meth labs, prostitution fronts. He proposed a sixteen million dollar renovation plan, bringing "new energy and opportunity to this traditionally blighted area." He announced support of a development firm that planned to build a huge apartment complex here. Several staffers smirked, assuming this was baloney, easy to ditch once the election was over (the polls had now tipped decisively in the mayor's favor). What they didn't know, and I did, was that this area bordered a soon-to-be-completed freeway, so the land value was bound to increase. I'd examined the documents in the city planning office. Even if the developers simply maintained low-income housing while waiting for the value to peak, the federal government would guarantee them $400,000 a month in subsidies, plus tax credits of over $1.5 million a year. And the mayor sat on the firm's board. In this light, some baffling Negro problems didn't seem so baffling, after all.

I was happy when the votes were counted, the black babies left alone—when my presence was no longer "useful," and I could resume dreaming of better cities.

———

The flashlight wavers again, a weak battery. I shut it off and stand at the alley's edge. Frogs chirp in humid fields nearby. I remember Mama telling Ariyeh and me good-night as frog *chrrs* drifted through open windows, then grew louder, softer, louder, a lulling night cycle. As she stood in our bedroom doorway, did Mama think of me as a "prize"? Mostly, I remember her correcting me as I grew older: "Get that mush out of your mouth. Speak clearly." Or: "Don't slouch like some grumbly ghetto kid. You're better than that."

Speak clearly. Lord. Another alley memory nudges me now. When I was eight or nine, and we'd returned to Houston for a visit, Mama sometimes walked me across here to a falling-down house at the edge of a culvert. There, I'd read to an elderly shut-in. I don't recall her name, just her appallingly large head, her concave temples as though she were a slowly leaking balloon, and her thatch of hair, as fervid as Frederick Douglass's 'fro in those famous sepia pictures of him. As I read aloud— articles from *Time, Ebony, Jet*—Mama sat in a corner of the bedroom (a lemony soap and talcum odor in the doilies, the rug) correcting me when I slipped up, urging me to speak more clearly, enunciate, louder,

louder. Who were these sessions really for, the old woman who needed distraction, or me, who apparently needed lessons in English usage? We were back in the old neighborhood, but this wasn't my old Mama. This was the Dallas matron, the "Northerner," training me to better myself, to shake off musty smells from dingy old rooms, to learn the rules of language and proper bearing. In the green-gold afternoon light, stream-ing through dirty windows past water-damaged curtains, Mama's face was as delicately stern as a piece of hand-painted china, beautiful but precise in a predictably strict way that diminished its loveliness. Even when she smiled she seemed on the verge of terror, as I did, facing the street. What did she fear? That I'd never learn to enunciate clearly? Or was she reliving her own girlhood, gazing at me, the lessons that took, the ones she ignored? What traps was she still trying to flee, through me?

We weren't alone with the grand old dame. By an old chifforobe, in a spoke-backed chair covered with a simple cotton quilt, a boy sat day after day, maybe fourteen or fifteen. I don't know who he was or what he was called. The old woman's nephew? Grandson? I must have been told these things, but they're lost to me now. He'd pull the quilt around his shoulders—though the room was a sweatbox—and watch my lips as I read. His stare was like the looking-at Ariyeh and I got from the old men when we walked home from church, a gaze that said *I want to do things to you,* and it made me feel both powerful and afraid. Look how I can make a boy set his jaw, I thought, fix his eyes on me, feverish, raw, but what else might he do if Mama weren't here? She saw this silent exchange, and it gave her even more to dread, I'm sure—reminded her, perhaps, of her own buzzy stirrings, her first longings, in the bayou heat. Is that why we finally stopped calling on the old woman? Did Mama not want me to connect Houston's swelter with the curious warmth just starting to prickle between my legs? Did she hope the old neighborhood would hold for me no romance?

If she caught me sloe-eyed on my bed, my hand drifting lazily down my belly, she'd tell me to sit up, get busy, do something useful. At night, I'd often dream of being smothered in one of her quilts, and I'd wake, gasping, then slip out of bed, careful not to stir Ariyeh. At least twice that I recall, I walked out to the alley, right to the edge of the chancy street, and sat in the dark, imagining the shut-in boy, as I thought of him, finding me here. I got goosebumps wondering what would happen if he did. I sat in the dirt, in my slippers and peppermint gown, rocking, rocking, my forearm stiff between my legs.

Now, I slide down the hot, dry culvert and cross a brambly lot. The old woman's house is gone. I never saw the boy again. Soon after the summer-of-reading-aloud, Mama stopped bringing me back to Houston.

Frog clicks. Crickets. Grackles, not bats. I sit in a damp patch of grass. The flashlight is dead so I set it aside, breathe deep. I'm sorry I wasn't a prize baby, Mama. I'm sorry I felt what I did in the old lady's room. But see? I've done all right. I've bettered myself. These days, I can read most anything, even boring statistical reports composed for the mayor, transportation plans, and land development codes. I can wear any mask and wear it well. *Black don't crack.*

But those old feelings . . . that lazy, dizzying heat . . . the breathlessness, the buzz . . .

I grip myself, rock in the dark, cover my mouth so all I hear are cricket songs, croaks.

4

U N C L E   B I T T E R wakes me, midmorning, tapping the door with his foot. "Got breakfast, Seam. You dress?"

"Hold on." I scramble from under the sheets, pull on a fresh pair of underwear, some jeans, and a Dallas Cowboys T-shirt. "Come in."

With crusty old oven mitts he's carrying a steaming bowl. He sets it on the floor, returns to the house, and comes back with a teapot and a cookie sheet brimming with soft brown rolls. "Made us some molasses bread and some oatmeal. You girls used to love this stuff, remember?"

I *do:* slow summer mornings, Ariyeh and I would beg to eat breakfast in the backyard—it was usually cooler outside, early in the day, than it was in the house. Uncle Bitter served us on the lawn.

"You ain't gonna win no popularity contests wearing *that,*" he says, pointing with one hand at my shirt, stirring the oatmeal with the other.

"I don't figure I'm going to be very popular around here, anyway," I say, smiling. "A coworker of mine was a finalist for the Cowboys cheerleading squad. She got a handful of promotional clothing and passed it out at work."

"Pretty blonde?"

"No. She was black, as a matter of fact." *Black like me. Day-black.*

"Hm. I only seen pretty blondes when I watch the games on the *tee-vee.*" As he stirs, he watches me comb my hair with my hands. It's shoulder length, straight, and seems to intrigue and appall him, equally.

"I used to get up early in the morning, 'fore you girls was awake, chop the walnuts and the apricots, flake a little coconut, sift the good brown sugar into the oats . . ."

"Where was Mama?"

"Your mama slept in a lot, them days." He pours us some weak red tea. "That where you want to start wit' your questions?"

The oatmeal's earthy smell joins grass and oak bark in the air, mint from Bitter's garden, and the sweet scent of apples from a neighbor's tree. Sunlight pokes through an open knothole in the shed's east wall, lands, parchment colored, on the red flannel nailed above the pillow.

"No. I *do* have lots of questions about Mama—and my dad," I say. "But let's start at the start."

He hands me a roll along with a bowl of oats. We sit cross-legged on the mattress, facing each other. Sparrows are wild in the trees. I notice an empty cicada shell in a corner, brittle as spun sugar.

"*All* the way back? What you know?"

"Mama never told me a thing. Beyond the rape story, I mean."

"*I'da* told you, when you's of an age to truly take it in. But you never come back."

"Mama didn't want—"

"When you reach a certain point, it ain't your mama no more. It was you. *You* decided we wasn't no part of your life."

"You're right. I'm sorry."

He rubs his chest.

"I missed you so much, and Ariyeh, in junior high and high school. When Mama married Mr. Licht, I knew she intended for me to become a good suburban kid. White bread. Well-to-do. I rebelled for a while, claiming my heritage. Reading Maya Angelou." I laugh. "But by the time I got to college—I don't know, maybe it *took,* finally. Mama's pressure. Or maybe I got tired of fighting. Not fitting in. Maybe I opted for the easy way out. I figured, 'I look white. Why not take advantage of that? It's the way to get ahead.' So that's what I did."

"I always worried for you. At war with yourself. It showed in your body, your play. You and Ariyeh be drawing, she churning out one finished picture after another, you rubbing everything out, starting over all the time."

"Start me again, Uncle Bitter. With the gallows. Please."

He sets his bowl on the ground, wipes his mouth with his wide, callused palm. "All right. You know the name Cletus Hayes?"

"Yes sir." I tell him I learned the *official* story from the trial transcripts. I tell him about C's letter and the *Crisis.*

He grins. "So she kept that stuff, did she?"

"Piecing it together, then . . . I figure it *wasn't* rape. Right? Or not exactly. Maybe he forced himself on her *that* night, flushed from the

riot, but . . . I figure Cletus Hayes and Sarah Morgan had a relationship—"

"Fancy talk. They's in love."

I brush bread crumbs from my fingers. "How do you know this?"

"Sahry told me."

"You knew Sarah Morgan?"

He nods.

"And Mama? *Her* blood? Cletus Hayes?"

"In part. From messing with Cletus, Sahry birthed your grandma
Jean—"

"Wait wait wait, Uncle, please. Before begetting and begetting, like
the Bible—"

Bitter raises his hands. "Let me start again. I's working the oil rigs
just outside Texas City. This was '43, '44. Place was booming 'cause of
the war. Oil. Cotton. Chemicals. Lotsa black famblies living there, hir-
ing out for labor. Me and my old lady, Maeve, we move into this tinkery
old building downtown, near dockside."

I'm startled by the mention of his "old lady"; ever since I've known
him he's been on his own. I never even wondered where Ariyeh came
from: a consequence of being plucked too soon from this world. As for
Bitter's own origins, I remember him saying once he grew up in a
"hoodoo alley in the Vieux Carré" before his family moved to Texas.

"At home, I mostly kept to myself after work," he says. "I smelt like
a damn gusher all the time, oil and shit on my hands. I'd scrub and
scrub and seem like I never could shuck that *jelly*-smell. But Maeve,
she's a real go-getter in them days, friendlied-up with everyone in the
building. She's especially close to this pair of comely ladies upstairs.
Didn't have no menfolk around. Both waitressed or something. They's
raising this little eight-year-old girly—whirlwind. I'd hear her clomping
up and down the stairs after supper, screaming to go play in the park."
He sips his tea. "The parks in Texas City was more like abandoned
refineries. 'Stead of a jungle gym, you know, you'd have a cat cracker to
climb on."

I watch spiders weave their webs; I'm impatient for him to return to
the garden. But I learned a long time ago, Bitter has his own pace, spinning stories.

"Wellsir, the day come when the *Grandcamp* caught afire. It was a
French Liberty ship, pretty thing; just pulled into port, hauling cotton,

tobacco, peanuts, twine, guns, and a shitload of ammonium nitrate fertilizer—'bout two thousand tons of it, someone told me later. One of the crewmen noticed a plume of smoke in the hold early one morning, went down and tried to douse it with a jug of drinking water, but no go. The captain ordered the hatch covers sealed, figuring to smother the fire, you know. But the pressure blew the damn covers off. By that time, the volunteer firemen had come, but the poor boat was so het up now, it vaporized the water.

"I 'member I's already manning a rig, edge of town—it's about nine o'clock in the morning—when I heard the *ker-boom,* looked up and saw this smoky ol' mushroom rolling over the port, saw wood and ship's rigging sailing through the air, raining like brimstone on the Monsanto plant and the dockside housing where Maeve was still in bed. I dropped everything, went running right home. Maevey was okay, but the blast had tore off part of the roof, shattered all the pipes. Water spraying like high tide. Real hairy. I stayed home rest of the day, helping famblies rescue their pictures and stuff, cleaning up. The ladies and their eight-year-old scrambled down to our place, 'cause their 'partment was puredee flooded. All day we's patching pipes, clearing wood, and we heard rumors 'bout dockside. Fellas said forty firemen had disintegrated. A hunnert and fifty workers missing at Monsanto. Terrible, terrible. Little girly crying—you could hear her up and down the stairwell, 'long with the *shush* of busted toilets.

"Middle of this unholy mess, no one cottoned to the fact that the *High Flyer,* another Liberty ship docked in port, was also stocked with nitrate. And sulfur. It had come through the blast all right—or so everyone figured. We was wrong.

"Long story short: middle of the night, Texas City become an inferno. Flames, wood, steel rushing our way from the water like a windstorm from Hell. Oil tanks popping all over town and up and down the coast. Quarter of the city perished that night. Ashes and bone.

"Maeve and I scurried out the building, rubbing sleep from our eyes, stairs tumbling right behind us. She's squeezing the girly to her chest. But them other two ladies, who'd sacked out on our floor, bless them, we never saw them again."

He stops, presses his chest with his fingertips like a man playing accordion, then spoons more oatmeal for himself.

"So that's when we move into Freedmen's Town," he says. "I went to work for a carpentry shop, Maevey kept our home till the cancer got her in '59. She raised the girly, which weren't easy, let me tell you. Fire put the fear of Hell into that poor little soul. She'd wake middle of the night, screaming like she's scorched."

He sticks his spoon into his mouth and holds it there. The shed is getting hotter as the sun lifts. My patience is melting away. I get up, open the door, pull the towels back from the windows. "I'm confused, Uncle Bitter. What does all this have to do with—"

"Your mama," he says, placing the spoon in his bowl, fanning his fingers over his heart. His shirt is so thin, I can see his darkness beneath it. "That little flame-frightened girly."

I stand, staring down at him. Bees flit against the windows.

"Them ladies that perished. Sahry Morgan and your grandma Jean. I didn't know them well as Maevey did, but I'd sit with them sometimes on the stairs, drinking lemonade late in the evening, you know. I's embarrassed around them, smelling so bad like I did all the time, but they's easy enough with me, eventually, to tell me a thing or two." He straightens his legs. "Now, I don't know the particulars, you understand, but I *can* tell you Sahry was on the outs with her fambly 'cause she decided to go ahead and keep the baby."

"Cletus Hayes's baby?"

"That's right. Jean."

"Did she talk about Cletus?"

"Not much. I cain't tell you whether she got knocked up, riot night, or whether she's already carrying. She'd been seeing Cletus on the sly since the soldiers first come to town."

"She told you this?"

"She did."

I slide back onto the mattress, rumpling the sheet. A spider catches a ladybug, just above the door. In my research into Cletus's background, I'd discovered in the archives of the Texas Freedman's Bureau a claim by an ex-slave named Leticia Hayes. Her boy, Cletus, had been taken from her by a wealthy white man, a cotton baron north of Houston. The Freedman's Bureau was established after the Civil War so sundered families could locate one another. Mostly, it tried to help women find their kids. Leticia Hayes's claim is dated August 1868—an earlier Cletus. But there's more. She swears her son was stolen and whisked away to an East

Texas cotton plantation while she was forced to remain in the city as a domestic aide.

The bureau *did* locate him and issued a written order for the boy's release. The very next day, however, it authorized his holder to keep Cletus in return for the "young man's continuing care, culture, and education." I found no reason for the reversal and no further mention of Leticia Hayes. The state of Texas denied her fifteen hundred dollar reparation claim. I'm guessing she died of grief. Or hunger, if she couldn't provide for her boy. Could *this* Cletus be the soldier's father? Most members of the Twenty-fourth Infantry were recruited up north, but Private Hayes was a Houston native. Riot trial transcripts confirm this, though they say nothing else about his background.

Another thing: Leticia Hayes's son was bound over to a man named Morgan. Son of a slave, then? At home in the old stomping grounds? Feeling his oats? This is the figure I'd patched together, *my* Cletus: a badly made quilt.

I ask Bitter, "Was Cletus's father a slave on the Morgan farm, before they moved to town?"

He shakes his head. "I know squat about Cletus 'cept he didn't rape nobody. That was Sahry's fambly, embarrassed by their daughter, looking for someone to blame. She told me Cletus was trying to leave her, and she was pissed about it."

"Why did he want to break things off?"

"Cain't answer that."

"Why did she decide to keep the baby?"

"Don't know that, neither, Seam."

My forehead is sweating. "And my grandma? Jean?"

"Jean struck me as a lost young lady, tell you the god's honest truth. She had that light skin, like your mama and you. Flirted with all the boys in the building—found her exotic, I guess."

I grip my knees.

"Well. Lord knows who your mama's father was. Some roughneck in the oil fields."

"Black?"

"We didn't mix with no whites. 'Cept Sahry. Poor ol' misfit, shoved out on her own." He reaches for the teapot and winces. His hand shakes, and he sits back, wheezing.

"Are you all right, Uncle Bitter?"

"Getting old, that's all."

"What is it?"

"Damn chest squeezing me lately." He rubs his elbow.

"Is the pain in your arm, too?"

"I don't need no nurse."

"Uncle, those are heart symptoms—"

"On'iest thing wrong with my goddam heart is it's *broke,* way your mama run from us." He reaches again for the pot, pours himself some tea, and sips it sullenly. I'm ashamed that, along with concern for him, I feel a spike of resentment: after caring so long for Mama, then coming all this way, now I've got to care for *Bitter* too? He's supposed to watch after *me.* Another shameful thought: like the "uncle" routine, pain is expected of him, so of course he displays it. He's *always* provided what's called for. And to an extent, that's really what's paining him now, I think—the confines of a ready-made identity. Watching his fingers and the gnarled veins in the backs of his hands, I realize for the first time I've never seen him as a *man,* or as a worker, a father. He's always been just "Uncle" to me, always one of the "old ones." I've taken him for granted, yes; on the other hand, as a child, I thought certain old men, like Bitter, were the only men of feeling. They were the only people I trusted. Unlike the boys I saw, most of them didn't drink in the middle of the day (Bitter was an exception). They actually listened and talked. They carried hankies in their pockets and were quick to offer one if you cried. They went to church. They knew amazing skills: carpentry, plumbing.

He looks better now.

"Do you want to stop?" I say.

"Go ahead. Ask."

"You're sure?"

"Seam—"

"Not if you're—"

"Goddammit, girl—"

"Okay, okay. Mama."

"What about her?"

"She ran because of my father? Something to do with a man?" I watch the rhythm of his breathing.

"That's what we figgered. She never did say directly." He's still wheezing. "She's awful unhappy here. Missed Maevey something fierce. I married again for a short spell—Ariyeh's ma—woman name Cass. You 'member her?"

"No."

"Neither does Ariyeh, much. Both too young when she left. Your mama and Cass never did square with each other."

"And my dad?"

He sits up on his knees, kneading his calves. His joints creak. "You want it all at once, do you?"

"Your answers just leave me with more questions."

"It's always gonna be that way. You know that."

"Please."

"It's hard for me to talk about your dad."

"Why's that?"

He scratches his head. "Jim Clay Washington was his name." Simple. Flat. The awful secret all these years. Just a pair of words, *Jim Clay*, a couple of lost buttons in the dust beneath a bed. Damn it, Mama, what was so hard about two words? "Worked as a wildcatter, played the juke joints at night. I didn't like him when he first come sniffing around Helen. Real arrogant manner. I come to see, later, he's mostly bluff. Scared puppy, like the rest of us. Scared of the Man. Scared of being poor. He had some greatness in him as a singer. Frittered it all away. Booze and such. You know. The old story."

"Did he play at Etta's?"

"Sometime."

"He met Mama there?"

"Might have."

"They never married?"

"No."

"And I was just a mistake. A bottle baby."

Bitter squeezes my hand. "He run off about the time Cass did. I wish I had more to tell you."

"Why don't you like to talk about him?"

"It's just painful for us all. 'Specially Helen. She stuck around awhile, helping me raise Ariyeh and you. Then she up and took you north."

I snort. "She was going to better herself."

"No. Well, sure. But she wasn't like the others who left once they got a little money or once the white-owned businesses started moving in and taking over. You know"—a rueful laugh—"we used to have high standards around here. You could 'better yourself' 'thout leaving home. But since the integration and such, that's all been lost. Pride in the *neighborhood* been lost. Anyways, your mama, she was running *sad,* like she knew no 'betterment' could save her. At first, I talked her into visits—mostly for you kids, pining for each other so. Then: nothing. Till you show up two days ago."

"I'm sorry, Uncle Bitter." I pause. "Can I still call you Uncle?"

"We fambly, Seam. Not by blood, maybe, but by circumstance. I don't know about you, but I look around, all I *see* is circumstance."

I smile. "Thank you for breakfast."

"You get what you come for?"

"Like you said, there'll always be more questions." I pull my damp T-shirt away from my skin. "And I don't really *know* what I came for. A break in my routine, maybe." *Running sad,* I think. *Damn straight.*

"How'd you start trailing Cletus?"

"In college, I tried to study the Houston riot. There wasn't much on it anywhere. Finally, from a federal records center, I got hold of the trial transcripts . . . all I knew from Mama—*her* version of things—was that a black soldier had raped my great-grandma. I knew she wasn't telling me everything. I figured that incident, whatever its truth, had to be the beginning of *me.* The black and the white." My head spins from the heat—and the news Bitter has brought me. Suddenly, I need to go. To be on my own for a while. "I have a lot to chew on, Uncle."

"That you do."

"If you don't mind, I think I'll take a drive. Then I'll stop by and see Ariyeh."

"You okay, Seam?"

"Yeah. You? Your chest?"

"Healthy as a radish. How long you got here? Your Sabbath-leave?"

I stand and reach for my purse. "I don't really know. I took a month off from work, but I hadn't given it much thought . . . why?"

"I's just thinking it's good to see you."

I nod. Opening the door, I catch a red flash. "Uncle, what's that flannel for? Nailed to the wall?"

"Wards off hurt. My buddies who sleep here—fellas at Etta's—they feeling, you know, pretty *hurt* most the time."

"I thought maybe you were trying to get rid of me." I grin at him.

"Hell, I already *been* rid of you, girl. You'd think I'd throwed a black chicken over your head. *That's* how you chase folks off." He laughs, wheezing. "When I's a boy, to make the cats come home, we used to spoon sugar into they mouths every morning, then make 'em look in the mirror. They's back at sunset, never fail. I gotta do that to *you?*"

I bend and kiss his forehead. "I'll be home this evening. I'll go shopping and bring us some supper, okay?"

"I be jinks swing!" He kisses my hand. "Might be I could get used to you being here, Chere."

———

Noon sun, reflecting off law firms and banks, ripples past power lines. I adjust my visor. The skyscrapers' windows are magnifying lenses focusing heat onto tiny rental homes. I pass a landfill—"Mount Trashmore," Uncle used to call it, "one of Houston's few hills"—seething with flies next to an elderly woman's house. She's rocking in a porch swing as if meditating on rotting paper, food, clothes.

A city bus chuffs past the cemetery. Its roundness reminds me of a barbecue grill, passengers sizzling like ribs inside. The buses in Dallas seem bigger, nicer, cleaner than these, and I think, *I'm back in the South now, where a bus is not just a bus, but a ghost of the old social order.*

And I think of Bitter's patter, his stories and jokes: if it *was* all a mask at first—now hardened into flesh—who could blame him for hiding behind it? Whites didn't feel threatened by an "uncle"; in our own community, old men and uncle types were second only to babies in the amount of affection they received from the women.

As for his "hoo-raw," his tale of my family, twisted and murky as the bayou, the more I ponder it, the more I lose it. Bitter used to take me to the water, hold my hand on the bank, grab a stick and point out catfish and carp, wriggling among algae, paper cups, hubcaps, and broken toasters dumped into the stream. I'd glimpse the fish then lose them, never sure if I'd seen or imagined them.

It's like that now, with my family.

In this part of town, weeds, moisture, and heat gnaw concrete and wood, and you can see the hellish swamp this really is without motors and steel, pulleys, glass, and Our Blessed Lord and Savior, central air-conditioning. Uncle once told me Mexicans and Negroes cleared the land because whites couldn't have survived the mosquitoes, malaria, snake bites, and dirty water involved in erecting the city.

Now, billboards and buildings form flimsy, elaborate masks covering the chaos, ready to suck us down if we stand too still—a precariousness I've known all my life. Bitter may have adopted a safe routine; I've stayed camouflaged too. In college, freshman and sophomore years, I masked myself as wealthy, white, partying on the weekends, studying on the run. I'd received an academic scholarship to Southern Methodist in Dallas, one of the state's most expensive private schools, pleasing Mama no end (if the Affirmative Action officers, whose files listed me as African American, had ever seen me, they would have accused me of running a scam). Classes were easy and boring, until one term in English the teacher assigned us Ralph Ellison's *Invisible Man.* "Ellison once wrote, 'Whatever else the true American is, he is also somehow black.' What did he mean by that?" the instructor, a young Bostonian with an Irish accent, asked.

A limber blonde, who always annoyed me, preening in the back row, drawled, "'Cause we're all human beings, okay, when you get right down to it. We're not all that different. We all, like, fall in love and stuff."

"Bullshit," said Keshawn Jackson, the only obvious black pupil in the class, one of the few minority males on campus not riding an athletic scholarship. "What's the most you ever suffered, dear? When your mama snatched away your charge card?"

Both these answers were lazy, too easy, mired in stereotypes, but they had the effect on me of sniper fire. I sank in my seat. Keshawn reminded me of my old crush, Troy, intense, argumentative, rough around the edges. He'd shaved his head—before M. J. had popularized the style—and he looked exotic, sleek, a little dangerous. Was his baldness a slap at the fat afros of the seventies? A logical next step for someone seeking distinction?

"Anyway, Ellison's just a house nigger," Keshawn growled. He enjoyed tweaking the ofays. "He wants to be part of the American tradition, right? Twain, Hawthorne, Melville, James, T. S. Eliot, for Christ's sake—he's sucking Jim Crow's dick. 'Yessir. Okay, sir. I'll write it the way you say.' It's bullshit. A black novelist, if he's going to tell us anything new about ourselves, has got to *tear down* the tradition, blow it up and start over from a fresh perspective."

"So then . . . what? You'll have anarchy? That doesn't help anybody," said a usually quiet kid up front.

"Gotta start somewhere, pal."

"Maybe we live closer to anarchy than we think," the teacher said, trying to focus the talk. "Listen. Ellison also wrote, 'The Civil War is still in the balance, and only our enchantment by the spell of the possible, our endless optimism, has led us to assume that it ever really ended.'"

By now, I had learned to read *ideologically*, as Troy had asked me to do, but I was no longer seeking my heritage. I was after acceptance and success—a quick, easy out, away from Mama toward independence and peace of mind. That meant White Lane, right down the middle. It meant rejecting Maya Angelou and Nikki Giovanni. It meant masking myself, which was simple for me. Keshawn had no idea that, behind my rouged sorority face, I knew exactly what Ellison was up to. I'd caught the blues pacing in his sentences, the serious mockery. Still, I got Bs on the two short papers I wrote on the book; I wasn't about to give myself away, a peasant here in Paradise. Like my classmates, I tried just hard enough to get through the course.

At first, the sororities on campus weren't interested in me, not because they suspected my race, but because I was quiet, shy, not a quick joiner. My short hair and angularity gave me a "bit of a masculine thing"—several dorm-mates told me this, trying to "help" me. Finally, a girl whose ass I'd saved once or twice, aiding her with her calculus homework, invited me to the Tri Delt house. I wound up pledging, declaring myself a business major with a minor in marketing: the Yellow Brick Road to America's soul.

I wasn't the only one compromising for purely pragmatic reasons. One day, in one of my marketing classes, a pretty black girl told us she'd had a rib removed so she could be thinner; she was "going the beauty pageant route" so she could parley her winnings and attention into a career as a TV personality, maybe as a news anchor or a talk show host. "This isn't vanity," she insisted. "It's a business decision. Being beautiful is the only way a woman can make it in television—especially a black woman." Fiercely, the class debated her strategy, the selling of her beauty, her skin. "What's the difference between what you're doing and what a stripper does or a hooker?" a shocked boy asked. The girl just smiled, and I thought, She's tougher than I am. I was too intimidated to approach her after that, though initially I'd hoped we might be friends.

Surviving as a Tri Delt took tremendous energy, a cynical edge

cloaked as wit about trivial matters (in the house, concern over anything serious was "way *not* cool"). I hated my sisters' records—Fleet-
wood Mac, Pink Floyd—plodding, dippy music, overly earnest without
a whiff of irony or self-awareness, dead water compared with the *rush* of
the blues (though in those days, Mama's good little girl, I didn't allow
Uncle Bitter to muddy my thoughts).

By junior year I was exhausted, maintaining the act. One day, after
physics class, I found a quiet corner of the Meadows Museum on campus, a dimly lit gallery full of Goya's *Caprichos,* wild pen-and-ink drawings of twisted creatures. The sketches were too disturbing to lure many
viewers; the room was almost always deserted, and I started going there
each afternoon, sitting and reading, hiding out, the way I used to escape
to the junior high restroom.

The museum catalog said that Goya, when he made the *Caprichos,*
was fascinated by a Swiss theorist named Johann Kaspar Lavater, who
insisted that an individual's moral nature is shaped by his physical fea-
tures. A "degenerate" lower jaw was a sign of "brutal corruption"; a
"slavish devotion to pure reason" could lead to a "warped and bony forehead." In this, I heard echoes of Bitter's bayou superstitions, as well as
more sinister strains of genetic engineering and racial typing. Still, for
all their horror, Goya's sketches were madly funny. My favorite was a
drawing of two stumbling sleepwalkers hoisting braying asses—*I get it!*
I thought. *Man's donkeylike behavior! I* know *this stuff!*

In a history class that year, I learned that Spain, where Goya lived,
was a blend of both European and African influences, a bastard mix, a
slumgullion. Maybe that's where Goya's turmoil came from—why I was
so attracted to his work. I liked history classes so much, I switched
majors. This didn't please Mama or my stepdad, who disdained the
"impractical" liberal arts. By this time, tired of the Tri Delt house, bored
with three-chord rock and roll—bored with *myself*—I began, at last, to
think once more of the past, to smell, in memory, the bayou's sweet,
compelling rot. I pressed Mama again about our flight from Houston,
her aversion to blacks, the blackness in herself. I wanted to know about
Sarah Morgan. One day her husband Dale yelled at me to "leave your
poor mother alone, can't you? Christ, you'd think you'd want to live in
Queen City"—a poor, inner-city neighborhood—"instead of enjoying
the good things here. Your daddy couldn't have given you a life like this.
You know that, don't you?"

Aggravated by Mama's silence, I sought my answers at school. Sarah Morgan. Insubordinate soldiers. Eventually, these threads led me to the Houston race riot. I became obsessed with it and would have remained a history major if the professors hadn't discouraged me. Women weren't really welcome in the profession. I saw this in subtle games of intellectual one-upsmanship at socials. Men competed for the big prizes—the American Revolution, the Civil War, the New Deal—animals fighting over meat. African American history barely surfaced on campus—the field's few black scholars had earned their degrees at obscure institutions and were forced to spend most of their careers overworked in the classroom, woefully underpaid.

When I proposed writing on Houston history for my favorite teacher, he looked at me skeptically. "There's no collective memory in that city," he said finally. "It's been in such a hurry to grow, ever since its founding, it hasn't bothered to retain its past. It only cares about *Tomorrow*. I'm afraid 'Houston history' is an oxymoron."

He was right. Records from Houston's past had often been sloppily kept, misplaced, eaten by bugs, burned up, thrown out. The city's heat and humidity were natural enemies of paper, where much of history resides. In researching the place, I kept running into silence. It was eerily like talking to Mama.

In the end, I stuck with business and marketing, reading history on my own in the Goya room, surrounded not by short-ribbed TV beauties, but by humpbacks, birdmen, cannibals eating angels, children with hoary, feathered bodies. Slumgullions, all. I felt at ease with them. Happy. Since my freshman English class, Ralph Ellison's blues-prose had spun, flashing, in my head, and I returned to him now, this time studying his essays, his concern that "practically missing from America . . . since *Huckleberry Finn*" was a "search for images of black and white fraternity."

One day I ran across this phrase: "The American Negro [has an] impulse toward self-annihilation and 'going-under-ground.'" The words brought tears to my eyes, unexpectedly. I looked up at one of Goya's grotesques, a tortured creature writhing on the earth, and this time, instead of seeing myself, I recognized poor Mama, running, frightened, stumbling from her past.

———

On our visits back to Freedmen's Town, she walked with me down

magnolia-shaded roads or past pecan trees on the far side of the cemetery. She didn't talk much but seemed content to be with me. Web-
worms spun silk, patterned like musical staves, among the leaves. On
the hottest days, worms dropped, shriveled, from the limbs: old lady
fingers. People crushed them underfoot, accidentally, until the walks
were slick with chili-like paste. I didn't mind. I loved being with Mama.

Silk waves in the oaks today in front of Ariyeh's school. The neighborhood has been bulldozed and burned to near-extinction. An old
man in a hooded jacket—he must be broiling!—pushes an empty shopping cart past the campus. On the playground, three girls stop to whisper about him, staring and laughing, then resume their game. Closer, I
see they're using TV cable as a jump rope. Garbage bags flap in broken
windows on the building's second floor. An inspection sheet taped to
the wall near a boarded-up basement door says, "NO ACCESS TO BUILD-
ING HERE," and the remaining safety form is blank. A third- or fourth-
grade boy saunters past me, puffing on a plastic inhaler, wrestling a
backpack almost as big as he is. As they skip rope, the girls chant, "SSI,
SSI / Give it to Granny / So Granny won't die!" I'm astonished. SSI is a
federal program for the sick and disabled, and just about everybody—
including these laughing girls, it seems—knows it's worthless. Last
month, a woman who mistook my office for one of the social service
outlets burst in, yelling, "How sick you gotta be to get on SSI? I've had
AIDS for six months now, and the bastards still won't cut me a check!"

The school's main door gives me trouble. It's metal, painted green,
and sticks near the uppermost hinge. I tug hard, imagining how difficult it must be for a child to budge this thing. What would happen in a
fire? Fungus, old paper in the halls. Kids shuffle through them, quieter
than I would have anticipated, gloomy even. This morning, before I left
the shed, Uncle Bitter told me, "Three kids disappeared there lately,
over a span of six weeks. Ain't been found. Folks worried the Needle
Men is back."

In the sweltering front office I ask for Ariyeh. A big woman fanning
her face with a *Newsweek* ("George W.'s Run for the White House")
points out a cracked, dirty window to a concrete courtyard about the
size of a doctor's waiting room. "There she is, eating her sandwich." The
woman she means is slender, long-armed, in a red dress. Dark as
bookprint. I don't recognize my cousin until . . . yes, yes. Oval mouth.
Small nose, like a thread spool. Talk about a *remake!*

At the courtyard entrance, a sign on the wall says NO SKATEBOARD-ING. Below it, someone has scribbled *No Guns*.

Ariyeh's surprising appearance, along with Bitter's information about my family, has made me shy. We're strangers now, really. Not even real cousins. I'm slow to approach. "Excuse me," I say. "Ariyeh?"

She looks up, startled, and knows me immediately. A pleasure-twitch crosses her lips, tamped down instantly by anger, hurt, resentment? Who has she become in the last fifteen years? What burdens does she carry? "T," she says softly, looking away, setting her cheese sandwich on a square of wax paper in her lap.

"Look at you. You're beautiful," I say.

Wry smile. "Not fat, you mean. I hit a growth spurt around four-teen, sprouted like a dandelion. No more Ugly Duckling."

"You were never an Ugly Duckling."

"*You* haven't changed." A sting. A Needle Man prick. *Maybe some brown shoe polish on your cheekbones, little bit there, would help . . .*

"Uncle Bitter told me I could find you here. Can I sit for a minute?" She moves over, making room on the wobbly concrete bench. Her sweat smells like sage. "I'm sorry to interrupt your lunch."

"What brings you back after all this time?" She's playing it cool, the way Uncle did two nights ago when I showed up on his porch.

"My mama died."

"Yeah, Daddy told me. I guess he got a funeral notice."

"I had them send him one. She left me, you know, with a lot of ques-tions. I needed to be here to study up on them. So . . ." A quiet minute. She nibbles her sandwich. "How long have you been teaching?" I ask.

"Six years."

"You like it?"

"Pays the rent."

"I figured you'd be married with a passel of kids by the time you were twenty. Playing house was always your favorite."

"I'm not married." Another minute. "Got a boyfriend. You?"

"No."

She stamps a cockroach at her feet. Crushed, it keeps crawling away, trailing what looks like sticky coconut. "Your hair's still naturally straight like that?" she says, a little shyly.

"Mostly. In my teens, it thickened up some. Now, it seems to be relaxing again."

"Lucky. 'Round the time I lost my fat, I started going to the hairdresser to get pressed—two, two-and-a-half hours—forty dollars a pop. Daddy wasn't happy about *that,* let me tell you. I tried the snatch-back look for a while, but finally the chemicals turned everything into, like, these gnarly old plaits, so I gave up."

"It looks lovely."

She pats her short curls. "You're one of those women who, late at night in the clubs, makes the rest of us crazy," she says. "In the heat, when all our 'dos have wilted and fallen flat, you're still just perfect."

A tall girl in overalls comes running up to us. In *her* hair, a plump yellow scrunchie. She eyes me suspiciously, then whispers to Ariyeh, but not so softly I can't hear, "I be having my periot now, and the *Ko*teck thingy in the bat'room is *broke.*"

Ariyeh reaches into her big leather bag, produces a tampon with an applicator. The girl grabs it, greedily, then hurries off. "Fourth grader," Ariyeh says.

"You're kidding. How old is she?"

"Thirteen. We stopped social promotions here a few years ago, so some of these kids stay stuck."

A grackle lands in the courtyard, plucks at the gooey bug. In its throat, the bird makes a leaky air hose sound.

"Uncle told me you've lost some kids lately."

"Three. All boys. Ten-year-olds." She bites into an apple, talks as she chews. "Police checked all the unguarded construction sites in the area, the crack houses, vacant lots. Nothing."

"Needle Men?" I smile, though as soon as I've said it, I know it's in bad taste.

Of course she won't share the humor. Or memories of our childhood on Bitter's lap. "If Reggie—my boyfriend—ever heard Bitter spinning that tale, he'd hit the roof. He doesn't have any patience for superstition or folklore. I guess I don't either, anymore."

I decide not to tell her I passed the Flower Man's house last night and thought of us. A man in a gray custodian's uniform fast-walks through the courtyard, scolding a boy for apparently setting fire to paper in a trash can. "Send you to boot camp, boy, how you like that?"

Ariyeh balls up her lunch bag. "I need to get back."

"Ariyeh."

She stands, then turns to me, waits.

"Ariyeh, I'm sorry I didn't stay in better touch. I know Bitter thinks I was being a snob. Maybe you do, too. I was just . . . my mama didn't want me to . . . anyway, anyway, I missed you. I thought about you a lot."

She taps the bag against her thigh. It sounds like a torn tambourine. "I didn't think you were being a snob," she says softly. "I just thought you were being *white*."

I look at my hands. My very pink palms. Then Ariyeh starts to laugh. I stand, smile nervously. I laugh with her, slowly at first, finally in great, sobbing waves of relief. I want to hug her, but she doesn't look ready for that. She *is* beautiful. And dignified. "How long are you going to be here?" she asks.

"A few days, at least. Right now I'm staying with Uncle, but I may give him a break and move to a motel."

"I'll stop by. Maybe you can meet Reggie."

"I'd like that." She squeezes my arm. "Ariyeh," I say, grasping her hand. "How well do you remember my mama? If you don't mind me asking?"

She chews her lower lip. "Pretty well. I remember she always seemed sad to me."

"She never talked to you about my daddy, did she?"

"No."

"What do you remember about your own mother?"

"Cass? I remember her yelling all the time. That's all."

"What about?"

"Anything. Everything."

I nod and let her go. She disappears behind a big metal door, catty-corner to the one I came through, in a wall scored by scorch marks. Green fungus mottles a window frame next to the door; with nail polish, someone has painted on the glass "Uh-*Huh*." Two boys, about ten, with sneakers as big as banana floats, pass through the courtyard, glancing at me, snickering.

———

In the Safeway parking lot, as I'm loading my trunk with grocery bags, a car passes palpitating to a rap beat. I turn, expecting black teenagers. Instead, two white boys in a brand-new BMW cruise with the windows down, thrashed by the tune in their speakers.

Bitter isn't home, so I unload our supper supplies, snatch a beer, and walk across the street to the cemetery. Sunflowers, snapdragons, and hollyhocks curl around headstones of mothers, fathers, children, baseball players, street singers, salesmen. The snapdragons smell like ashtrays. I remember picking flowers for Mama as a girl. She never thanked me for them; she'd take them from my hands with a seriousness that indicated she deserved this lovely tribute. *Maybe some brown shoe polish on your cheekbones, little bit there . . .* the day Ariyeh suggested this to me (some boys, passing Bitter's yard, had laughed at me), I bawled fiercely. Mama, stirring chicken soup on the stove, said, "Go pick me some flowers. Hurry up now." When I came back, she arranged the roses, lilies, and violets in a jar, poured me a glass of milk, and sat with me at the kitchen table. "Aren't they pretty?" she said, turning the jar around and around. "And they're all different, each attractive in its own unique way."

I knew what she was trying to tell me. "Mama, don't you wish you had darker skin?"

"I most certainly do not."

"Why?"

"Honey, you can spend your life wishing you were someone you're not, and it won't do you a lick of good. Look at Ariyeh. Don't you think she wishes she were as thin as you are?"

"I guess."

"But she's beautiful, too. With her own style, right?"

"But—"

"Sweetie, you don't know how lucky you are. One day you'll recognize the advantages in looking like you do."

Her face sagged. She'd been up at dawn, as she was every day, making hotcakes for Bitter, Ariyeh, and me. Was my daddy ever there? Cass? I don't remember them. Lunch and supper, she was at the stove again. Her straightened hair straggled into her eyes. She was thin as well—probably *too* thin, I think now.

Another evening (just after we'd moved and had returned to Houston for a visit), she was walking home from the store carrying two big bags of food. Fresh vegetables had moistened one of the bags; when she reached the yard, a neighbor dog, a little schnauzer, bounded over to her, startling her. She swung away from him and the bag ripped. She fell to her knees in the dead grass, sobbing—from exhaustion, I realize now. I approached her quietly from where I'd been playing. She didn't ask me to help her. She tried to smile through her tears. "Hello, honey," was all she said. I felt scared, seeing her vulnerable, unhappy. I picked up a cabbage, a carton of eggs (only two had cracked), a spaghetti package. "You're a sweet girl," she said. "That quality's going to get you anything you want in life."

"What do you mean?"

"I mean you won't have to live in a ratty old neighborhood like this when you grow up."

"I like it here. More than Dallas," I admitted.

"You'll do better than this, believe me." She tucked a banana bunch under her arm.

"Ariyeh and me—"

"Ariyeh and *I*."

"—we're going to live in a tent with our husbands and children and be famous."

"For what?"

"Just for having our pictures on magazines."

She frowned at me, balanced a jam jar on her hip. "When's the last time you saw someone who looked like Ariyeh on a magazine cover?"

"I don't know."

"That's right. Remember that."

I didn't know what she meant, and I don't know now where her self-hatred started, or how. The fall from the garden. Shame at her own naked self, leading to her long rest, too soon, under a headstone just like one of these.

And my *own* shame? Recalling the girl today who needed a tampon, I remember sitting in my Dallas bedroom, cramping, trying to read the Modess box while Aretha sang on the radio, "R-E-S-P-E-C-T. . . ." I longed for Ariyeh then. Was the same thing happening to her? This messy flow . . . it wasn't just another fault of mine, was it, a flaw in the package, like my off-kilter skin?

I rise, brush leaves and dirt from my pants, and pick a sunflower for the supper table.

———

Bitter sucks a beer while I sauté onions and garlic in a crusted old pan, maybe the pan Mama used at this very same stove. Robins chortle in the trees, and I miss my parrots; dogs bark, children shout. The garlic quashes the old-bathrobe smell floating through the house. Bitter's put jazz on the phonograph, slow, sad piano, something I don't recognize. Sunset, filtered through bumps and flaws in the kitchen's thick window, is a pink-purple patch on the dirty yellow wall.

"So. You give Ariyeh a heart attack, showing up out the blue?"

I smile, drain the vegetable oil, add soy sauce and a teaspoon of sesame oil to the pan. "She's looking good. Tough job, though."

"'Bout all she can do with them kids is keep them off the streets a while—which they're gonna end up there, anyways. Some of them pretty smart, I guess. But they ain't going nowhere—less'n their mamas just up and move them out."

I let that pass. "Still, you must be proud of her."

"I am." He picks at the label on his bottle. "That Northern mayor of yours. He put any money in the colored schools? You know, we hear y'all *enlightened* up North."

"I hate to tell you, Uncle, but Dallas isn't far from here. In spirit, as well as space."

He laughs. "Tell you the truth, sad as it made me, I didn't blame Helen for sneaking you out of here. Look what she done for you. You a educated girl. Self-possess. Good job. Nice car. Hell, she done the right thing. Shoulda takened Ariyeh with her."

"Ariyeh's done just fine." I slice a catfish fillet into checkerboard squares, then lay the squares in the marinade. I boil water for frozen peas, start the rice.

Groaning, Uncle Bitter rises from his chair, walks to a scarred oak hutch. From a shelf he plucks an object, then comes and puts an arm around my shoulder. He shows me a red card, old, softened now almost to the texture of paper. Its corners have crumbled away. Faded, typed letters say, "Nigger—stay away from the polls." "Nineteen forty-eight," Bitter says. "Our second year here in Freedmen's Town. One morning a prop plane come buzzing over our streets, dropping these cards by the thousands. Bloody snow. You best believe I didn't vote that election. None of us did. We knew what it took to keep a roof over our heads, in peace. So Henry Wallace had to do without us." He taps the card on his fingernails. "Things improve some over the years, little by little, but by the time you and Ariyeh born, we still didn't have no library in this area, other than Buck Jackson, the barber's, paperback collection, which he lent out to folks from the back of his shop. What I mean is, yeah.

Ariyeh done well, all right. She a hard-working gal, smart as a whip. But it's all been *in spite of.* You know what I'm say'n? What you got, when your mama move you north, Ariyeh got *in spite of.*"

"I know," I say. I pour vegetable oil into a fresh pan, slide the fish in, and cook it over high heat. "But I lost something, too, Uncle Bitter. You and Ariyeh. After a certain point, yes, it was my choice—okay, I admit that—but by that time I'd been taught I was someone else, not the little girl who'd started to grow up here. It was hard to keep thinking independently. I didn't know how to *act* around black people anymore—not that I ever learned how to act around *whites.* Can you grab us a couple of forks? We're ready here."

We settle at the table and I light a candle. "I lost whatever chance I might have had to find my daddy while I could."

Bitter nods. He says, "This sure is nice, Seam. I ain't et this fancy since Maevey died," and we eat our meal quietly, awkward at first, then relaxed. He chews in a rapture. As we're finishing up, I ask him about his childhood in the French Quarter. "Is that where you first learned to appreciate good food—and gris-gris?"

"Sure enough." He swipes a napkin across his lips. "We lived in a little oyster-shell alley back of St. Ann Street, where the ol' hoodoo queen Marie Laveau used to live. My mama said she 'membered rich white folks pulling up in their carriages middle of the night, asking Marie for love potions." He leans back and picks his teeth with a finger. "First job I ever had was hanging outside the produce warehouses down by the river, stealing spoilt 'taters and onions. The shippers threw them away, see. I'd cut off the spoilt parts and sell them to restaurants for a nickel apiece or to the old ladies in the neighborhood, who always had 'em some incense burning on an altar. I learnt a lotta spells making my rounds." He laughs. "Back then, I thought the height of success was to be a street crier. I 'member the watermelon man coming 'round early in the morning, shouting,

I got water with the melon, red to the rind!
If you don't believe it, just pull down your blind!
I sells to the rich.
I sells to the po'.
I'mone sells to that lady
standing in the do'!

"When I's a little older, I graduated to selling coal off a wagon. We'd go to Storyville—all the red-light ladies slinking 'round the doorways, freezing they asses, wearing them teddies, you know. Needed coal for they cribs, burn it down to ash. Lots of *them* practiced the hoodoo, too. And we'd sell to the gin joints. The Funky Butt Club, where Buddy Bolden played. And I 'member hearing Satchmo for the first time when he's just a pup—*lots* of good hot air. You know Satchmo?"

"Sure. Axeman's Jazz?"

He grins. "We called him Dippermouth them days, he had such a wide ol' smile."

"So you really believe in those spells?"

He looks confused or offended. Or both. "'Course I do, Seam. I seen 'em work. There used to be a ghost on St. Ann Street. I swear. I seen her—hollow eyes, snowy hair. She'd hang out on the steps of the old opera house and, at night, disappear into a rooming place over to St. Ann and Royal. One of the ladies I sold 'taters to told me this particular haint was a woman who'd kilt herself after finding her man with a lover. She rose from the grave one night, snuck into the lovers' room, and turned on the gas, 'phyxiating 'em both. The lady who told me this, I went with her one afternoon, right into the haunted room. She had her some goofer dust and sprinkled it all over the place. None of us ever saw that ol' ghost again."

I pour him another beer. He sits quietly now. Whether or not his tales are even remotely true, he has a past he can call on, I think. Maybe that's what Cletus Hayes means to me. Whatever the reality of his relations with Sarah Morgan, whatever his connection to me, I can make him my personal ghost, a badge here in a community haunted by tragic luck. I squeeze Bitter's hand.

After rinsing the dishes we sit in the yard near the mud-dauber shack, splitting another beer. Stars spackle the sky. "If you're thinking of staying awhile, maybe it's time you move inside," he says. So. My probation's over. "Shack's good for a night or two, but it ain't no long-term deal."

"I was considering a motel—"

"Hush. I got a big, fat couch in there."

It's not all that big, but I thank him anyway.

"*If you black, stay back; if you brown, stick around; if you white, you right,*" Bitter says. "That's a saying we used to have here, kind of a joke on how the honkies saw us. Your mama knew it. O'niest explanation she ever give me for why she move." He massages his chest, just below his collarbone. "I think she thought she was gonna save you. And maybe she did, who knows?"

"Well—"

"It took bravery for her to change her whole life, Seam."

"I suppose."

"And maybe you ain't lost all that much, after all. You here now, right? Something I didn't 'member this morning, come to me later. There's a fella knew your daddy real well, name of Elias Woods. Used to hang out at Etta's 'fore he move south of town. I got his address 'cause I done some carpentry work for him once upon a time. Don't have no phone, I know of, but you might want to go see him. Might be he could tell you more'n I can 'bout your pa."

"Wonderful. What's his story?"

"Cain't rightly say. Ain't seen him in years."

I rub my eyes. "While I'm down this way, I'd also like to see the field where Cletus Hayes was hanged. Seems like it's part of *my* story, somehow. Something I ought to witness."

"Pretty grim vacation. You know where it is?"

"I've got a vague idea—though for years the army tried to hide it. A few intrepid historians have managed to pinpoint it, generally."

"Well now, you start using them fancy words, it's time for me to go inside and get that couch ready for you."

I nearly tell him *Enough of the "uncle" routine; you understand my "fancy" words perfectly well,* but I'd only upset him, and I'm not sure it's just a routine, after all. Maybe I'm wrong about that. Not everyone wears a mask.

He sprinkles out our beer dregs. Frogs chirp in the bayou a few miles away. Crickets *treak.* He bends down, pressing his chest, then picks something loose from the lawn: a mistletoe sprig, dropped from a tree. He dangles it over my head, leans close, pecks my cheek. "Glad you here, Seam."

I take his hand. Lord, he's frail. It occurs to me I've returned to Houston too late—when the most tangible link to my past may be about to collapse. "Me too, Uncle Bitter. Thanks."

5

LOCUST TREES throb with cicadas. The city's old grid pattern gives way to the new: the faded remnants of east-west streets poke through grass and weeds, petering out where fresh roads, following the latest commercial lures, tug the city in whole new directions. Driving south through Houston, on my way to find Elias Woods, I'm reminded why I was drawn to city planning, a job that combined my love of history with memories of my first bruised neighborhood.

My first boss used to quote Le Corbusier to me: "Architecture or revolution. Revolution can be avoided," meaning if we build better buildings, we'll shape happier lives. An unfeasible ideal but, as the boss used to say, worth fighting for.

"When's the last time you saw a decent porch?" a planner once asked me. "Your grandma's house, right? Homebuilders nowadays, they don't know a porch from their own patooties." His unfeasible goal was to save Dallas by heralding the second coming of the porch. "I don't know how we'll do it," he said, "but I'll bet we can lock in some porch incentives in the land development code." He sent me out to measure distances between sidewalks and front doors, to count porches or note their absence, to see whether space existed for chairs or a swing . . . he wanted me to research blackberries; he remembered a blackberry vine around his own grandmother's porch and was convinced the plant could humanize our neighborhoods. The first field guide I turned to said "BLACKBERRY: any of various erect-growing perennial brambles that bear black or sometimes whitish fruits." *Black or sometimes whitish:* unlocking that phrase, it seemed to me, was the key to humanizing our cities, but I couldn't explain this to my planner.

I loved doing research at night: passing houses in the dark, seeing the lighted windows, the warm shadows of those inside. The city seemed cozy, then, safe.

One night, I drove through a tired neighborhood across the Trinity River from downtown Dallas. One of the older areas. Skyscrapers blazed like free-standing chandeliers. The air was hot. Frogs *chrr*-ed. The river smelled both fetid and sweet, like apples gone bad. I was counting porches—quite a few over here, though most were ancient and saggy—when something moved on a parked car in the street. I glanced over: a mud-brown owl the size of an open accordion. It swiveled its head to watch me. Eyes yellow as fall leaves. Ruffled air, a soft chop: another owl landed nearby. Then another appeared, settling on a bent, unreadable sign. All around me, feathered beats grew thick as walls; the night became a house of wings. A Goya dream. I felt exhilarated, frightened. The birds called to one another, a chorus so mournful, I thought a sob had escaped the sky. The birds blinked at me as I inched the car down the street. Their calm, after my initial shock at their presence, relaxed me. I didn't feel judged. Or even quite *real*. A piercing detachment suffused their gazes, as though they saw past surfaces. I felt stripped of my body and skin—no bothersome hair, no menstrual spotting to worry about—reduced (in their eyes) to pure, natural movement. I couldn't sustain it, but for a moment I felt more at home in the world than I ever had: a current of light or heat. A pickup turned the corner, loose headlights swaying like dance-floor strobes. The owls scattered.

Now I pass rickety porches, reminders of that night. A smell of coffee on the breeze, from a nearby processing plant. Rust. Car exhaust.

Reinerman Street is on my way, so I turn and park by the yellow house. Corn leaves rustle in the old lady's vegetable patch. Teenagers circle Brock's Combo Burger in dirty, dented cars, yelling at one another, flirting. Bitter's hoo-raw hasn't changed the neighborhood's looks for me or given me a clearer glimpse of history, but as with the owls, I feel an uneasy shifting in the air, as though the present weren't quite real. It's the same sensation that overcame me when, on return visits here, Mama told me, "You don't belong here anymore. This is not your place now." I could almost feel my identity slip, like a cheap, tossed-off mask—but what was beneath it, I hadn't a clue. The teenagers' voices grow murky, a rush of underwater bubbles. Sweat soaks the back of my shirt. I picture Cletus's face and feel myself melting into him, a thrilling freedom, a scary drift. Eyes closed, I know myself to be walking, walking . . . my body heavier, more massive in the upper arms and thighs, burdened, tight . . . the day's a scorcher so I remove my cap. My buddies do the same. A streetcar clatters behind us, but we prefer to stroll rather than sit in the back of a car, enduring a white conductor's contemptuous stare. It's the morning of Thursday, August 23, twelve hours before the riot for which we'll eventually hang. For now, on R&R, we're carefree and happy. Unarmed.

Charlie—Corporal Baltimore, a provost guard and model soldier—suggests we head up San Felipe to get a cool soda. We notice two mounted policemen down the block; I know one of them, a mammoth named Rufus Daniels. The colored housekeepers here refer to him as "Dan'l Boone, a nigger-baiter, one of the meanest cops around." I tell Charlie and Ben, my other companion, we should stay to one side of the street and keep our heads down. The officers see us. They turn their stallions to keep us in view, straighten in their saddles. We pass an alley, and my stomach clenches. A pair of colored teens is kneeling in the dirt, throwing dice. *Canned goods,* the community calls its boys. *Don't matter what they do—even if they doing nothing—they just canned goods for the cops.* Lately, the police have mounted an intense campaign against crap-shooting, citywide, increasing neighborhood tension. I quicken my stride, so if Daniel Boone stops to inspect us, we'll be past the alley and he won't see the boys. But the boys look up, hear the hoofbeats, and hightail it out of there. Charlie, Ben, and I fall back, startled, as the kids run foolishly up the street, in plain sight. The stallions crackle past us, knocking us over; a tail whips my face, a breath-stealing sting.

The kids swing past a woman at a clothesline. She's wearing a man's T-shirt and shorts, her brown skin wet with sweat. The cops dismount; Daniels fires his pistol at a slat fence the boys have leaped. The woman screams and falls to the grass, covering her ears. Daniels's partner, a thin, box-faced man, peers around the fence, shakes his head. "Little devils are gone," he says. "Quick as damn greyhounds." Daniels jerks the woman to her feet. "You know them nigger kids, hm? Tell me where they live!" She shivers in his grip. The T-shirt rides up her waist. Daniels laughs. "I'm waiting, Mammy. Where they at?"

Charlie steps forward, toward the yard. I lay my hand on his arm, whisper, "No."

"You . . . you raised your six-shooter," the woman stammers. "They was just *kids!*"

"No ma'am," Daniels says. "I fired into the ground. It was only a warning shot. Right?"

She stares at him as if at a haint.

"*Right?*"

"Charlie, *no!*" I hiss, but it's too late. "Excuse me, officer," Charlie says, stepping onto the lawn. On the clothesline behind him, bedsheets flutter like herons. "I think it's pretty clear this woman doesn't know anything."

Daniels shoves her to the ground. "You uppity son of a bitch," he says, planting his feet, a dime-novel gunslinger. "You questioning an officer of the law?"

"No sir. I'm just saying—"

"You uppity son of a bitch," he says again. "Ever' since you goddam soldiers got here, biggety nigger women like this one trying to *take* the town. Feeling confident and brave with y'all around, eh? Well, I'll show you *confident.*" He swings his pistol, clipping Charlie on the cheek. Charlie staggers back. Daniels is on him again, clubbing his forehead. The other cop trains his gun on Ben and me. Daniels hovers over Charlie now, kicking his ribs. "What say we send this cow to the Pea Farm, eh? Give her ninety days to think about refusing to aid justice. And as for you, you uppity son of a bitch, I guess I gotta keep hitting you till your heart's right." He kicks Charlie twice in the groin.

According to testimony I'll offer later at the trial—all of which Daniels's partner will refute—the big cop turns to me, then. "You and your friend get the hell out of here now, and don't never come back to this neighborhood, hear? Spread the word at that monkey's nest. We don't want to see you monkeys no more."

His partner raises his pistol and breaks the air twice. Ben sprints down the alley. I walk slowly—the only defiance I can muster—glancing back at Charlie, motionless on the grass, his head a bloody pulp. My knees are weak, and I tremble like a puppet. With each step I feel earth hammering my heel bones, up my legs and spine, into the base of my brain. My comrades at the camp will swarm like hornets when they hear the cops have killed Charlie. For no reason. No reason at all. Sweat streaks my neck as I'm walking, crying, walking, walking . . . into Brock's Combo Burger to order a sandwich to go. A teenage girl wearing braces hands me a Coke and a straw. I must look dazed; she exaggerates her movements to catch my attention, and I take the drink from her. The smell of sizzling meat and melted cheese, the rank intimacy of human sweat, churns my stomach. I wipe my eyes, spill coins near the register. The girl has to count them for me. When I walk back outside, gripping my food bag, the heat slaps me in the face. Across the street, the old woman turns a hose on her garden.

————

The Gulf Coast seethes in the sun. In scorched rice paddies, still water steams lightly, brown and mud-thickened, rippling with finger-thin snakes and waterstriders, mosquito larvae, chiggers. Gator country. The air smells like burnt paper. Ahead of me, just off the highway, I see the edge of hundreds of miles of oil refineries and chemical storage tanks ringing the coast, a skeletal city. I eat my burger quickly, before the odors get worse. Clouds bank against the blue, foamy as sea waves.

The address Bitter gave me for Elias Woods is in a cheap housing development for oil workers, boxes built on a swamp. As I slow, looking for street names, I'm aware of more and more water seeping boisterously onto the asphalt, until finally I can go no farther. The neighborhood is submerged. Ahead of me, roofs poke out of slimy brown whirlpools; treetops—big, arthritic hands—twist from algae swells. An empty boat bumps against a basketball goal whose backboard barely breaks the muddy surface. Two dogs paddle through willows, past a listing hound's-tooth couch snagged on something metal. A wooden sign propped against a chimney says DAMN. Or DAMNED.

I get out of my car and stand at the mess's lip. Water laps at my shoes, scummy, a green and purple film in its center. The back of my mouth aches in the ashy air. Through mistletoe limbs, clustered on the eastern horizon, I see refinery flames wrinkling the air like cellophane. Texas City. Seagulls startle me, cawing overhead, sounding like scared little girls, and I imagine Mama running through a mushroom cloud.

If Elias Woods lives here, he uses a scuba tank. The address paper sticks to my palm like a delicate dogwood blossom. I return to the car, back out, and head for the first functioning building I see, a filling station, Blake's Service and Handi Lube. A gray-haired man in a dirty green suit kneels by the gas pumps, tracing their shadows on cracked cement with a piece of blue chalk. He grins, embarrassed, when I pull up. "Bid'ness slow today," he says through my open window. "Just trying to stay occupied. Fill 'er up?"

"No, actually, I'm looking for this address."

He studies the runny numbers. "Sunk," he says.

"What happened?"

"Hurrican'. Blew through here two, three year ago, just about drownded us all. City promising to drain and rebuild, but we ain't seen nothing yet."

"Where did people go?"

"God knows. Wherever they could. Grabbed up whatever was left and skeedaddled."

"Did you know a man named Elias Woods?"

He scratches his head with the chalk, etching a blue line in his hair above his right ear. "Seem kindly familiar but I ain't rightly sure. Tell you what, there's a man might could he'p you, down this road a ways. Junkyard-looking place on the right, 'bout three mile."

I thank him and leave him coloring the concrete. The road narrows between fields of green reeds and some kind of cane. It winds beneath a freeway then turns into gravel and dirt. Huge apple trees, tangled in dewberry vines, lean as if weary to the ground. Rusty barrels (fertilizer? oil?). Gardens gone to seed. An ad for SERPENTS. THREE MI. EAST. Someone's hung a sign in an oak: JESUS IS COMING. Someone else has changed it; now it reads JESUS HAS COME. On the right, another wooden sign, painted white: ANTIQUES AND INFORMAL MULTICULTURAL MUSEUM, and below that, KWAKO DOBIE-BEDICHECK JONES, PROP. I park beneath the leafy fans of a fat banana tree.

Wooden Coke bottle boxes lie scattered among collard greens in the yard. Sculptures welded from car parts, boat motors, and plumbing supplies line a white, broken-shell path toward a small wooden house. Seagulls trot contentedly in the high grass. Saxophone jazz swells inside the house. In the doorway, a small woman in a red scarf and light blue muumuu hammers a loose picture frame. She's light-skinned but darker than I am, the color of pine bark. Rounded cheeks, narrow eyes. She looks up and smiles at me, but keeps her arms in, close to her body, a defensive posture. "Hello. You're here for a tour?" she asks. Before I can answer, she's pointing to a gate west of the house. "Museum grounds are that way. It's a dollar donation—you can stick it in the coffee can nailed to the fence over there. I'll be here when you're done." She resumes her hammering.

I'm not sure what to do, but then I think, It's only a dollar. What does an "Informal Multicultural Museum" look like? I can wait fifteen minutes to ask my questions.

So I slip a bill into the can, step past the gate and into an overgrown pasture filled with junk. Bathtubs, sinks with drains the color of sunset; hubcaps and tires; an old phone booth, glass shattered, bell insignia painted on its side; dishes, martini glasses, garlic stalks; street signs in Spanish and English; garden tools, rusty rifles, flagpoles, plastic toy swords; a toilet bowl turned into a planter, African violets spilling over its sides. I've been scammed out of a buck. I glance back at the house, a shack really, barely upright in a jungle of vines, salt air, refinery fumes, and hurricane threats. What's a dollar? Good luck to these folks. I watch the woman hammer the frame. She's like the Flower Man, saving it all, especially the ugly, stupid stuff . . . finding beauty in it. If you live in a wasteland—a poor neighborhood, soon to be extinct—what choice but to celebrate the trash? Shoring fragments against the ruin . . .

A bird statue, tall as I am, made of table legs and fenders, with two umbrellas for wings, greets me at the end of my tour. Multicultural, I don't know. Multitextured, certainly. The sax spits fire at the sky. *Them that ain't jazzing, beware!* I approach the house. "See anything you want?" the woman asks, setting aside the frame. I notice, now, a scrap bag of blue and white cotton slung across her shoulder. My mama used to own a bag just like it, to keep her piecework in.

"Oh . . . no. But it's all very interesting."

"I'm Barbara. My husband, Kwako, he's the artist, the sculptor. There's more inside." She nods at the house.

"Actually, I'd like to ask you . . . do you know a man named Elias Woods?" She turns rigid, suspicious of me, so I spill it all fast. "I think he knew my daddy, who I never met. My uncle gave me his name. I'd like to ask him some questions."

"Hm. Let's go see Kwako," she says, still stiff. She leads me, past rain barrels, wooden TV cable spools, and carburetor parts, to the back of the house. There, beneath a green canvas awning on the porch, surrounded by glass wind chimes, a man in a steel mask welds an S-shaped pipe to a tiny freezer. He's tall and thin, wearing gray overalls. Barbara calls to him over the flame's howling breath. He looks up, snuffs the torch. A last burst of sparks jitters into the yard: a lightning bug swarm. An adobe-colored quilt hangs across a porch rail behind him. He ditches the mask, smiles. Sparse, crooked teeth. A gray goatee, hair dense and matted, like transistor radio wiring. "Welcome, sister," he says. "You're a lover of our culture's great diversity, are you?"

I don't know what to say. "Sure."

"It's okay, sister, no call to be scared. You know, our whole society, it's based on fear," he says aggressively, as though I've asked him the Secret of Life. He wipes his hands on a rag. "They sell you threats and illusions, lies about each other, all the different races and such, keep us separate. But here at the Multicultural Museum, we strip away the lies, celebrate God's bounty *as it is*." God's bounty being castoffs, broken plumbing, old axles and tires, I guess. "This freeway over here?" He points past drooping banana leaves. "S'posed to been built forty years ago, ever since I's a boy. They *still* ain't finished it. So you think politicians gon' take care *your* future? No ma'am." His verbal shifts rattle me. Barbara's heard it all before, I can tell—part sermon, part stump speech, part sales pitch. She stands patiently, a bored, polite smile on her face. Bees flit through a willow behind her. The sax sputters, feints, jabs.

"Now me, I ain't had no schooling," Kwako continues, "but I made up for that with travel and with *comparative thinking*. I seen the way things are, see, I seen past the lies. I freed myself. Now, I don't want to step on your heart, sister, as a Caucasian woman and all, but I know it's the truth: Caucasians need to ask themselves, 'Am I willing to let go some of that sneak-gotten wealth?'—see, *you* didn't oppose African Americans, maybe, but your ancestors did, and you benefited from that." As he talks, he pulls on a pair of gloves, picks up a brush, and begins slathering black wax on his sculpture. "Now me, as a man of color, I know my responsibility is to prepare myself to understand my brothers and sisters worldwide. English, Spanish, French, Creole, Garifuna—I gots to learn these tongues so I ain't, you know, *alienated* from the others. We're all influenced with the African DNA. That makes us kin. Global communication, it's the key to mankind's unity."

I'm spinning with heat and the speed of his talk. His sentences mirror his art, I think: fragments from here and there, stuck wildly together to form . . . God knows. Maybe it doesn't matter. Maybe the whole point is just to form *something*. Is this the way my daddy sang his songs? Lived his life? Improvising, shifting place to place, from family to family, maybe, leaving behind all his messes, his women . . .

Barbara maintains her patient expression. It must be exhausting to be married to a self-styled visionary. She's still gripping the hammer.

Crazy white woman, no business here, who knows what she'll do? "She wants to know, do we know Elias Woods?" she says when Kwako stops to clean his brush.

He cocks his head at me. "Why's that?"

"He might be a friend of my daddy's," I say.

"Who she never met," Barbara adds.

"My uncle gave me his address, but apparently the house is underwater."

"Who's your daddy?"

"Jim Washington. Old blues player around here, some time ago?"

"Well now." Kwako bobs his head to the bebop sax. He looks me over, more closely. "I guess you *are* a lover of diversity, then. Mm-hm. I gotta tell you, though, Elias, he's gone."

"Dead?"

"More or less. They got him up in Huntsville. Deaf row. Kilt his wife."

"Oh."

"Sorry to bear you bad tides."

Barbara, softening, watching my face, finally sets the hammer down. "Would you like some coffee or tea?"

"No. Thank you. I think I . . . I think I should get back to my uncle now. Let him know." Truth is, I don't know what to do with myself, and this is plain to the couple.

"You sure?" Barbara asks.

I'm not sure of anything anymore. "Yes." It's like when Mama told me I didn't have a place here now. A girl with no trails to follow, in, out, anywhere. A whore for warmth and certainty, but not deserving any . . .

Kwako pulls a card from his shirt pocket. "All right, then, if you say so. Phone don't always work," he says. "Seem like every time it rains or the wind blows, the lines come down 'round here. But give a call if you want to. Sound like 'multicultural' right up your alley."

I take the card. *These fragments I shore . . .*

"And I'm fulla talk, as you hear." He laughs.

"Thank you. I appreciate your time."

Barbara sees me glance at her quilt. "You do piecework, sugar?"

"My mama did. This reminds me of her. It's beautiful. Yours?"

"Yes. Got more inside. You're welcome to look."

"Not today, thanks. I really should go."

"Come back sometime, will you?" Kwako says. "Tell us about your fambly. Look at more quilts. We'll give you a good price on one."

"I will." I shake their hands. My arm feels as weightless as cork.

————

From my angle on the freeway, driving back to town, Houston's sky-scrapers blaze like Zippos. Mirrored glass buildings soak up the sun. I'm still pondering Elias Woods when I cross the San Jacinto River and remember that several years ago, under this bridge, a squatter's camp formed—"Tent City," the media called it. Out-of-work oil laborers, desperate steel men who'd hit the road once the northern mills shut down, gathered in the mud here, living off garbage. Newspaper photographers loved it. But Tent City wasn't the image Houston's city planners wanted loose in the world. Along with the Chamber of Commerce, they talked the cops into chasing the squatters away.

I imagine tents, now, made of old quilts; then army tents. The river's curves through mossy magnolias remind me of the Twenty-fourth Infantry's camp. How must Cletus have felt after leaving Corporal Baltimore—dead, for all he knew—at the feet of the brutal cops? How must he have felt, returning to camp, breaking the news to his comrades? How did he react when Sergeant Vida Henry swore they'd taken enough shit in this cracker city, and it was time for the troops to show some balls? What did he think, later, lifting his rifle, marching into the dark?

The trial transcripts say nothing about why Vida Henry snapped, or how he was able to sway others into bucking their training and common sense. At first, in the heady fury over the cops' behavior, the troops must have felt their cause was righteous ("To hell with fighting in France! We got to stick by our own and clean up *this* city, right here, right now!"). But at some point, after shots had been fired, houses damaged, people killed—including Rufus Daniels, the "nigger-baiting" cop who'd beaten Charlie Baltimore—horror must have set in, fear over what they'd done. It must have occurred to Cletus Hayes that Vida Henry had lost his mind.

I imagine them together by the bayou. I'm drifting again; I slow down, concentrate on the road, but even so, my skin no longer holds me . . . the night is drizzling rain. Most of the soldiers have scattered by now, hoping to make it back to camp before they're caught. "Ain't going back, Cletus," Vida Henry says. He leans against a chinaberry tree and rolls a cigarette. "You know what'll happen, we go back."

All around us, frogs are as loud as bass drums, making it hard to think. "Maybe not," I say. "Maybe they won't know it was us."

Henry laughs. "Yeah, and maybe you'll wake up tomorrow morning white as chalk."

"I'm not going on, Sarge. It's foolishness. Won't bring Charlie back."

"*You're* the one saw him sprawled there. How can you not fight for him?"

"How is *this* fighting for him? Shooting at houses?" My head's as heavy as a crate of boots. I smell like mud. "I'm done."

"Do me a favor, then."

"What's that?"

He offers me his rifle.

"No."

"Save me the trouble of shooting myself. Please."

I stand, unsteadily, start to walk away. Owls bellow in the trees. "Good luck to you, Cletus," Henry says. "You're going to need it."

I stumble through blackberry brambles, bayou water sloshing in my boots. A loud click, then a lid slamming shut. The rifle report freezes my spine, but I force myself to move. Nothing can salvage this night or redeem my shameful behavior, but crossing rails past empty, uncoupled boxcars, I think of Sarah Morgan. One last time, I think of *planting seeds.*

———

Can't we all just get along? A planner I worked with, a liberal white man who grew up in L.A. and who was profoundly disturbed by the Rodney King riots, once proposed a multifamily public housing project built around courtyards, with lush landscaping and bright ceramic tiles. His idea was that each family would sacrifice ten percent of its interior square footage to create a shared neighborhood center: mailboxes, washers and dryers, a community kitchen, a child-care room. "The shared public space will enforce a sense of collective responsibility," he reasoned. "It'll be perfect, especially for single-parent families, who need all the help they can get. I mean, let's face it, right now, our public housing sucks. We have inner cities that aren't worth caring about. That leads to a nation not worth defending. At the very least, a nation vulnerable to black rage."

I liked him. He used to quote Walt Whitman in the office. "You know what Walt used to say? He asked America to become a vast 'city of friends' basking in 'robust love.' Now *that's* a vision of city planning!"

Like all utopians I've known, he was crushed when others ruled his dreams unfeasible. He quit his job and became a VISTA volunteer. Later, I heard he was killed one night in a drive-by, serving food outside a homeless shelter in a dying neighborhood, still trying to breathe life into his vision.

I went through a phase of promoting *getting along.* I'd hear an ofay make a racist joke, then spring the news on him I was black. Inevitably, instead of apologizing, he'd make an excuse, usually a long-winded list of *his* hardships. Failed athletic careers. Lost rock-and-roll dreams. School rejections. "The whole damn world's elitist, all right?" a fellow told me once. "*You* people don't have a patent on suffering." I learned to keep my mouth shut. To *expect* misunderstandings and fear. To approach planning with skepticism and diminished expectations. To relinquish Eden, a city of friends.

6

AT ARIYEH'S suggestion, I meet her and Reggie at a place called the Ragin' Cajun. Last night at Bitter's, when she came to arrange the lunch, she told me Reggie and Bitter didn't get along. Reggie was a tireless community activist. He'd raised funds to salvage collapsing row houses, fix them up, and convert them into a public art project.

When I arrive at the restaurant, he and Ariyeh are already seated. He's small, the color of peanut brittle, with shoulder-length dreads. He's leaning over the table, gesturing with strong, slender hands. "Even if all they do is play games, the cost is justified."

"How?" Ariyeh says.

"Baby, I gotta go through this *again?*"

"How is it justified?"

"See, even *before* the American Revolution, this country locked a power structure into place—"

"Reggie, seriously, what do your damn conspiracies have to do with computer games?"

"Hi," I say.

Ariyeh smiles, stands, introduces us. "Good to meet you," Reggie says. "I'd just like to finish this point, okay?"

I nod. We all sit down. A plastic cover overlays the table, red and white checks.

"South Carolina, 1739, all right?"

"Oh Christ, Reggie, don't *history* me again—"

"It's the *facts,* baby. Listen to me, now. What did the legislators do?"

"Let me guess."

"Banned reading and writing for coloreds, that's what, and even out-lawed talking drums."

"Okay, Preacher-Man."

"The point I'm making is, the Internet is the new talking drum. In the twenty-first century, guaranteed, baby, every important social connection is going to be on-line—"

"But *one* computer—"

"It's a start, sugar. I showed you those stats, right? Thirty-three percent middle-income whites own PCs, compared with nineteen percent blacks. *Nineteen percent.*"

"All right, but—"

"We're two separate nations: white and wired, black and unplugged. Seventeen thirty-nine all over again."

Ariyeh tells me, "Reggie wants to buy a computer for the Row House Project, get the neighborhood kids comfortable with technology. I think what he and the boys really want to do is sit around and play Doom Master or Master Doom or whatever the hell it's called."

Reggie grins. "Part of the education. You hungry?"

We stand in a long line at the counter. The walls are covered with beer signs, football posters, cartoon armadillos, Louisiana license plates. A sign above the men's room door says CRAWFISH GIVE GOOD HEAD. We order cornbread, corn on the cob, and a large bucket of crawfish. The room is pungent and hot, buzzing with talk and the sizzle of frying foods. At a table next to us, two white men the size of Frigidaires, in white shirts and blue ties, paw through a basket of hush puppies. On our other side, three black men wearing oily gas station uniforms bite the heads off their crawfish. They suck the meat.

Ariyeh is tense. Another child has disappeared from her school. "That makes four boys in two months," she says. She tucks her napkin into her light blue blouse. "Cops are getting nowhere, and the kids are scared to death. I mean, what if there's some wacko on the loose? I don't know how to protect—"

"You conk your hair?" Reggie asks me, pointing at my head with his chewed-up corncob.

"Reggie!"

"Not anymore," I say, flushing. "But I used to." I'm holding a crawfish in my hand; it feels alive to me, its stiff legs wedged between my fingers. The food is spicy. It's like swallowing straight pins.

"What about the kitchen?" He fingers the nape of his neck. "You know, this real kinky part here. Must be tough to keep straight."

"Not so much nowadays."

"Ever Jheri-Curl it?"

Ariyeh says, "Reggie, that's enough."

"You can pass, can't you?" he says.

"Yes."

"It's how you get by."

"Sometimes. Most of the time."

He nods thoughtfully. Encouraged by his bluntness, I ask him, "How come you don't like Bitter?"

Ariyeh squirms.

"Shit, that shuffle-and-jive he does, that 'uncle' business, it's the kind of self-hating crap let whites dog brothers from the start. I can't fucking stand it." He touches Ariyeh's arm. "I'm sorry, baby. I know he's your daddy. But she asked."

"It bothers me too," I admit. Ariyeh turns to me, surprised. "I mean, I didn't know any better as a kid, but since I've come back this time . . . still, it's who he is now, isn't it? For men his age—"

"Don't tell me he didn't have a choice. He did. Just like you do. You're not the 'anguished mixed-blood child,' are you? Tell me you haven't accepted a stereotype as the way to carry yourself?"

Again, I feel my face go hot. "And you? The 'angry black militant'?"

He smiles. "You're right. I like your pluck, girl. And you're right on target. It's damn hard to escape the boxes hammered out for us." He leans forward. "Who are the biggest consumers of television in this country? Black folks. And what kind of pictures of themselves do they see there? But I tell the neighborhood kids: self-awareness—especially awareness of your own clichés or the ideas the culture *wants* you to swallow—is the answer to kicking all the shit. The way to shoot past whatever the Man expects of you. You, I don't know," he says to me. "You seem smart about yourself. But your uncle Bitter's faith in mother-wit and soft-shoeing it . . . I think that old man lost his soul a long time ago."

"I don't agree," Ariyeh says. "Let's change the subject."

"I can't imagine you two growing up together."

Ariyeh and I look at each other and laugh—because *we* can't believe it now, either. The big men beside us rate the Houston Rockets. "Olajuwon's lost a step." "Barkley's been slacking for three seasons now." "Drexler's legs was good for one more run."

"What about you?" I ask Reggie. "Where did you grow up?"

"In the Fifth Ward here. Me and my walkies, my cornerboys, you know, we were groomed to do bids. Ass out. Convicted before we were born. It's just luck I'm not serving time. Went to a school that should have been condemned for safety violations in the fifties. Scrubbed each night with Pencor Soap. Funny how I still remember its name. My mama told me, 'This here soap is made by guys in the penitentiary, which is where you're going to end up.' *Destiny.* So I learned to live for props—"

"What's that?"

"Props. You know. Proper respect. You earned it on the street by doing something cool. We all knew who'd earned the most props. Taking something. Ripping someone off. All the way *live.* We knew we were eighty-sixed from the good life, see, so we figured we were owed whatever we could steal. Let me tell you, BMT—"

"Black Man Talking," Ariyeh interprets for me. "Means, 'Listen up.'"

"That's right. We learned to express only one emotion, sister: rage."

As he talks, Ariyeh wears the same bored expression Barbara Jones did, listening to Kwako. She, too, has hooked up with a visionary, a man who's changed his frustrations into creative energy, but who, in his grandiosity (I'm guessing), overlooks daily chores and the immediate needs of others. But maybe I'm judging unfairly.

"On my ninth birthday, to impress my cornerboys, I swiped a starter pistol from the school gym—one of those guns they fire to begin a race? After classes I caught a guy from another gang—we all marked ourselves with different-colored rags. I knocked him down and shoved the pistol into his mouth. When I pulled the trigger, it flashed and broiled about half his face. Teachers caught me, and that was my ticket to the system. They sent me to YSC, Youth Study Center—first of about half a dozen trips. After that it was BCC, the Bureau for Colored Children. These are prep schools for the pen, you dig? I was learning to be a criminal."

The gas station guys are laughing. "No, I *ain't* fucking wit' you," one says to another in a tone that indicates *Of course I'm fucking with you but I'm too cool to admit it.* The white men still debate basketball. "Rodman's a showboat, man, bad for the game, ought to be banned from the league." The voice says, *Crazy nigger, I'd love to see him get what he deserves,* but with a thrilled edge that also indicates, *I love it when he's bad, I wish I had the balls to be bad.*

"So what broke the cycle for you?" I ask Reggie. "Your luck. What was it?"

"Books. In BCC a guy gave me Maya Angelou."

I smile.

"W. E. B. Du Bois, *The Souls of Black Folk*. Elijah Muhammad's *Message to the Blackman in America*. See, on the street, props had never been handed out for intellectual development. But in the system, where you had lots of time, some guys started using their minds, their imaginations. So the irony was, prison freed these fellows, let them pick in high cotton. Gave them power their white captors never intended them to have. I'm living proof of that."

Reading ideologically.

"I hate to say it, but I've got to get back," Ariyeh says, wiping her hands on a shredded napkin. A busboy swishes by, knocking crawfish shells from our table onto wet paper on the floor. He scoops the paper up and dunks it into a trash can. "Why don't you go with Reggie to see the Row House Project, T? I think you'll be impressed."

I glance at her, then him. His energy makes me nervous.

Ariyeh senses my hesitation. "It's an example of what can be done to salvage old black neighborhoods. It's what ought to be happening in Freedmen's Town. I think it's something a city planner should see."

"All right," I say, falsely bright. "Lead the way."

"No no, I disagree," one of the big men says. "Michael Jordan earned every penny. I mean, the man wasn't *human*. I swear he had *wings* in his butt—"

Reggie leans their way. "The NBA throws an obscene amount of money at a few hundred brothers to compensate for the collective guilt you ofays feel, but you know what? There's not enough money between here and Africa to *ever* atone for the lethal shit dumped on my people."

The men tremble; tartar sauce greases their thumbs. The gas station gang hoots, bumping shoulders. Ariyeh tugs Reggie's arm. He walks away without leaving a tip: *we were owed whatever we could steal.*

Outside the restaurant, he chuckles, pleased with himself. Clouds fat with seawater bubble up in the east, turning the afternoon light a pleasant blue-green. The passing traffic smells toasted: hot brakes, broiling metal. "I have to go back to school now and face dozens of frightened children, who wonder why their friends have disappeared. I don't want to have to worry about *you* doing a ghost too," Ariyeh tells Reggie.

"They're all talk and blubber," he says. "Living vicariously through black, athletic bodies. And hating them at the same time. Pathetic."

She kisses him curtly on the cheek. "We'll talk about it later." She takes my hand. "I'll drop by Bitter's again soon. You're staying a while longer?"

"A while."

"Follow me," Reggie says and steps into a red Honda. I wave good-bye to the woman I used to think was my cousin, back when I believed I knew my family, my home. My own true colors.

———

The Row House Restoration Project, twenty-two shotgun houses built in the twenties and thirties, braced, refurbished, repainted, occupies two city blocks on Alabama Street, ten minutes south of Freedmen's Town. With local arts grants and a smattering of corporate support, Reggie has turned the abandoned homes into a series of galleries displaying the work of black, Chicano, Asian, and other minority artists. In one house, lining the floor, I find a collection of snapshots in canning jars. The artist's statement explains that she distributed 150 disposable cameras at schools and churches in Houston's blighted neighborhoods and asked kids to take pictures of whatever they wanted. She placed the results in over three thousand jars, beneath a banner that reads, "What will we choose to preserve?" The pictures show broken fire escapes, drug needles glinting in gravel parking lots, old people sleeping, undernourished babies.

In another house, life-sized cardboard figures stand, faceless, in the center of the room. Huddled against the walls, in shadow, cutouts of children. The artist hoped to dramatize the trauma of child abuse, she writes, by showing "something is horribly wrong in this house."

A third artist has used her space to "celebrate pattern making, a tradition passed down through generations of African American families—using a variety of surfaces and materials to record events and thus claim our place in the universal order." On the walls, torn newspaper strips covered with crayon drawings, elaborate maps made on napkins and cardboard boxes, photographs pinned to tapestries sewn out of bedsheets. They remind me of my mama's old quilts.

I'm delighted to see one of Kwako's car-bumper birds perched on a porch. "I just met this guy," I tell Reggie. Lunch still burns my mouth. "Yesterday. I drove to his museum."

"Good man. One of Houston's finest folk artists." Sunlight and shade sculpt his face: crystalline brown panes. I understand what Ariyeh sees in him: dignity, pride, an impressive commitment to his community. But the arrogance! It doesn't help that he reminds me of another beautiful young man in dreads, Dwayne Jefferson, a former coworker who fucked me over last year. These damned self-made men! *Don't look back,* Mama warned me when we abandoned our old life. But ever since—haven't I longed for whatever's off-limits? I vow to myself, for Ariyeh's sake as well as my own, to keep a cool distance from Reggie.

The last house on the block is still being renovated. Its stripped walls smell of piney woods. Reggie warns me to be careful of the flooring— "Some of those planks are just splinters." I stand in the little room, breathing in dust, the tinge of rusty nails, the imagined odors of muddy clothes, shoes, boiling potatoes, spit-up, and milk—the sweet and bitter smells of a cramped sharecropper life. And I wonder if my daddy, whoever he was, once lived in a room like this, huddled in candlelight on cold nights, running a pocketknife over rain-tightened strings, coaxing sad sounds out of the worn old wood.

"I'm amazed at what you've done here," I tell Reggie. "Ariyeh was right. This is a model of good city planning."

"I wanted to preserve history and our heritage and at the same time make it an active, living place, a resource for the people here—"

"The neighborhood's soul?"

He smiles at me, and I recall Dwayne's roguish charm, remember the shut-in boy, all those years ago, staring at me from across a quiet room. "It's been a political and financial nightmare, as you can imagine. But we're holding our own for now. Come on. Let me walk you down to the office, show you what I'm proudest of."

A rap song grunts from a passing car. The sun has turned the ground into a hard, baked crust. Reggie's sweating lightly beside me. Yeasty, warm. As we walk, I move away from him, slightly. "So, Ariyeh was telling me. You're here to find your daddy?"

"Not *find* him, exactly. He's long gone, from what I can gather. But I wanted to hear from Bitter who he was. Who they *all* were. My family."

"And once you know?"

"I thought it might bring me some kind of peace." I laugh. "I see now I was wrong about that. Besides which, I'll never know it all. Too much time has passed. Too much lost."

"Like this neighborhood," he says. "It doesn't matter so much what you recover from the past as what you do with yourself now."

"Spoken like a true renovator."

He grins. We come to a house with the word OFFICE painted in red on its side. Two boys, about ten, in do-rags and basketball shirts, shoot hoops at a goal on the corner. They quit their trash-talking long enough to stare at me. "Reg-*gee*," one calls. "'S up, man?" His sneakers glow in the sunlight. His loose drawers look like grocery bags slipped down over his knees.

Reggie nods at the boys, and we step inside the office. It's cool; a rusty blade fan hustles in the corner. The wooden floor creaks. A cricket by the door trills now and then, like a smoke alarm losing its juice. The room smells of egg rolls, doughnuts—fast food sacks clutter the trash can. Next to it, a box of CDs: DMX, Swizz Beatz, Method Man. Above a small desk, framed on the wall, a Frederick Douglass quote: "What, to the American slave, is your 4th of July? I answer: a day that reveals to him, more than all other days in the year, the gross injustice and cruelty to which he is the constant victim. To him, your celebration is a sham; your boasted liberty, an unholy license; your national greatness, swelling vanity." Next to it, pinned with a nail, Psalm 100:

Make a joyful noise to the Lord, all ye lands. Serve the Lord with gladness: come before his presence with singing. Know ye that the Lord he is God: it is he that hath made us and not we ourselves; we are his people and the sheep of his pasture.

A list of donors also appears on the wall: Lannan Foundation, Amoco Corporation, Cultural Arts Council of Houston, Wells Fargo Foundation, Philip Morris.

"I know, I know," Reggie says, watching my eyes. "I felt funny, at first, taking dead presidents from a tobacco company, but they were happy to give—"

"Poor neighborhoods are a rich market for them," I counter softly. "Blacks smoke more and suffer higher lung cancer rates—"

"Shit, girl. You get these figures from the mayor's office?"

I realize I sound the way *he* did, lecturing Ariyeh. "Yes, as a matter of fact."

"So you frown on—"

"It's just that, working for the mayor, I see black and Hispanic officials bought off all the time. They're usually the only Democratic leaders opposed to smoking bans, because of grants like yours—'good-will' gestures to neighborhoods like this."

"Say what you will, I needed five thousand dollars for a community Thanksgiving dinner last fall," Reggie says. "It would have taken me months of paperwork, a bumper-car ride through the usual aids agencies, with no guarantees. Smoke-folks made the eagle fly right away, no questions asked." He points out the window to another house, right behind the office. Wet blouses droop on a line. "That's our Young Mothers Residential Program. We offer one-year residencies to single mothers and their kids. They get to live in this nice, refurbished place while they work and further their education. Our aim is to help them become self-sufficient and pull themselves out of poverty."

"That's wonderful, Reggie."

"So. Does it really *matter* where the money comes from?"

"I don't know," I admit, buzzing from our banter.

"The biggest problem around here is teenage moms with no jobs, no husbands in the house—most of the neighborhood boys wind up in jail. We got a woman living here now, Natalie, former hooker, crack addicted—clean eighteen months. Two children, a little girl, three, and her boy Michael there." He points out the window at the kids shooting baskets. "The blue shorts."

He steps outside, motioning me to follow, and knocks on Natalie's door. A thin woman, dark and as sleek as Kwako's metal sculptures, answers, blinking painfully in the sunlight. "How you doing?" Reggie asks.

She scratches her ribs. The straps of her red cotton halter slide down her shoulders. "Fine." A croak and a whisper. She clears her throat. "Studying my economics book. Sasha's asleep."

Reggie introduces us just as a bright black BMW lurches to a stop in the street, blasting rap. "Skeezer! Say mama!" a young man yells from the car. "Got some Wild Cat here, or how 'bout some Kibbles and Bits? I know you be wanting some, sugar. Your *name* on it, right chere. Take a look."

Natalie lifts a hand to her mouth.

"Easy, now," Reggie says to her. "Ignore them."

"Assholes. They come by here every day in some new G-ride. I worry about Michael."

As she says this, the young man waves to her boy. "Yo, Air Jordan!

Special today, just for you, some *mighty* African Woodbine. Ax your mommy is it payday. A twinkie'll do."

Michael looks like he's going to hurl the basketball at the shouter's face. "Get the hell out of here!" he screams. "Leave my mama alone, you sorry-ass—"

"Michael!" Natalie calls.

"Scotty got your mama bad, bitch-boy. Foe-one-one. Skeezer, best teach this little bitch-boy some manners. Might be he be a dead rag someday."

Reggie moves toward the street and stands with folded arms. The car pulls away, but not before the young man spots me and yells, "Miss Ann! Miss Thang! What up?"

I try to get a better glimpse of his face.

Reggie rubs Michael's head. "Let me know if you see them again, okay?"

"Bus a cap in that nickel-slick peckerwood—"

"Michael, just let me know if you see them, all right?"

"Sho."

Reggie tells Natalie not to worry, keep studying, she'll be fine.

"Take care," I offer lamely. She stares at me, then Reggie, then cuts back to me with what appears to be a nasty little sneer of suspicion.

Back in the office, Reggie says the young man in the car is a "small-time asshole, Rue Morgue's his street name, thinks he's a world-class bad-ass." He tells me Wild Cat is coke mixed with methcathinone. Kibbles and Bits, crack rocks.

"And African Woodbine?"

"Pot. Cheap as hell these days. Kids half Michael's age are selling and using the shit. See what we're up against?"

"You're very brave."

He laughs. "I'm just trying to keep a few of us alive. What you just saw—it's why I can't stand Ariyeh's old man. She and I fight about it all the time. He's living in the past, dig, no *idea* what's happening in our community today, the pressures the kids are under. He bought this notion, long ago, that if a black man just shuffles sweetly, mumbling, 'Yessir' and 'Nosir,' he'll do all right. And those fucking spells of his, as if he could just *magic* away all the trouble on the streets . . ."

"He did what he had to, in *his* time, to stay alive. At least he never wound up in prison."

"And you. You got your own magic, eh?" He touches my arm. "High yella. Lets you pass through walls."

I ignore this. "It was good to meet you, Reggie. I hope to see you again before I leave."

"Wait, wait, wait," he says. "I didn't piss you off just now, did I?"

"No."

"You're not leaving mad?"

"Not at all." I smile, to reassure us both.

"Friends, then?"

"Friends."

"Okay. Good. I'm glad. Ariyeh's really happy you're back."

"I missed her, too."

"I hope you find your daddy."

Probably ran off with some Skeezer. "Thank you. I appreciate the tour."

"Bring your best game!" Michael taunts his pal beneath the basket. "Come on, G, show me something! Bring it on!" Tires squeal in the distance; I hurry back to the silence and safety of my car. Reggie joins the boys: a grinning, lanky charmer. Is that how my daddy struck my mama? An irresistible force? Burnished and glowing? Did she feel like a whore, maybe taking him from some other woman? My chest tightens as Reggie spins, laughing, graceful, and I think of Ariyeh. I slip on my shades, turn the key.

———

As if to affirm Reggie's judgment of him, Bitter is wearing a poultice on his neck: six strips of raw bacon sprinkled with cayenne pepper wrapped in a lemon-drizzled towel. He's sitting on his porch when I arrive, sipping tea, staring at the boneyard. I've brought us some KFC for dinner. I sit on the top step, dizzied by the late-season honeysuckle scent in the air. A choir practices in the church down the street. *Coming home, Lord, coming home.* "What happened?" I ask.

"'Nother chest-squeeze. I's cleaning out the mud-dauber shack— Grady, one of my buddies, got sick in there this afternoon—and it feel like the fist of some ghost reach right into me, past my ribs, and crush my poor ol' heart. Had to sit a spell, catch my breath. So I got me this poultice, open up my arteries some."

"You need to see a doctor, Uncle Bitter."

He shoos away my words. I feel flesh-heavy, sniffing chicken, smelling rolls. Paint is peeling off the front door, the porch sags. It occurs to me to ask, "Do you have medical insurance?"

"I don't need no doctor. Hush now."

I can't afford to get stuck with his bills. The thought shames me; immediately, I assure myself: Of course I'll do what I can. And so will Ariyeh. Still, this doesn't kill my panic. We sit and listen to cicadas thrum and throb.

Bitter rubs his chest. "I been thinking all day 'bout Elias, the news you brung me. Hard to credit. I didn't know the man too good, but he seemed harmless enough to me. Guess you never know. Sorry it didn't work out for you."

"I was thinking of driving to Huntsville. See if I can visit him in prison."

"Got to get your name on a list. The waiting takes a month or so, I hear. When he scheduled to die?"

"Don't know."

Bitter shrugs. "Sorry, Seam. Tell me. What brung you here *now?* Was it your mama dying?"

"Yes, in part. Going through her stuff. Cletus's letter to Sarah Morgan."

"Stubborn woman, your mama. Never even told me she was sick."

I almost say, *Who's stubborn now?* Instead I ask, "When's the last time you heard from her?"

"Years ago. We was dead to her."

"She was dead to herself. I mean"—do I really want to say this? do I believe it?—"she wasn't happy in that white man's house. I don't think so, anyway. It was just a path out for her, a way to find physical comfort and to secure a life of advantage for me, which I didn't really want. Or I did and didn't." My throat's parched and I reach for Uncle's tea. I remember an afternoon, about a year ago, dropping by for tea with Mama and finding her in tears. I asked her, "What's the matter?" but she only shook her head. I wonder, now, if she felt the cancer's first grip that day. She looked as weary as she did those early mornings in Houston, cooking for us all. We sat in her living room, on her white couch, in white sunlight, sinking our feet into a plush beige carpet. Even the air smelled vanilla. I wanted to laugh, but my mama was weeping. Finally she said, "Have you had a good life, Telisha? Have I given you a good life?" "Of course, Mama." I held her hands; they were cold. An ice cream truck passed in the street, tinkling, through a speaker on its roof, "Pop Goes the Weasel." "I just wanted you to be happy," Mama said. "That's all." "I'm happy, Mama. Really."

But that day I'd been in tears myself. The night before, my coworker Dwayne had asked me out. He was a research aide; we'd been friendly and flirty in the office in the three months he'd been there. He was arrogant and handsome, off-putting and charming all at once. Even his idle stares looked smart-ass and fierce. One day we were poring over maps, gathering data on inner-city neighborhoods. "Ever notice the word *ghetto* has disappeared from our language?" he asked me. "When's the last time you saw that word in the paper? Nowadays it's 'inner-city' this, 'inner-city' that. *Ghetto*'s too racially charged, so we got to bury it." We talked a while longer, and I don't know why—maybe because he was so passionate, like cocky, ninth-grade Troy—I admitted to him my messy family stew. He looked at me differently, then, as though I were a genie just risen from a run-of-the-mill bottle. A week later he asked me to dinner and drinks.

The evening began pleasantly, with Mexican food at a new place on Greenville—"Yuppie Row," Dwayne called the avenue, pointing out the chic new cars in front of glittering restaurants. "I'll bet, at some of these places, you could hear the best watered-down blues in Dallas."

"If you don't like it, why are *we* here?"

"Oh, I like it. Who said I'm not a yuppie?"

I laughed. I liked it, too. I hadn't worn a dress in months, and I felt good in my blue pullover.

"The *real* blues is in Deep Ellum—what's left of it, undeveloped. Ever been there?"

"Nope."

"I think you need to see it." He dropped his voice: an exaggerated Darth Vader. "Get in touch with your *dark* side."

I laughed again but uncomfortably this time. Later, on our third round of drinks at our second bar of the night, he pushed the dark side. "See, I've got you figured this way," he slurred. He'd been drinking martinis. "For you—as for everyone else, really—white is linked to goodness and purity. Black with the nasty." He pushed his dreads out of his face.

"The nasty?"

"*Anything* nasty." He reached over and rubbed my belly. "But you got it inside you, girl." I scooched back on my stool, away from his hand. What had I done to make him think he could touch me this way? My skin tingled.

I wouldn't let him take me to Deep Ellum so late. "All right, then. A compromise," he said. "Let me show you a spot I know. It's a white joint, but the music's real."

We wound up at the Strictly Tabu Room on Lemmon Avenue, a smoky little bar stuffed with yuppies, but Dwayne was right about the music. An old Negro—*Negro* seemed the proper word for him; he'd stepped out of another era, with a long barber shirt, gray cotton pants with cuffs, and white-spatted shoes—played the vibes, all by himself in a corner. Gentle Lionel Hampton riffs, melodies folding into one another, water over pebbles. I ordered a chardonnay and relaxed into his loose improvisations.

Dwayne wouldn't let it go. The dark side. The nasty. Like a chant, one of Bitter's old spells. It had a hypnotic effect on me. Sex had been missing from my life for a couple of years. Uneasy in my own skin, I avoided touch. For a long time I'd known this about myself. Some of my sorority sisters in college had even called me "lezzie" (after I'd told them I wasn't like them and begun to withdraw) because I didn't go on many dates, because I looked "like a boy." Dwayne nibbled my ear. "Please stop," I said. "My place," he said. "No," I said, shivering. "I'd like you to take me home now."

In the car, in front of my apartment, he dropped all pretense. He wouldn't let me loose. "The dark part of you wants it," he panted, pulling my dress up over my knees. I would have laughed at him if I hadn't been so frightened—and unsure, thinking, Maybe it's true, maybe the old neighborhood got into my blood, a bayou fever, those crickety nights I'd sneak out of bed—*a bad, bad girl*—and tickle myself down below, sitting in the culvert, dreaming of the shut-in boy. Maybe none of Mama's efforts made a difference. I hadn't bettered myself at all. Despite a shiny surface and years of education, I was still at bottom a dark, nasty child. A bubbling, boggy slough.

I smelled the olives Dwayne had swallowed with his drinks, smelled his aftershave, heavy and musky like a thick banana grove, and nearly passed out. "I've never had a *white* black woman," he wheezed against my ear.

That day in Mama's house, cushioning her sobs against my chest, I cried too, for the ache in my body, for the insult Dwayne had left in me, festering, for the bad girl I could never escape. "It's all right," I whispered to us both. Mama held me tight. "It's going to be all right."

Now Bitter chews the ice from his glass. "If she weren't happy, she on'y had herself to blame," he says, and for an instant I think he means me. He readjusts the poultice on his neck. "I 'member, right before she took you away up north, she got broody, keeping to herself. I'd ask her what's wrong, she'd pull inside herself. Used to drive down to Galveston, leaving you with me, just to stare at the ocean and them big ol' Victorian houses near the seawall. Said she liked to imagine living in them mansions, with they gardens and the gingerbread trim 'round the windows." He rubs his chest some more. "Way I see it, she grew up in Hell, in the fires of Texas City, and spent her whole life running from it. Sea weren't big enough to douse the flames." He holds out his hand and I take it. "I wished she'd let me help her some. I wished I coulda seen her 'fore she passed."

"I'm sorry, Uncle Bitter."

He sniffles. "Well, my own mama used to tell me, 'Don't never put your hand on a young tree just bearing fruit or the fruit'll fall off.' When your mama come to us she was a young tree. Maybe we handled her wrong."

"You saved her life."

"Oughta sprinkled hummingbird heart on her head. Fine powder, right 'fore she left. *That* woulda kept her with us. Powerful gris-gris."

I squeeze his fingers. "Uncle, I'm worried about you. I don't think gris-gris is enough to stop these chest pains. Something's wrong. You need to see to it."

"Tomorrow I get me some nutmeg. Tie it 'round my neck."

As though the talk of spells had summoned them out of the late-evening light, two green and purple hummingbirds flare in and around Bitter's rose bushes. They tip their beaks at us, almost in greeting, then vanish is if through a rip in the air. *Coming home, Lord, coming home.* "I'll go heat up this chicken," I say.

"Forgive me, Seam."

"What for, Uncle?"

"For not taking better care your mama."

I kiss the top of his head. "You said it yourself. She wouldn't let us near."

In the church, someone shouts, "Praise Jesus!"

Bitter holds my hand to his shoulder. We watch the sun set behind the twisted apple trees just beyond the graveyard.

7

ARIYEH USUALLY sleeps late on Saturdays, her one day off (she's active in church on Sundays), but today she's agreed to come with me to the hanging field where Cletus Hayes died. She believes my interest in the place is morbid—I suppose it is—and has no desire to see it. But the time we'll have in the car will let us catch up with each other. I pull into her driveway at eight. She lives in Montrose, an old but slowly gentrifying area of town, just two miles from her daddy's home. "Generic house, generic furniture," she says, laughing, showing me around. "That's what it means to join the middle class, isn't it—you become just like everyone else?" She's packed turkey sandwiches and some barbecued potato chips for us. On the road, she helps navigate me through a puzzle of cloverleafs, and soon we're on open highway, heading west toward San Antonio. I feel us both relax.

"You really are looking good," I tell her.

"You too. For a *white* girl." She chuckles. She knows she can needle me and get away with it. Already, like the marshy lands here resettling after long winter rains, we've reestablished our balance. I tremble with anger at Mama, denying me this lovely friendship all those years.

"I'll tell you who I'm worried about, and that's your father," I say, setting the cruise control. "He's having chest pains."

She blanches. "Again? I caught him a few months back, feeling poorly, but he swore to me the trouble had gone away."

"Is he afraid of doctors? Does he have insurance?"

"He's covered on my policy, through the school." She chews her lower lip. "But you're right. Getting him to a clinic will be like jumpstarting a mule."

Bluebonnet fields, past blooming, blaze green all around us. The bluebonnet is the Lone Star State's official flower; every Sunday painter in Texas has whipped out acres of bad landscapes. It's a hackneyed sight by now, but the blossoms *are* beautiful, little mirrors of the sky, and I'm grateful to be reminded of them.

I seem to have depressed Ariyeh, talking about Bitter. She's spent more years than I have, trying to find cracks in his mask—*if* it's a mask. "Reggie's energy is astonishing," I say. "It's a wonderful thing he's doing with the Row Houses."

"It is. It's hard for me to get him to slow down. But he's such a relief after all the frogs I dated before. Lot of lazy black men in the city. I don't know if you know that."

I laugh.

"What *about* you?" she asks. "Any men?"

"Not any good ones." I tell her about Dwayne—it feels natural to confess to her, the way we did as girls, gossiping and laughing all night.

"Jesus, T. Did you report him?"

"Not to the cops. I knew he'd claim the sex was consensual . . . and I wasn't sure it wasn't, up to a point—"

"Oh, don't do that to yourself. Guilt-tripping and stuff. The man *raped* you, honey. And because of your *skin*. Sick son of a bitch. I hope you got him fired, at least."

"Transferred to another city office. I told him I couldn't work with him anymore."

"He escaped lightly. And you've been feeling guilty about it ever since, hm?"

"Mama took a turn for the worse soon after that, so I didn't have much time to dwell on him."

In fact, the week of Mama's funeral, going through her things, I found Sarah Morgan's letter from C and began to piece together what really might have happened between my great-grandfolks. I thought the night with Dwayne, a fresh chill in my mind, would help me clarify— or at least vividly imagine—the relationship. The attraction/repulsion of forbidden skin. The fine line, sometimes, between violence and mutual passion. Surely, because of what had happened to me, I could see Cletus a little clearer, from Sarah Morgan's perspective? But really, the opposite occurred. I felt a swell of panic whenever I considered Cletus and Sarah's rendezvous. I knew my alarm was more about Dwayne and me than family history, but knowing this didn't help. I couldn't calm my anxiety, and it's part of what set me on the run, I suspect, back to what Bitter could tell me. How *do* black couples behave toward one another? And why?

"So what got this bee under your bonnet, to find your family?" Ariyeh asks. "Your mama's passing?"

"Partly. Though I'd been curious for a long time. Sounds funny, I suppose, but I got tired of being white. Tired of the 'burbs. The thing is, I remembered Houston, you know, though Mama had tried to erase it from me. I missed you and Bitter. You were like old songs I'd hear on the radio, tugging on me from far away."

"I remember your mama crying in a back bedroom, in the dark, all by herself. It's one of my strongest childhood memories. I don't know why. She used to scare me, she was sad so much."

"I wish I could cry for *her*. I mean, I know she had a hard life, I know she moved us to give me opportunities she never had . . . but I feel such rage at her, now, for *orchestrating* my life."

Ariyeh reaches over, takes my hand, and holds it on the seat between us. We pass a pair of hitchhikers, a long-haired couple with bedrolls and a cardboard sign saying ALBUQUERQUE. I'm still thinking of Mama, and the hitchhikers remind me of the one time I had to bum a ride—on the day she died. I'd stayed upset with Dwayne, with everything that had happened the night of our date. I kept hearing in my head, "The dark side. The dark side." One Monday, on my lunch break, I decided to exorcise this voice, to cancel Dwayne's challenge to me and tackle what he so clearly felt I wasn't facing.

But that wasn't all. I was running from Mama, too, that day—not so much her sickness and the duties it required . . . refilling prescriptions, bathing her, reading to her. I was happy to do those things. It was the *pretense*. The get well cards from friends. By now, we all knew she wasn't going to get well. The flowers. The move back home from the hospital, as though nothing had ever happened. The bedsheets her husband washed *every damn day*, as though she lay in a fancy hotel suite rather than a sickbed (she didn't sweat and barely moved enough to soil the linens). Dale told me he was doing everything he knew to "make her feel comfortable." But it seemed to me that he and Mama did everything they could to deny what was happening, the way Mama had disavowed our past. Just another whitewash. I wanted no part of it. I didn't mean to be cruel. But I *did* want to grieve—openly, and with Mama. Apparently, that wasn't allowed in Dale Licht's subdivision.

So one Monday—though I knew Mama had worsened, and I should stick by a phone—I headed for Deep Ellum. I *hoped* it would be a dark and dreary place, that it would remind me of Houston, that it would confirm for me that my beginnings were as awful as I thought (that day) they were . . . as wretched as my Dwayne-and-Dale-infected mood.

Rain and wind buffeted the trees, made the streets hard to negotiate. I checked a map and soon found myself crossing railroad tracks, bumping along old brick roads. Since the night with Dwayne, I'd been reading about Deep Ellum—the history buff in me—and had come across a description of the neighborhood in an old black weekly, on microfilm in the public library: "Down on 'Deep Ellum' in Dallas, where Central Avenue empties onto Elm Street, is where Ethiopia stretches forth her hands. It is the one spot in the city that needs no daylight savings time because there is no bedtime, and working hours have no limits. The only place recorded on earth where business, religion, hoodooism, gambling and stealing go on at the same time without friction."

I saw an empty train caboose, a streetcar shell, and several soft brick buildings, many of them burned, with faded signs on what remained of their walls: TOOL SHOP AND LOANS, INDIAN HERB EMPORIUM, SHOWS NIGHTLY. But mostly I saw slick new department stores, fern bars, antique shops. The neighborhood was rapidly redeveloping—the city didn't want to face its dark past, either. Whatever secret places Dwayne knew, holdovers from the old days, I wouldn't be able to find on my own in this driving rain. Discouraged, angry, still aching between my legs (more psychological now than physical), I turned around, tears in my eyes, to head back to work, and the car began to sputter. The "oil" light came on. I chugged another block or two before the engine died altogether. I didn't have an umbrella, so as I walked, looking for a gas station or a pay phone, I sought shelter in doorways, under awnings. Inadvertently, I'd looped back onto one of the undeveloped blocks. Broken glass, metal strips torn from dead buildings curled across the walks. Drunks huddled on porches or under boarded-up windows, begging change. *The nasty.* This is what I'd come to find—to degrade myself out of spite, out of anger at Mama, Dwayne, Dale—but it didn't make me feel any better. I heard a saxophone stutter somewhere inside an echoey room. Steam coiled from rusty grates in the concrete.

I was shivering and soaked when an old Ford Fairlane, dented and red, pulled up beside me, splashing my feet. It was as scratched and weathered as an old horse. A young black woman on the passenger side rolled down her window. "Need a lift?" I got in back, wary but grateful, and asked to be dropped at the nearest service station. Behind the wheel, a big, gruff man, bearded and with an afro the size of a bowling ball. The car smelled of French fries and talcum powder. We drove for several blocks, none of us speaking. Finally, at a stoplight, the guy turned to me. "I want you to know, I don't normally stop for white folks," he said. "It's only on account of my old lady here that I'm giving you this ride." I nodded and croaked, "Thank you." He let me off at a Shell station. I had the car towed and wound up back at work around four. I called to check on Mama, and Dale, weeping, told me she'd passed away unexpectedly an hour ago (*who* wasn't expecting it, you poor, pathetic . . .).

I sat at my desk, gripping the phone till my hand hurt. I'd been playing in the dark while my mama died. And the dark wasn't really there anymore. Everything was a lousy, stupid joke. This is what I'd thought I wanted to happen—for the truth to burst through the laundered veneer of our lives, but no, it wasn't what I wanted at all, not at all. What I *really* wanted, I knew now, was to return from Deep Ellum with the "dark side" all over my skin—inside-out, upside down—enough to shock Mama out of her sickbed stupor and force her to tell me everything, everything, right from the start. But now she was gone. How much of me, I wondered, went with her? I tried to weep, then and for several days afterward, but by now I was well-trained. Whatever's inside, I'd learned, you keep back, like an old dollar bill in a mint tin.

By coincidence I see a Shell station and pull off the highway to fill up. Ariyeh has been quiet for several miles. As the young attendant wipes my windshield, she turns to me and says softly, "I've just been thinking. Trying to decide whether I'm making this up or not, and I don't think so. I believe I remember your daddy coming to the house one day."

I sit up straight. The smell of gas through my open window dizzies me. The car shivers in the breeze of passing trucks.

"We would have been . . . oh, I don't know, five or six? Can that be right? I'm not sure where you were. Off with your mama somewhere. I remember my own mama, Cass, was yelling and screaming about money or some-such, giving Daddy hell over something, and I'm just trying to stay out of the way, you know, when this strange man walks up on the porch, real slim, puffing a cigarette, and asks Daddy can he borrow a sawbuck or two? This is the part that seems like I'm making it up, 'cause for all her yelling, Cass was never really violent . . . but it's also the part that catches in my mind like an actual memory, it was so unusual. Cass rears back and hurls an open honey jar at the screen door, right where the man is standing, shaking sort of, like he's sick, and she shouts at him, 'Ain't a dime in this house, and if'n there was, *you'd* never see it!' I see him slouching there on the porch, spattered with gold, shaking his head and mumbling—I can't believe I remember this now—'Heads or tails, either way you lose.' I asked Daddy about him later, and something he said made me think he was your dad."

I try to picture the man. "You never told me."

"Eighteen bucks even, ma'am," the attendant says, startling me. I give him a twenty. My hand shakes.

"Didn't I? Then maybe . . . I don't know . . . maybe I'm dreaming—"

"Oh hell, it doesn't matter. Either way, he's just an old ghost to me."

"A ghost who won't leave you in peace."

I admit to her I put a call in to Huntsville, requesting a visit with Elias Woods. The official I reached said he'd get back to me. He was afraid I was a journalist. "No more death row interviews, all right? You goddam liberal writers *always* make us out to be monsters. We're only doing our jobs."

The attendant returns with my change, and we're off again, through pecan groves and scrub oak, dewberry fields, gnarled old magnolias, moss-covered, leaves applauding in the wind. The air smells of mint. Just off the highway a drive-in movie screen looms in a field, an immense sheet hung out to dry. Bitter took me and Ariyeh to a drive-in once when we were little; I remember thinking, "Bitter's the only dad I have"; remember popcorn and Cokes spilling over our dresses; remember Bitter sighing. I even remember the movie because I saw it again years later, this time in a suburban Dallas theater, a second-run place, with an all-white, upper-class audience. The film was *Pinky,* about a poor mulatta who decides not to "violate her race" by marrying a white man and inheriting a wealthy plantation; instead, she chooses to remain a Negro and opens a school for dark-skinned kids. The drive-in audience, mostly young, mostly black, howled with derision at the melodramatic, sentimental plot and at the woman's stupidity, passing up the good life. Years later, the white audience in Dallas wept at the young woman's selflessness. I recall glancing at Mama, who sat impassively beside me as Dale and her new white friends dabbed their eyes, careful not to topple soft drinks into their laps. (What was she thinking? Was the movie a surprise to her? Would she have gone if she'd known what it was about?) And I recalled the low, dark chortles in the night from long ago, the smells of sweat and food and sex (though I didn't know that's what it was, then) rising from the cars, the smell of the nearby bayou, rotty and dank, frog chirps competing with actors' voices from the scratchy drive-in speakers, and I wanted to return to the noise and the stink and the mess, to *real life* (my lost daddy's home), which seemed to me buried now under Mama's department store catalogs, bedspreads, and furnishings. Her scented toilet paper.

"Yeah, I remember that drive-in," Ariyeh says now. "It's the first place I saw people fucking, though I thought they were hurting each other or something. I think Daddy *wanted* us to see it. Sex education."

"Right." I laugh. "When I was twelve, Mama took me to a series of films at the YWCA. Each week, cartoon cutaways of uteruses, penises, gumdrop sperm. No one said a word, all these mothers and daughters sitting stiffly in cold folding chairs. And in the car, on the way home, she kept her eyes pinned to the road. When I asked her what in the world we'd just been watching, she'd say, 'Why don't we get some ice cream?' Or she'd stop and buy me comic books—*Silver Surfer, Fantastic Four,* these boys' books, you know, that I didn't have the slightest interest in, though they weren't any more outlandish than the sex-toons—and I'd wind up gorging myself at Baskin-Robbins. To this day, I associate conception with the taste of chocolate-chocolate chip."

Ariyeh cracks up, and we recall all the places we sneaked off to as girls to talk about boys. The mud-dauber shack. A spot along the bayou, where someone had tossed an old stove and it lay rusting in the mud, tangled in poison ivy and tree roots. And of course, our favorite, the Flower Man's house. Sometimes we'd see him nailing up a new treasure—a child's tutu, a clay butterfly, a G.I. Joe doll—on the outer walls of his home.

"Is he crazy, the Flower Man?" I ask.

"Who knows? Maybe he's just got a genius for junk. Like I do for lunch. Can we stop soon?" She smiles, embarrassed. She was *always* the first to get hungry.

I pull off near a billboard advertising mysterious ancient caves. A cow watches us unwrap our sandwiches. We sit on the hood of the car. "A developer's dream," I say, gazing at the fields. "I try to remember what it was like to enjoy nature's beauty. Surely, at one time, I could just soak it up. Now, I can't look at any place without imagining feasibility studies, cost estimates . . ."

"Do you *like* your job?" Ariyeh asks.

Sparrows gossip in the trees. Diesel smoke in the wind.

"I'm good at it. Is that the same as liking?"

"I don't think so, sweetie."

"I have an aquarium at home. The catfish always stays at the bottom, cleaning up the others' leftovers. They're darting around at the top, picking food off the water's surface. He's catching whatever falls between the cracks. I call him Hoover."

"You feel like him, is that it?"

I waggle my head, neither yes or no.

"Sounds like he works too hard. Like he's trying to hide."

I open the potato chip bag. "You?"

"Jesus. Me? I'm a Band-Aid stretched across an open chest." A rueful laugh. "We don't have enough resources to give these kids a first-rate education. Or even a *third*-rate one. They're going to wind up on the streets, killing each other, most of them. We all know it. The kids know it, too, so they don't even try."

"Are there any whites in your school?"

"Only a handful. Busing's been repealed."

"You're very brave. You and Reggie both. I told him that."

She nibbles her bread. "Daddy thinks we're crazy, trying so hard to improve things. We fight about it all the time, and he and Reggie can hardly speak to each other. He says he's lived long enough to see most ideals wither and die. 'Pie in the sky don't do black folk no good,' he tells me. You know the way he talks. I admit, sometimes I think he's right. I get so tired."

I hug her. She sags, and I realize how tense she is most of the time.

"Well. We'd best get to this gloomy old field of yours," she says, falsely bright.

"You sure?" I say, rubbing her back.

She nods, narrows her eyes. "I'm sure. It's Saturday, for God's sakes. What am I doing worrying about work?"

She's done talking now. I won't push her. I learned a long time ago not to do that. "Okay. Let's see what we can see." But I'll watch her closely the rest of the day.

Just east of San Antonio I take a cutoff onto a narrow gravel road. My directions are makeshift, a slew of landmarks and locations from various historical sources, all incomplete, testifying to the fact that nothing remains to distinguish the hanging field from other meadows. In all likelihood, I won't even know it if I see it. We bump over ruts and rocks. Billboards for foot powder, insecticide, Yankee Motor Oil. Hillocks of hay. Jutting stone. To the west, a line of pines, stiff but somewhat crooked: sloppy troops at parade rest. Behind them, sloping down the barest suggestion of a hill, mesquite trees tangled in dewberry vines. "This is it," I say uncertainly. My face goes hot. "I think this is it."

Ariyeh looks at the field, boredom in her eyes: a child disappointed at the fair. At least she's forgotten her own troubles for now. "*This?* What makes you think so?"

"Those trees. That little hill. It's got to be."

"There's nothing here."

"Exactly. The army erased all traces of what it did."

"Why?"

"Well, naturally the officers knew it was incendiary, lynching thirteen black men. They wanted to make an example for other Negro soldiers, but they didn't want to incite more rioting in Houston. So they carried out the execution in secret away from the city and only announced it afterwards. Even then, they said it had taken place at a nearby fort in accordance with strict military procedure."

"What do you hope to find here today?"

I shake my head, step from the car. Grass scratches my ankles. I make sure the Taurus is okay in the high weeds, not too hot underneath, no danger of flame. Ariyeh follows me, a few tentative steps, then stops to swat mosquitoes. Her boredom has turned into annoyance. The field is soft in places, then hard, like leftover food not fully frozen. It *smells* leftover, too: smoky, green, slightly spoiled. The pines are dry in the late summer heat, green-going-to-yellow. Red and purple dabs of flowers. Shadows move across the limp stalks as a warm breeze blows the trees, silhouettes huddled in soil clumps, praying men, bones bent by grief.

I survey the field the way I imagine the commander did that day, sweeping my eyes across its borders against the bronze and azure light, and I feel myself slip—out of my skin, out of time. Green bugs pop from the dirt. A khaki-clad guard, gripping his rifle, turns his collar up against a sudden early-morning chill. The folding chairs creak. A whiff of sweat and shit. *Coming home, Lord, coming home.* I can even smell the ropes, several yards away, resinous, dusty, redolent of earth and passing time. They sound violent, like disease must sound inside the body, eating it away. The hangman adjusts the knots. A train whistle echoes to the north, clacking wheels, roaring wind, goods speeding through the woods, sustenance for communities of fortunate men, far away. Sweat rivers my ribs. I call, "Attention!" and ask my god to forgive me. As the prisoners shuffle up the scaffolding, I turn my head away, and there, shivering in the shadows at the fringe, a pathetic white figure in a rumpled blue dress, hands clasped, her gaze darting, ratchety, quick as a hummingbird. Her presence unsettles, even angers, me. She has no business here. The army does not conduct charity work. Best to send her home with various physics, herbs, broths, with sympathetic sighs and the narcotic advice of talk-cure men. A thump. A shout. One of the doomed has tripped on the gallows steps. I flick my eyes to glimpse him . . .

. . . *to see if he is safe.* Is it he who is down? Shaken, tugged, kicked by a guard. My eyes sting. I pull a kerchief from my dress pocket. What does it matter if Cletus twists an ankle? Within minutes his soul will be lost. He stands stiffly now at the platform's edge, his long arms, capable of such tenderness and warmth, neatly by his side as if he were about to be decorated for valor. I have felt the soldier in him, a slight formality as though his commander were judging him, even in our intimacies: his kisses little forays into unsecured territory, cautious, efficient. For all he has risked to spend a few unbuttoned moments with me, he is still a deeply proper man, his bravery dutiful, expected. *I* am the rebel, careless in my prim trappings (perhaps a tad ungrateful, unappreciative of how easy life has been till now), aching to secede . . .

Until last night, when the city fragmented. Sudden spasms like a Roman candle. The noise awakened me over my parents' murky snoring. Gunshots. Guttural voices. Immediately I knew there was trouble at the camp, perhaps because Cletus had been nervous for days, sensing unease among his comrades, simmering anger. I rose quietly, buttoned my dress. Cletus and I . . . did we have a regular meeting time? Each night? Three nights a week? In my mama's garden? Why not in a safer spot? How was he able to escape from his bunk? Did he tell his commanding officer he wanted to rise before dawn to lend us a hand, before his own chores began at the camp? Was he granted permission to be charitable to this stumbling white family for whom his father once worked?

And tonight, what had happened to him? Mud-spattered, soaked, frightened, and wild. "Cletus?" I whispered. "For God's sakes, what is it?" He trembled as though his ribs were a spinning turbine. He gripped my arms, tearing a sleeve. He was at war. The causes were unclear to me, the reasons for sacrifice ambiguous, but I felt the conviction in his clench. He hadn't waited to be shipped to France. "Cletus?" "Forgive me," he said. Then my buttons spilled into the furrows at our feet, bitter seeds among the sproutings of weeds, and I was enemy, hostage, land to be seized . . . in a lurch, my perspective leaps again; I smell olives, gin, stale automobile upholstery; Dwayne's face hovers above me; "The dark part of you wants it" . . . *Coming home, Lord, coming home.* Another leap. Cletus wears the rope now like a horse's harness. He holds his dignity. Or he doesn't. The soldiers pull the triggers. "Cletus! For God's sakes!"

Ariyeh folds her arms, scratches an ankle with her foot. An edgy sound, insisting on the moment. "So?" she says, imploring me to be done with this place.

I bow my head to clear it, walk to the fringe, where the field starts to curve like a toppled bowl. I struggle to focus. "This must be where they had the coffins waiting. And there, where the Mexicans stood. The hired men who'd actually do the burying."

"What do you get from this?" Ariyeh asks, not unkindly. She slaps another mosquito. "Looking around? Speculating?"

A whisper in the trees. Birds. Wind. "More questions," I admit. "I think the only resolution I can hope for is to accept I'll know only so much. Maybe I know as much, already, as I ever will. But to be convinced of that, I need to see this. To see it's nothing. Does that make sense?"

"Of course. Yes."

"Too many perspectives . . ."

"What do you mean?"

"I wish I could settle on a single approach to the story . . ." A train—an *actual* one—goes speeding through the woods. "I've always blamed it on the women. Instability. A weakness of mind, even of soul. Mama and Grandma, neither black nor white, here nor there . . . and Great-Grandma, I can't even pin *her* story down . . . but that's not what I'm getting at. Sometimes I lose myself in other people. People from the past. It's the weirdest thing, Ariyeh. It's like my whole ego . . . I don't know . . . just *spills* into others . . ."

"It's a gift. A vision. The ability to see through the cracks."

"I fear it means I've got no center."

"No, really. Think of slaves," Ariyeh says. "Living in shacks but gaining access to the big house, the masters' bedrooms and kitchens. They had the whole perspective, in a way even their owners didn't. Saw it all, top to bottom, inside and out. Maybe that's the gift you have, T. I mean, I believe that stuff."

"If so, it's a bitch to carry."

"I know."

"Sometimes I think I'm going nuts. Hearing voices, you know, like some crazy bag lady on the street." I want to linger in the field, to breathe it inside me, but Ariyeh is getting more and more impatient. I smile at her. "Okay, what do you say? Dairy Queen? Time for an ice cream sundae?" I hear the false cheeriness in my voice, and I'm sure she's aware of it too.

"Sure. I'll buy."

We move toward the car, listening to the insect buzz in the field. Back on the highway, signs for bail bondsmen, a semipro baseball team, an Arthur Murray dance studio. I'm disoriented; I grip the wheel until my fingers ache.

Ariyeh laughs, capping our uncomfortable quiet. "You ever take dance lessons?"

"No." I feel the pull, still, of another world, another time. "I have enough trouble keeping my balance as it is."

"I tried once, at ten or eleven. Talked Daddy into shelling out the cash—he still had his carpentry practice then. Right away I discovered ballet was *not* for black girls! Those pink tights? Supposed to blend in with the white girls' skin, but my ass showed right through. Chocolate syrup in a strawberry sundae! And the movements, all shoulders, and *tall,* stiff postures—not for us low-slung types. Teacher used to scream at me, 'Pull your hips up,' and I'd tell her, 'Lady, these hips ain't going *nowhere!'* It was the one time Daddy yelled at me when I was a kid, the day I wanted to quit. I'd pestered and pestered him for the lessons, and he'd wasted good money. Told me I had to put up with the embarrassment. That's the way it is for folks like us. He'd done it all his life. It's the kind of attitude Reggie can't stand in him." She slumps in the seat. The outing is over for her; her world has come pressing back in. "I don't know. I guess it worked in Daddy's time—up to a point. Most fellas didn't get hurt, putting on a silly clown act for the buckras. Reggie had the Movement, you know. It was on TV every night. Malcolm and H. Rap. He learned to clench his fist. And that worked too—up to a point."

I spot a DQ sign and exit. "What about now?"

"Now?" She sags again.

In the Dairy Queen, Mexican kids clamber over mustard-smeared tables. Their father, tiny, in a straw hat and dirty shirt, stands helplessly by the napkin dispensers. A woman I take to be his wife balances four or five soft drinks in a mushy cardboard container and yells at the kids in Spanish. Ice cream drips like Elmer's glue from a silver machine just behind the counter. The cashiers are either high school kids in braces or grandma types who can't hide their contempt for their young partners, who will probably work here only for the summer. "You can supersize that for only sixty more cents," a girl behind a register tells an overweight woman desperately counting her change. While Ariyeh buys our treats I'm standing back trying not to lose the hanging field. Its soft light, its moldering mulch smell. But even as I tighten my mental grip, it's slipping away from me. The present is too damned insistent. Cletus shatters again, and Sarah Morgan. As ever, I'm left on my own. It's *now,* it's August, Ariyeh needs thirty-six—no, thirty-eight—more cents. I scrabble in my purse and hand her the coins.

8

WE'RE BACK at Etta's on a Sunday night. Ariyeh has talked Reggie into showing up, and he sits across the table from me, sullen, gripping a leather bag as though it's his last earthly possession. Earl and his boys are taking their sweet time setting up. Bitter's buddies trickle in, one by one—overalls, straw hats, ratty cotton shirts (only the women are dressed to the nines)—and make their way to the bar.

"Hey man, what up?"

"End of the world."

"I can co-sign that."

"Mickey Mouse in the house and Donald Duck don't give a fuck."

"Etta darling, how 'bout a Forty or an Eight Ball?"

"Hen Dog for me, and some of them hog maws."

"Pass the pluck-wine."

Like last week, the brandy women settle regally at a table, placing their paper sacks in a delicate row, and as before, Earl, dressed in green and purple silk, courts them lewdly. "Mmm-*mmm!* Looka the box on that fox! Sugar, you sharing them cakes?"

The women ignore him, but they're trying hard not to smile.

A man at the bar, knocking back cup after yellow cup of what he calls "do-it fluid," ogles Ariyeh. "You jingling, babe," he says, swaying. "You ain't no haincty bitch, is you?"

Reggie scowls, and another man says to the first, "Parlay, slick. Don't be beaming on the brother's girl. He liable to jump salty on you."

"You damn skippy," Reggie growls.

The first man turns to me. "Fried, dyed, and laid to the side," he says, pointing at my hair. "Am I right? You muh-rhine-ee, ain't you?"

"Dead it, slick. Git ghost," the man's friend says, watching Reggie nervously, and both men move away toward the Coors crates stacked against the wall.

"Charming place," Reggie tells Ariyeh. "A throwback to the twenties, when the only ambitions allowed the black man were to get drunk and get laid."

"Chill, Reggie. Please. And try to be nice to Daddy."

The old scarecrow leans against a wall holding a malt liquor can, grinning in private ecstasy. Etta shivers past rows of ripped, cotton-spitting chairs, ferrying a tray of Olde English 800s. I'm struck, again, by everyone's age. Reggie, Ariyeh, and I, along with the bass player and drummer, are the only under-fifties. Reggie has noticed this too, I suspect—he glares distastefully, sizing up the room. In the malarial light from the bar's beer signs, Bitter and his posse appear ancient, wrinkled, and discarded. Packed-away paper. They crowd our table now, bearing drinks: OEs and Hennessy's "Very Special" cognac. The old men smell of aftershave and peanuts. Reggie gestures at the band members, who are talking and laughing with one another while their guitars remain in cases and the drummer's cymbals lay stacked on the floor like extrathin cake layers. "It's after ten already," he mutters harshly.

"Listen him," says a short man next to Bitter. "I think he wearing a white man's watch, eh Bitter? Best sit back and relax, brother. We on CP Time in here."

The men—three of them, and Uncle—all laugh.

"When you live by your hands, the way we done, you learn to 'ppreciate a *slower pace,* know'm saying?" the man continues. I've heard Bitter call him Grady. The two of them worked together in Texas City, roughnecking and unloading bananas from Peruvian freighters. "Last job I had, canning shrimp down in Galveston, ever' three day or so, the factory upped its niggamation—you know, speeding up the 'ssembly line so we'd work harder and faster for the same amount of pay. Now, that timepiece you wearing and that impatient scowl on your face, brother, they based on niggamation. White man's tricknology. You feel a whole lot better, you let it go."

Reggie's fists tremble on the bag in his lap. "I've spent the last three years renovating twenty-three row houses on Alabama Street, using only hammers, screwdrivers, and saws," he says, low and precise. "Don't assume I haven't worked with my hands."

A tall man whistles and laughs. "Ooh-ee, Grady, better watch yo' ass. He be thinking he the Head Nigger in Charge!"

"Mack Daddy!"

"Word to the mother!"

Ariyeh's hand moves like a blown leaf up Reggie's arm. He frowns, squirms in his chair, but doesn't say anything. Finally, the band rolls into its first tune. Earl is already sweating. The drummer *flick-flicks* the hi hat—a sassy skirt-switch—and the bass fills in with *betcha bottom dollar, betcha bottom dollar.* The lead riffs *lonesome me,* and Earl scats and grunts like a catfight. *You get them every morning when that train whistle blows and the factory doors burst open; you get them at lunch when the bugs are so bad you can't sit still and eat your bread; you get them in the evening when the pint bottle's empty and that greased steel blows once-a-more, once-a-more, once-a-more, ah, I'm talking about the blues . . .*

The scarecrow closes his eyes and goes into his solo dance; politely, folks shove back their chairs to make room. The brandy ladies order setups and ice, squeeze their plastic limes. *You get them every night when the bedbugs start to bite.* The room smells sweet and sour: gin and cologne, perfume, food, and sweat. Black faces, brown faces, yellow, gold, and tan. I'm glad for Bitter's lanky old frame, hunched just a few feet away; glad for Ariyeh's beauty and Reggie's indulgence on her behalf; glad for Earl's graceful bulk. In only my second time here, the place feels deeply familiar, like a rag doll from childhood rediscovered in an attic, stained with years-old dog slobber, spit-up, and dirt, smelling faintly of all those nights you clutched it in bed as a girl, tucked between your legs or tight beneath your arm. I sip some of Uncle's cognac. It warms my mouth and throat.

Reggie rises, unlatching his leather bag. Ariyeh glances at him, anxious. From the bag he pulls a handful of orange fliers—melty and pale in the bar's yellow light—and begins to pace the room, leaving them on tables or beer crates within people's reach. Folks stare at them, then him, lips twisted, angry, as though they've just been ordered to leave.

You get them at midnight all alone in your bed when the body goes cold and the no-noise of your house wakes you like a smoke alarm, alarm, alarm, ah, you know what I'm talking about, I'm talking about the blues . . .

I pluck one of the fliers from a beer puddle:

Free Mumia Abu-Jamal
The Voice of the Voiceless

Free All Political Prisoners
and Prisoners of War

Bitter also peruses one of the sheets. "Hey!" he shouts at Reggie, grimacing, squinting. "What's all this Mumia-Jumbo?" Ariyeh shakes her head.

"Read it," Reggie tells him.

"Don't make no sense."

"Mumia's on death row in Pennsylvania, wrongly accused of killing a cop. The government wants to silence him."

"Oh, the gov'ment, huh?" Bitter tugs his bottom lip. "And why's that?"

"He was a founding member and minister of information of the Black Panther Party of Philadelphia. He had a radio show, and he exposed the cops' racism in bombing the MOVE house, burning all those children—"

"Brother 'bout the *people's* business," Grady says, grinning. He slurps his malt liquor.

"That's right, *brother,*" Reggie hisses. "While you old poot-butts sit here getting wasted night after night, listening to this retro shit"—he nods at Earl—"some of us worry about the fact that the government is about to murder a prominent black revolutionary—"

"Reggie," Ariyeh sighs, her face behind her hands.

"Whoa, boy, watch it now, watch it, you 'bout to mess up with a capital *F!*"

"Sho that's right. Bet a fat man going through a doughnut hole!"

"—some of us worry that the informal executions of the sixties— Fred Hampton, Martin—have become, in the nineties, *formal* executions. Legal lynchings, dig? You know how many black kids are sitting on death row right now?"

"Ooh, he an E-Light, Bitter. Best back off him, man!"

"He got da butta from the duck!"

"Man say, 'Gimme some dap!'"

You get them when you lick the sweet honey and you know you shouldn't have even opened the jar.

Bitter smiles patiently. "Let me drop some science on you, Reggie," he says. "You an earnest, sincere fella—I've never doubted that—but this Black Nationalism shit is strictly po-ass. Generation just ahead of you learned that during the civil rights years. You only cut yourself off, you make it *us-against-them,* see, start believing the gov'ment out to crush us all. Gov'ment don't have that much imagination."

"Government is about power, pure and simple. And you're an ignorant old fool if you think it's not out to absolutely annihilate the black man."

"Geek sho got a hellified way of 'splaining thangs," Grady says.

"Look at the Crime Bill Congress passed, hm?"

The men just stare.

"Makes joining a gang an 'aggravated circumstance,'" Reggie says. "Who you think that's aimed at? White folks? And who are the Congress and the army? *Gangs!* Rich ofays who felt free to steal a *whole continent* from its original inhabitants—"

"Shit, boy—"

"—to rape girls and sell poppy all over Southeast Asia, or to bomb kids in Philly—"

You get them in rain and fog, in sunshine and snow. Wherever you go, the blues'll surely know.

"Imagination tops power, ever' time," Bitter insists. "Fellas my age, we know this, 'cause it's how we've got by. And you know imagination's secret? It *integrates,* man. Mixes memories, songs, poetry, ideas—little bit here, little bit there. From the white man's world, from the black man's world, making us all a little richer. You cut yourself off, pretty soon you use up all your own air. See, me, in my time . . . I may have been barred from certain places *physically,* but I saw *black style* making its way into white dress, white talk, white music. Slow but sure, our imagination chipping holes in that wall. And wherever I worked, I was sneaking access to white spaces, man, seeing more of them than they could ever see of me, studying up on them, learning, gaining *power* to go 'long with my dreaming, don't you know? You give away your best advantage, boy, you prance and shout, 'Black is beautiful!' Keep it on the down-low, is all I'm saying."

"Old man, you can talk from appetite to asshole, and I still won't buy it. You're not on the street the way I am, sifting through the wreckage. Nine-year-olds hooked on crack. Last week, Ariyeh's school? Pair of fifth-graders caught freebasing in the boy's room." He swings his head; his dreads look enameled in the room's streaky light. "Better recognize the *structure* of the fix."

"What you talk'm 'bout?"

"All right, one example? Just one, 'cause I know that's all you can hump."

Bitter snorts.

"Listen up. Used to be, powder coke went for two hundred bucks a gram—it's a rich man's drug—till the government and the drug cartels figured they could score a hefty profit *and* kill our kids, flooding the ghettos with that same shit in rock form. Now a rock sells for ten bucks. Dig—most *coke* users are still fat-cat ofays, all right, lee people, but most the jail time's done by our brothers doing crack. Follow me here."

Oh, he's got the *spirit* now. Cooking with propane. I can't keep my eyes off him.

"Feds allow probation for first-time possession of five grams of coke. For the same amount of crack—the street version, the *black* version— it's five years, automatic. That's *power,* my man. A cold, deliberate attempt to crush our families, our youth, our future, and our hope."

Bitter runs a hand across his chest, wrinkling his shirt. "Young'uns with 'tude, tight as Jimmy's hatband, think they invented it all. Injustice, righteous anger. Don't know they own history. You think like lit, boy. Don't come into my house trying to Martin-and-Malcolm me."

"Well, don't *you* mammy-and-uncle *me,* old man."

Ariyeh is anguished, listening to her lover and her father go at it, but me . . . despite my fears of Reggie's temper and my worries about Bitter's health, I find myself exhilarated by their exchange. I know what Reggie's talking about: I've seen stone-cold power-plays in the mayor's office. And I've survived on Bitter's "down-low."

But more than this, I realize I really *was* cut off—airless, alone—in my stepdaddy's home. Dale Licht couldn't imagine two black men disagreeing. Or a black generation gap. To him, all dark-skinned folk were a monolith, thinking alike, acting alike, a fearful enemy when freed from their proper place (serving well-done rib eye in the country club). I remember one day, during O. J. Simpson's trial, I stopped by the house to lunch with Mama. Dale was home from the law office that afternoon, studying briefs at the kitchen table. Next to the microwave, sound low, a portable TV showed Johnnie Cochran talking about the bloody glove found on Simpson's property. "If it doesn't fit, you must acquit," he said, electrifying me, echoing the slightly mocking, singsong signifying language I remembered from Houston street corners. Dale's neck turned red (Cochran wasn't speaking to *him*). "*How* can all the blacks think this man is innocent?" he said. I wanted to tell him, "*All* blacks don't think that," but it's a measure of how much I'd sponged up his world that the same question had plagued me. Eventually, Dale's fury dwindled into sadness. He looked old and defeated, his gray hair rumpled into quills. In moments like this, when I saw his vulnerabilities or when he was kind to Mama or me, which was most of the time—he was, is, a nice man—I could concede he was a more complicated package than I gave him credit for being. He'd call the country club waiters—men his own age—"boys" and think nothing of it, but he'd also married my mama, whose dusky past he knew all about. He put up with my sullenness, even when, half the time, *I* didn't know why I felt sulky. Since I've been on my own I've avoided him, and surely he feels the bitterness of my rejection. Still, if I were to call him, he'd do anything I asked. Like it or not, I understand his world is also mine. I don't know how to square this with the fact that, if he were sitting with me here, he'd be trembling with fear and disgust. At the moment, I'm shaking with pleasure.

But Ariyeh has had enough. "Stop it, both of you," she tells Bitter and Reggie. Her eyes shine. "I'm trying to hear the music."

"Fine," Reggie says, throwing up his hands. "Wasn't *my* idea to come."

Bitter settles in his chair, stroking his chest. I squeeze his arm.

Sweat's flying off Earl: a busted fire hydrant. "We styling and profiling!" he shouts. He leans over the brandy ladies' table. "Yo' mama do the lawdy lawd!" he croons, rasping, breathy. We're jazzing on a Sunday night. If the Axeman is out there—I glance at the door—he's pacing in frustration. I sip some more Hen Dog, close my eyes, and tilt my head, whirling with its rusty warmth. It tastes like an old door hinge.

"Have you heard? The bird, bird, bird—bird's the word." I open my eyes on the strutting man who'd spooned over Ariyeh earlier. Reggie stiffens, but she isn't even aware of the guy. She's watching Etta stuff bottles and wet paper towels into a Hefty bag. "What's the matter, sweetie?" I ask. She looks horrified.

"It's like . . . a child's body," she says, one hand to her mouth, the other pointing at the bag. "I keep picturing them, you know. The missing boys from our school."

"See? It wasn't a good idea to come here tonight," Reggie says, smoothing her shoulder. "Let's book, how 'bout?"

"No, no. I like the music. I like sitting here with my cousin." I lock my fingers in hers.

In the open doorway, now, the Axeman looms, raising his blade . . . but it's only Bayou Slim, squinting through the smoke, bumping his old guitar case into the room. Earl and the boys step back. The crowd quietens. "Looks like death eating a sodey cracker," Grady whispers, trembling, bony—he's licked a few crumbs himself.

Slim doesn't bother to tune. He thumbs his strings as if skimming stiff pages. "Heads or tails, you lose," he croaks—not so much singing as *thrusting* his voice into the booze-fumed air. Only the old scarecrow is dancing now. Everyone else concentrates on the floor or the drinks in their hands. Even Etta turns away. "I am that I am!" Slim screams, holding his final chord. He whips off his frayed straw hat and collects a few dollars. When he slips out the door, the room resumes its buzz.

"Etta, doll, can we get a letter from home over here, please ma'am?" Grady calls.

She brings us a watermelon sliced into wide, red grins. I pass—again, I've had more to drink than I realized—and step outside to clear my head, though the air, even this late in the evening, is hardly a relief: dense, close, searing. It's like standing by a barbecue grill, inhaling the heat. Roaches, big as cigar butts, twist across the gravel parking lot. Smaller bugs *snick* and skitter at my feet. I rub the smoke from my eyes. The Big Dipper tilts above the Flower Man's house. An old song pulses through my head: "Follow the gourd . . ."

The streets are empty. I wonder where Slim could have got to.

"There you are." Reggie lounges in the doorway, holding his bag. "I had something I wanted to give you." He steps near, as warm as an old bed quilt.

"Oh? By the way," I say, "I'll be happy to write in support of Mumia."

He squints at me, a tough, guarded look. "Thank you." He pulls from his bag a fat paperback, gold and gray: *The Angela Davis Reader.* "Ariyeh told me about your run-in with your colleague."

I'm not sure what he's talking about. Dwayne? Before I can ask him, he nudges my hands with the book. "I've dog-eared a piece you should read."

All my life, smart black boys have been telling me what to think. I look up at him, questioning, lean toward his body a little. Ariyeh appears behind him in the doorway. "School tomorrow," she says, followed by a yawn. "I thought I could stay for a couple of sets—I really wanted to—but I guess I've got to call it a night. Can't keep my eyes open."

I thank them both for coming. "How often I get to spend time with my cousin?" Ariyeh answers.

"Are you okay?"

She nods unconvincingly. "You'll call me, now, before you leave town?"

Bitter and his buddies laugh raucously inside. The Flower Man's bottle tree chimes. "Sure," I say. She kisses my cheek. So does Reggie. They throw their arms around each other and weave away, through the gravel and glass of the parking lot.

9

A WHITE PINE building, three blocks from Bitter's house, GROCERY/RIBS painted on its side. There's a pay phone in a weedy lot out front. Across the street this morning, on the porch of a rickety row house, four old men guzzle Forties. In front of the store three b-boys with a boom box smoke blunts and give me a cocky once-over. LL Cool J is rapping about *knocking you out*. (Yeah, this white chick's heard Cool J, I could tell the boys. I don't live *entirely* on another planet.) Sausage sizzles inside; a wet, earthy smell rolls from the open doorway. Next to the phone, near a stack of rotting boxes, a rat pulls a shank bone into some shade.

I punch in my phone card code, then my friend Shirley's number. She's been feeding my fish and birds. I call her a friend, though I see her socially only at the happy hours after work (she's just down the hall, in Social Services). It rarely occurs to me to invite my coworkers home for dinner. I'm not sure why. Shirley is high yellow, too, so I feel comfortable with her, though we've never schmoozed about skin.

She answers on the third ring and seems happy to hear my voice. No problem, she says, take a few extra days. I promise to write her a check for the additional food when I get back. Maybe in the next two weeks I can talk Bitter into seeing a doctor. Maybe I can get my name on the prison's guest list. "How are Crockett and Bowie?" I ask.

"Such good birds. Crockett's picked up a couple new words. My fault, I'm afraid. I did like you said, made myself at home, spent a little time with them. The other night, while they ate, I stayed and watched *NYPD Blue*. Today, Crockett's going, 'Scumbag. Skel.' Sorry."

I laugh, though this *does* bother me. A barrage of insults when I walk in the door?

"Telisha, I wanted to ask you . . . you know Dwayne Jefferson, don't you? He said you were pals."

The name stings. "Yes. Why?"

"He's been calling me, asking me out. I think it turns him on, I was a finalist for the Cowboys cheerleading thing? I like him well enough, I guess, but there's something . . . a kind of arrogance . . ."

"Stay away from him." My own force shocks me.

"Really? What do you know?"

"Nothing, just . . . I agree with you. About the arrogance." Do I lay it all out for her? What purpose would that serve? Can I trust her, or would the story get out, all over the mayor's office? *I've never had a white black woman.* "Just be careful, Shirl. I don't think he's a good guy."

"Okay, thanks." She's disappointed.

She says she's run through the Terra Fin flake food. I tell her to make things easy for herself and get some long-term feeding tablets for the aquarium. My voice wobbles, saying good-bye. It's not Shirley's fault—she asked an innocent question—but I'm angry at her for unsettling me.

"Say, fly lady, I'm amp over here," one of the b-boys calls. "I ain't gaffling you, babe, come on over now and check out my hard, honey bozack. It's fiending for you. No shit, sugar."

His posse cracks up. "Aw, get off the woman's bra strap, G. She come backed up."

"I just want her to lamp wit' me."

"Look to me like a Mickey T."

I step through the weeds, watching for rats, annoyed at my thready jeans, which attract sticker burrs left and right, but grateful I didn't put on shorts this morning, which might have amped the boys even more. Hide as much flesh as you can—a habit with me. Cool J's rapping now about a "playette" with toe rings whose sexual prowess can turn a prince into a king. I cross the street, pause on a dirt path where a sidewalk should be, and pluck the thorns from my pants. At the happy hours with Shirley and others from work, in Fuddruckers or Fridays or Chilis, rock-and-roll muzak usually plays, but occasionally a rap tune will jump through the speakers. "You ever really listen to this shit, the hard-core stuff?" a mayor's aide asked the table one evening. "It's 'mothafucka mothafucka mothafucka.' That's it."

"Maybe they'll all kill themselves and save us the trouble," said a buddy of his.

The men on the porch are doing a pretty good job, right now, of erasing themselves. The yard is littered with drained malt liquor cans, blue as diamonds in the sunlight. The old scarecrow from the gut bucket is with them, swaying on the balls of his feet, eyes closed, grinning at the secrets in his head.

I cut through several more overgrown fields, back to Bitter's. Compared with Dallas, Houston is magnificently lush. Willows, pines, magnolias. Big D is mostly parking lots now, especially downtown, where all-day parking can cost as little as seventy-five cents, so many lots are competing—a consequence of the development addiction that kicked in during the eighties and hasn't let up since. I recall shopping one day, about six years ago, and realizing how much Dallas felt like Disneyland now, standardized and gaudy, not a place where real people lived and worked (though amazingly we *did* work there, stuffed into our power-lunch costumes—like so many smiling mice).

Bitter's not home—just a note saying, "Errands." I gather my laundry, pass through the kitchen to the back porch pantry and Bitter's old washer. Maybe I should buy a couple new T-shirts to tide me over, the next ten days or so. I check Bitter's room, to see if he's left any dirty clothes. A pair of boxers, socks, and a shirt. I snatch them up, glimpse by his bed, in a squatty bookshelf, half a dozen paperbacks: titles and authors I've never seen. Donald Goines, Iceberg Slim. *Trick Baby. Pimp: The Story of My Life.* Bookplates stiffen the back covers: "Property of Buck Jackson," the barber who Bitter said used to run a lending library out of his shop. The books look silly, but I stand for a minute absorbing their fusty smell, the scent of all the years I lost when I should have been here, reading the same trash Uncle read, listening to his music, eating his bad fried food.

On the top shelf of his open closet, a familiar white shape: one of Mama's quilts. My heartbeat quickens. I pull it down. It's fusty, too, a cloud of mothballs and lint. I never learned the patterns, though I remember Mama talking about Log Cabins, Bow Ties, Shooflies. On this one, uneven lines dodge through rough squares, triangles tipple over rows of heavy brown knots. The cotton backing is soft and cool.

"Follow the gourd . . ." She used to sing to me as she stuffed thick batting between fabric layers. I'd be sitting at her feet in Bitter's kitchen, watching. How did it go? "The river's bank" something something. "Dead trees . . ." I've lost it. I hummed the tune as she sang, rocking on the hardwood floor, delighting in the winglike movements of her hands, fluttering across jagged strips of brown, green, gold. "'Nother river on the other side . . ."

Later, in my teens, I felt ashamed of her work, its ripply lines and apparently random designs; embarrassed when company came and saw the quilts curled across the couch. I felt her amateurishness would reflect badly on me. In Dale Licht's house she sewed in a tiny room just off the kitchen overlooking her backyard flower garden, azaleas and purple irises. When I'd get home from school and rummage through the fridge for string cheese, pickles, or strawberries, she'd call to me from that sunny little room, ask me to come sit with her as she snipped thread or appliquéd beads to raffia cloth. Usually I refused, mumbling, "Homework." When I did linger, I was struck by how much her hands had slowed over the years, how tough it was for her to tie a simple knot. Still, she worked with patience, humming peacefully, and occasionally I'd feel pleasure in watching her bring something out of nothing, a magic as great as the spells Bitter extolled.

I sit on his bed now with the quilt across my knees, hoping to catch Mama's smell in the stitches, adding small tears to the patchwork.

———

Bitter's still not back. Probably he's doing what he always does when I'm not around, buying food, hanging out with his friends, *living his life,* but his health's got me so flummoxed, his every absence feels chancy. I fold the clean clothes, sweep and dust, straighten the sofa. *The Angela Davis Reader* sits, heat-curled, on the coffee table. I remember Reggie mentioning the other night he had meetings each morning this week, "lovefests with potential donors," but he'd be in his office at the Row Houses in the afternoons. In a couple of hours, then, I'll return his damn book to him.

I fix a cup of tea, then stroll past the Magnolia Blossom, along a low stone wall where Ariyeh and I used to capture frogs after rain. I recall this neighborhood, in the early seventies, as lazy and quiet, buzzing with cicadas, the low purring of mourning doves, mockingbirds' sneers. Doors remained open, always, offering odors of bacon and eggs, or ribs and potatoes in the evening; through them, you'd glimpse Bruce Lee posters on living room walls, platform shoes lined up in long hallways, people in dashikis sitting on the floor bobbing their heads to Stevie Wonder, Curtis Mayfield, or the hi hat hiss of Isaac Hayes's "Shaft."

Now, every other door is boarded up, weeds choke windows. The air trembles to hip-hop.

Am I romanticizing, or were men more polite back then? They'd lean over and spit in the street gutters instead of directly on the sidewalk where people had to step. They'd look you in the eye and say hello. "Hi there, sister," or "*A salaam alaikum.*"

But then, there were those, like the b-boys this morning—"Hey, big legs!" "Boo-*tay!*" "Look to me like she with the itty-bitty titty committee." "Well fuck you, bitch, won't talk to me. You ain't shit, nohow." It *is* easy—too easy, of course—to airbrush the past. Did Mama ever look back with longing, even for a moment? Did she ever regret stealing away? Worry about losing the accuracy of her memories?

The propped-up Caddy down the street, rusting on cinder blocks, is one of a handful of altars for preachers of the dozens. *You ain't got game, Lame, watch me, watch me work. I went to your house to ask for money, your mama rip off her drawers, say, "Fuck me, honey."*

Your mama eat shit.

Your mama eat dog yummies.

Word!

Some of the boys wear wool caps and hooded sweatshirts, despite the late-morning broil, or shuffle about in heavy winter boots. They wear dungaree jackets turned inside out. Others high-style it in black and silver L.A. Raiders shirts, Kangor caps, and Tommy Hilfiger jeans—which nearly slide off their butts. Even from a distance, their capped teeth gleam in the sun; knuckle rings, neck chains sizzle and flash. These are the fellows missing from Etta's on Sunday nights.

Every other corner's got a clocker with a beeper, every vacant lot a lost soul ready to beam up to Scotty. The old winos, the King Cobras I remember trying to avoid as a girl, seem quaint and harmless next to the freebasers and skeezers screaming to themselves, weaving through fields of broken glass. As I turn back toward Bitter's, a lanky kid in Kani's and Tims stumbles into me out of the boneyard, marble-eyed, drooling, haranguing the trees. Our collision knocks the cup from my hand, and it shatters on the wall.

"Miss Thang!" I turn to see a Beamer take the corner. The man Reggie called Rue Morgue. "Well well. We out cool chilling. You with that, babe?"

"Excuse me," I mumble, stepping around the car. It tails me. Rue waves and grins, hanging out the passenger window. An insignia on his baseball cap shows a guy caught in crosshairs. "Come chill wit' us, aight?"

I keep my head down. I remember overhearing a colleague of mine in Social Services say one morning, to a bruised young girl, "There's no *type* of woman who gets hit. We could *all* get hit, okay?"

Trailing us, the lanky kid calls, "Yo! Right *chere!*"

Rue laughs at him. "Yeah? And how I know you ain't some knocko, G?"

"Come on, man, *look* at me." He holds out a twenty dollar bill.

"Fucking pipehead. Go change it for singles. We meet you 'round the corner in five."

The kid ambles off. The driver mutters something to the Man in Charge. "Yeah yeah, aight," Rue says, mock-serious. "We got mo' business now," he tells me. "My crew is in effect. But later, cakes, hm?" He aims a gun-barrel finger my way. "Maybe we knock boots, Jiggy. Lay us some pipe." He cackles. The driver glides them down the street.

———

On my car radio, a woman says Houston has surpassed L.A. as the nation's smog capital. A caller says, "I agree with Governor Bush. It's not that I'm against clean air. I just don't think the *federales* should tell Texans what to do with their cars."

I park next to an abandoned taco stand and a boxing gym rumbling with youthful energy. My hands have been trembling ever since the Beamer. Reggie's office is open, but no one's around. He's got a new picture on his wall: an *Emerge* magazine sketch—Clarence Thomas as a lawn jockey. The place smells of tuna fish and potato salad. A desk fan stirs warm air.

A hip-hop groove drills through the back wall, from Natalie's apartment. In the open doorway, her boy, Michael, in a red Houston Rockets jersey, gyres and slashes the sunlight—*Listen up, suckers!* I step outside. He sees me and stops. "What's the haps?" he says, looking braver than he sounds.

"Reggie around?"

"Hang. He be here. Holding a meet for the 'hood."

"Looks like you're helping him get organized."

"Yeah. He axed me to grab him some records—wantsa talk up the talk. You cruising or what? I seen you here before."

"I'm Ariyeh's cousin."

"That right?" He looks skeptical. He turns back inside and stacks CDs: Puff Daddy, Low G, Rasheed.

"Your mom?"

"Down at the U. Economics class."

"Tupac?" I ask, a wild guess, nodding at his boom box.

"Wu-Tang Clan," he sneers, but his face perks up. "You like this shit?"

"Sure."

"A 'bout it 'bout it chick, eh? You a wigger? Flipping the script?"

"What do you mean?"

"White person wantsa be a niggah, know'm say'n?"

I laugh. "Show me. Who do you like?"

"*All right.* Really?"

"Really."

Seems he's a young performer, waiting for an audience, or maybe he's just happy to have someone listen to him talk about *anything*. "Here it is, then. In all the *o*-fficial talk, in the papers and shit, 'Fifth Ward' is what they say when they want to say 'niggah' 'thout really saying it," he says, lowering his voice like a DJ. "So these here the original voices of Fifth Ward, Texas: Bushwick Bill, Scarface, Willie D—the Geto Boys."

For a year, Willie D and Scarface had a falling-out, he tells me—Willie's name *shit* in Southside, and a few niggahs died—but things are cool again, and the music's as dope as ever. He plays me some cuts on the boom box: "Mind of a Lunatic," "No Nuts No Glory," "Murder after Midnight." Fifth Ward, Texas.

"Yeah," Michael says, watching my face. "This ain't no Cristal-sipping, Versace-wearing shit. Boys keeping it *real*."

As I listen I realize, more forcefully than before, that I'm stuck in the early seventies: civil rights / street agitation / black is beautiful: Uncle Bitter's world. Reggie is right—I feel it now in my gut. The world has moved beyond the mere *low-down* of the blues and into a bloody mess. Crack-capitalism rules the streets, not protest marches. Needles, not Ripple. I glance at Michael. Kids like him don't expect to live past twenty-five. I think of the boys disappearing from Ariyeh's school . . . a sacrifice of children, forfeiture of the future, *but why?* . . .

Suddenly, Bushwick is dwarfed by a louder beat from the street.

Michael runs to the door. "Motherfucker," he says. Over his shoulder I glimpse the Beamer.

"Little rag! Little bitch-boy! You got that twinkie for me yet?"

"Fuck you, motherfucker! You dealing with a niggah that's greater than you!"

Rue Morgue removes his baseball cap. He's got a wide bald head. Shades, small mouth. He doesn't smile. "Got a body bag waiting for you, little rag." He waves to me. "Miss Ann! You *everywhere*, boogee. I's thinking you just a tourist, enjoying our fine vacation grounds. You *living* here now?"

"Michael, come back inside."

"Wants to hang with a Big Willie, Miss Thang? See how it's done? I'm your man. Come on over here, hm?" My palm trembles on Michael's shoulder. He shrugs me away.

"Come on, baby, slide on over here now."

"No, thank you."

"Damn, she a *polite* dime piece," the driver says. Rue coos, "I know you want it, sugar."

Michael's shivering with fury. Just as I'm certain he's about to make a move, the car spins away. "I be looking for you, Ann! You too, little rag! The Lord gon' be *harvesting* you soon."

I turn. Reggie's standing, arms crossed, in front of his office. He offers me a grim smile, but says only, "Michael, you got those records for me? The meeting's about to start."

We move slowly, as if a spell has been snapped. Rue's expression, it occurs to me, was like the shut-in boy's years ago, gazing at me as if he knew me better than I did . . .

Boys Michael's age and a few years older gather in Reggie's office. They're wearing basketball jerseys and colorful, roomy shorts. One's T-shirt reads, "The bitch set me up." Quo Vadis and fade haircuts, old-fashioned baldie beans. Some of the boys sip noisily from 7-Eleven cups or sports drink bottles. Everyone defers to the two or three kids with knuckle rings.

Reggie's finishing up some business with a man in a gray suit, slender and tall, wearing a small silver earring. Dark. Patient smile. "Amazing stuff out there," he tells Reggie. "The other day I clicked onto a site about the brain—its reactions to skin color. Believe it or not, some researchers have found that glucose activity kicks in heavily, in a certain part of the brain, whenever a person sees someone of a different race."

"So . . . we're hard-wired for hate?"

The man grins. "Well, it's the kind of subject your boys here can debate once they're on-line."

"Right. I'm sorry I've got this meeting here—"

"I need to run, anyway. I'll hit you back later."

"See you over at the gallery tonight? We'll talk more then?"

"You got it." They shake hands. The man steps out the door.

Reggie swigs water from a plastic bottle. The boys are getting settled, laughing loudly in groups. I pull Angela Davis from my purse. My hands are jittery. "You disagree with Sister Davis?" Reggie says. He screws the cap onto his bottle, which hisses and pops.

"'The myth of the black rapist has been conjured up when recurrent waves of terror against the black community required a convincing explanation'?"

"Just thought you'd be interested."

"So any time a black man is accused of assault, the accuser is 'perpetuating a racial stereotype'?"

"She's a provocative writer, isn't she?"

"Talk about *stereotyped*—"

"I've got a meeting here." He taps the bottle on his knee. "Stick around."

"No thanks." I brush a hand across my eyes.

"Really. Hang for a while." Before I can slip away, he claps his hands and calls the meeting to order. The boys sit still, their faces wide with admiration, animation, curiosity. The neighborhood can't afford to lose them, I think, the way it lost me, or I lost hold of *it* . . .

Reggie tells Michael to play a record; Michael punches a button on the boom box. The Geto Boys rap about white cops in coffins. "These your homies, right?" Reggie says, smiling at the boys.

"You got it, you got it."

"Keeping it real."

"Word, man."

They juke their shoulders, dip their heads.

"But see, I listen this shit," Reggie says, "and—whether it's just words or not—what I hear is a black man telling other brothers they got to eighty-six each other. Prove who's king."

"Tha's the way it is, G. Get the niggah 'fore he get you."

"Ever hear of minstrel shows? 'Jasper Jack'? 'Zip Coon'?" Reggie asks. "You think Scarface something *new?*"

The boys look confused.

"He the same ol' imbecile Negro been entertaining white folks for centuries. 'Cause you know who's buying these records? I know *y'all* ain't losing money on them. You copping them from the stores."

Uneasy grins.

"It's the white kids in the 'burbs buying this shit. It's like, 'It's cool to be black,' but underneath that, it's 'Look at that imbecile Negro dance. Entertain me, boy.' Stone, you ain't with that?" He points to a tall, bald boy in the back of the room who looks at the floor, scratches his thigh. "Yeah, but . . . yeah, but . . ."

"Speak up, Stone. You ain't no dumb nigger, are you?"

"Fuck, no."

"Then talk like a man."

The boy stiffens his back. "Reggie, man, Scarface talking the talk. What it's like on the street. Not in no suburb."

"What it's like, or what some E-light record producer on his fat Beverly Hills ass *tells* you it's like?"

I'm with the boys on this one. How many Rue Morgues are out there cruising right now?

"What sells in the 'burbs is the thrill of black danger. White kids thinking they getting close to something scary, something real, just by listening to the music, without having to risk anything." He glances at me, then paces the room. "You think the smart record producers don't know that? You think Scarface out thugging all the time? Hell, he probably in some swank business office somewhere, in a strategy session, planning his next marketing campaign."

Michael crouches by the boom box, tight-lipped and still.

"Besides, you think you learning street life from these tunes? What you learning? Guns kill people? That's *news?*"

Despite my tiff with him, it's a pleasure watching a man take intellectual responsibility in front of other males, instead of playing dumb just to hang with the crowd. *That's* an act I've seen all too often in the mayor's office.

"But yo, Reggie, we *valid* when we respected."

"That's wack, guys. Real messed up."

"*You* was living large. *You* did bids."

"That I did, slick. And when I got out I was a fucking hero."

"Word."

"You'da thought I'd won an Academy Award. But I'm telling you, man, a felony rap, you *done.* Ass out. I'm lucky I savvied in time. Turn up the volume, flash your rings, you might get noticed for a while. But it's like shooting from the outside without a good inside game. Pretty soon, the world'll figure your ass out and shut you down. You got no extra moves, you nailed. And Wilson, what's *this* shit?" He plucks a green sports drink bottle from a pudgy boy's grip, whips off the top, and dumps a slushy, sour apple-smelling mixture onto the floor. "Tequila? Gin-and-something? You freeze it in the morning, let it melt all day till it's good and lethal? Who you think you fooling? You want to kill yourself, boy? That what you after?"

"Sorry, Reggie."

"You're going to clean up my floor when we're done here." He tosses the bottle onto the slush.

Michael stands up and jams his hands into his pockets. "Reggie, I thought you liked rap, man."

"I like it fine. All I'm saying is, it's just music, packaged to make a profit. It ain't a way of life, all right?"

The boys mumble.

"Let me leave you with this. What's gonna happen when all these white kids, these *image chameleons,* lose their hip-hop jones and go to work for Merrill Lynch, hm? Where *you* gonna be? You down with that? Stone? You down?"

"Yeah. Fuck yeah. I'm down wit' that."

"All right, then." Reggie tells them they'll meet again next week to learn why Clyde Drexler is the exception that proves the rule.

"*What* rule?" Stone asks.

"Hoops *ain't* your way out the 'hood."

"Shit, G, you spoiling all our fun."

"Better find a new jones," Reggie says, checking his watch. "Wilson, mop's in the closet over there."

"Aw, Reggie—"

"Go get it, now. And don't bring that shit into my house no more." To me he says, "Telisha, I've got another meeting in half an hour, downtown. Sorry. I'm afraid I haven't organized my afternoon very well.

Here's what I'm thinking. Come to this gallery tonight." He hands me a card. Brazos Fine Art. "We'll discuss Sister Davis."

"Wait—"

"It's a fund-raising party for the Row Houses. A few of our regular donors—"

"I don't think so, Reggie. Do your business, and—"

"Ariyeh will be there. Wine and cheese, very relaxed." He chugs water from his bottle. "And I promise I'll give you a chance to tell me what a prick I am. Seven o'clock. Check you then."

"Reggie—"

"Seven. Ariyeh'll be glad to see you." A quick wave and he's gone. Making me wait because he can. Arrogant bastard. But I have to smile. He's smooth.

I find the keys in my purse. Several of the boys are bouncing and passing a basketball outside, laughing and taunting one another. I'm nervous, watching them scatter down the street. What's waiting for them just around the corner? Behind Reggie's desk, beneath the list of donors on the wall, Michael, sullen, packs away his tunes.

———

Bitter and his friend Grady sit in the grass in front of the mud-dauber shack, picking dandelions. Grady looks like he's on a short furlough from the boneyard and is due back any minute.

"Hi," I say.

"Hangover," Grady says and plucks a flower. Bitter nods hello. With a kitchen knife he slices a catfish on the ground. He sets the knife down, dribbles fish blood on a pile of petals and stems, then rolls them into a ball in his hands. Some kind of gris-gris for the shakes? He doesn't explain and I don't bother asking.

I tell him I'll be eating out tonight, meeting Ariyeh and Reggie. Can I bring him anything?

"We be fine. Mosey down the block here after while, get some chicken or something."

"I washed and folded your clothes."

"Saw that. Thank you, Seam."

"I noticed you've got one of Mama's old quilts."

"Got two or three of 'em somewheres in the house."

"Do you remember the song she used to sing while she sewed?

Something about 'Follow the gourd'? I've been trying to recall it."

He grins. "Sure," he says and begins:

The riva's bank am a very good road,
The dead trees show the way,
Lef' foot, peg foot going on,
Foller the drinking gou'd.

"That's it!" I say. Grady sways in the grass, humming.

The riva ends a-tween two hills,
Foller the drinking gou'd;
'Nother riva on the other side,
Foller the drinking gou'd.

Wha the little riva
Meet the great big'un,
The ol' man waits—

Grady grips his belly. "Whoa now," Uncle says and squeezes his buddy's arm. He picks up the fish, shakes blood from a gash beneath its gills. With narrowed eyes he signals me to go.

I nod. "Thank you for the song," I say. "You brought her back to me there for a minute."

He looks like he might cry. "Say hi to Ariyeh. Oh, Seam—you got some kinda 'fficial-looking letter. Come today."

"Yeah?"

"Kitchen table."

"Thanks."

It's official, all right: Texas Department of Corrections. From the man I'd talked to on the phone. I'd told him I worked for Dallas's mayor, and that seems to have done the trick. He informs me that Elias Woods has granted me a visit and I should call the prison to set up an appointment. No pencil, paper, tape recorders, or cameras. "TDC rules prohibit inmates from receiving any gifts." Fine and dandy, I think, amazed at how easy this was. What did Uncle say about a waiting list? Mr. Woods must not get many guests.

I wash up and change: plum-colored skirt, light yellow blouse. My job requires a few gallery-hopping outfits, and it's become a habit with me to pack them whenever I travel. When I leave the house, Bitter is rocking Grady on the lawn, his hands around the fellow's arms. "You gointer be fine," he's saying. "Let it go. Just let it all go."

———

The Brazos Fine Art Gallery sits between a rare book dealer and a Guatemalan weaving shop on Bissonnet Street just down the block from the Contemporary Arts Museum, whose sleek metallic walls reflect the setting pink sunlight. Caddies and Beamers crowd the small parking lot. The cars are newer and cleaner than the ones in Freedmen's Town, but their purpose is the same, and I'm coming to recognize it has more to do with proclaiming power and prestige than with providing simple transportation. Claiming the highest ground of all, a bumper sticker on a gold LeBaron says, COMES THE RAPTURE / YOU CAN HAVE THIS CAR.

Tinted green windows frame the gallery's narrow front door. Red brick, white wooden trim. Inside, an aggressive odor of floor wax and blue cheese, grapes, expensive sweet perfume. A roomful of buppies. After a few days in Freedmen's Town, among the Nikes and back-ass-ward baseball caps, the filthy shoes and shirts, it's a shock to see blacks decked out in fine silk dresses and pearls, Ralph Lauren polo pants, and one or two wildly red and yellow Rush Limbaugh ties. I scold myself for typecasting my own folks.

The man serving wine has the darkest skin in the room. Some things don't change. I take a glass of merlot and squeeze into a corner between a pair of sharp metal sculptures. I don't see Reggie or Ariyeh, but the room is packed and I don't have the gumption yet to push through milling bodies. Thin fluorescent tubes—red, yellow, white, and blue—line the walls, spotlighting the ceiling, drawing it closer to the eye. A posted statement by the door says the tube sculpture is by Dan Flavin, a noted Minimalist who worked with mass-produced industrial materials to question the primacy of the artist's hand and to challenge traditional notions of art. I think of Kwako's beer can birds and car bumper serpents, improvised using mass-produced materials, not to make a "statement," but because that's all he can afford to use. I wonder how this crowd feels about the art at the Row Houses—primitive, I'm sure, by the gallery's standards. Quaint and naïve. But presumably these are a few of Reggie's donors, Houston's black upper class. They must have seen where their money goes.

A glimpse of Ariyeh's pretty smile. She's in the back, next to a framed abstraction, green and white. Her bright blue dress nicely complements the painting. Reggie, beside her, appears to be displaying Natalie as though she were a rare carving. Her grin wavers, and her whole body lunges awkwardly whenever she reaches to shake someone's hand. It will take me a few minutes to wend my way to them; from a table I snatch a cracker with some cheese, then begin my slide through the press of buttocks and backs, shoulders and arms.

". . . victimization," someone behind me insists. "In the magazines, the movies. When's the last time you saw a well-off black man in the media or on the news—aside from Bill Cosby or Michael Jordan?"

"Telling you, man, the camera loves black 'pathology.'"

I slip by a big bearded man, accidentally smearing brie on his coat. He doesn't notice and I can't turn around, now, to tell him. I move on.

". . . things'll play if Dubya makes it to Pennsylvania Avenue?"

"Seems to me he's been pretty fair on race."

"He's been *absent* on race."

"Hey, 'absent' is fair, in my book."

"I don't know. He likes having his picture taken eating tacos. That shows racial awareness."

Laughter. I clutch my cup.

". . . blab and blab all you want about the legacy of colonialism in Africa, but I'm sorry, you do *not* kill babies . . ."

". . . no, to me, *Art* is Romare Bearden . . ."

". . . afraid of the stock market? Why? You know what a million dollars is? It's just a stack of pennies like your grandma used to save . . ."

"God bless the child that's got his own."

"No problem, kissing ass. That's why God invented mouthwash!"

"T, glad you could make it." Ariyeh gives me a hug. Natalie nods hello. Reggie is deep in conversation with the tall, slender man I saw at the Row Houses today. ". . . on the Internet you have no *skin*," Reggie insists, punching the air for emphasis. He bumps the painting.

"Precisely. You can be whoever you want without fear of prejudice."

"So. Just so I'm straight on this. *Six* computers plus all the software—"

"Whatever you need. And we can cover the initial hookup with AOL. Now, for us . . . should *you* make the arrangements, or shall *I* talk to her?"

For the first time since I've met him, Reggie seems indecisive. He crosses his arms. The man turns to me. "Rufus Bowen," he says, extending a hand.

"Telisha is Ariyeh's cousin," Reggie says.

"Is that right?"

"A city planner in Dallas."

"Well now. Tell me. Is it too late to save Houston?"

"No, no . . ."

He laughs. "I run a small Internet firm here in town. Civic health is of great concern to me. What's your guiding principle as a planner? The New Urbanism? Village neighborhoods?"

Another smooth bastard. Gracious and poised. But he appears to offer a rare depth of attention that asks for a serious answer. Or maybe I just like rising to the challenge. I begin, slowly, "Aristotle? He said, 'It's most satisfactory to see any object whole, at a single glance, so that its unity can be understood.' I agree. I favor buildings on a human scale."

Rufus Bowen smiles. "Understanding unity. A good rule for sizing up people as well, would you say?" The crowd nudges Natalie closer to us; Bowen reaches past me to shake her hand. "I'm sorry, please excuse us for a moment," he tells me and pulls her aside. She looks like a doe in klieg lights. I want to tell Reggie, *Get her out of here.* He touches my shoulder. "So. I was telling Ariyeh about your little flare-up."

I take my eyes from Bowen. "It wasn't a flare-up."

"I don't blame you, honey," Ariyeh says. "I would have felt the same. I used to admire Angela Davis, but she's gotten too extreme."

"Look, I'm sorry I upset you. I don't know what happened between you and your colleague, all right?" Reggie says. "I'm not making any judgments. I was just using Angela to point out that 'black man' and 'rape' are paper and fire—"

I drain my wine. "Excuse me, Ariyeh, but I've got to say it. You *are* a prick," I tell him. "You think I don't know about racism—"

"Hold on now—"

"—and lynching? What do you think brought me back here, hm?"

"Bravo, honey." Ariyeh links her arm in his, teasing him with a grin. Reggie shrugs, an exaggerated surrender. "Okay, okay. But I got you to think, didn't I?"

"Jesus, Reggie."

"I'm quite capable of thinking on my own," I say.

"I see that. I'm glad."

"What's going on over here?" Ariyeh asks him.

Reggie glances at Natalie and Bowen. "A little discussion."

"She doesn't look pleased."

To say the least. Her eyes flick back and forth but her jaw is fixed, puffing her cheeks. Her shoulders droop. The man looks taller in her presence, all upper arms and chest: an enormous held breath, ready to blow down the room. He's Reggie without the attitude, Dwayne with Visa Gold, Rue Morgue on a higher evolutionary scale. Whatever arrangement is being made, a woman this uncertain has no business next to a man so assured. The power imbalance is as palpable as the cheese smell in the room. Nothing abstract here: hunter and prey, stark and real as hell. Is this how I looked in Dwayne's cramped car, with his hands all over my tits? Is this how I carry my own vulnerability, an invitation like a bared neck? I turn away.

Ariyeh tells me this little soiree will wind up soon; she and Reggie and a few of the donors he's working will then head over to Blind Billy's, a blues joint near the Ragin' Cajun. "Come along. You and I can relax and chat."

Bowen squeezes Natalie's arm, then swivels and shakes Reggie's hand. "I'll be in touch," he says. He tells Ariyeh he was charmed to meet her. "Human scale." He winks at me. "I'll remember that." Then he saunters through the crowd and out the door, earring flashing. Natalie slumps against the wall—hungering, I'll wager, for Kibbles and Bits.

"You understand, you don't have to do anything you don't want to do," Reggie tells her.

"It's a job, I guess." She primps her hair and wipes some sweat from her chin. "Anyways. I gotta go pick up my daughter now. The babysitter needs to get home."

"Sure, sure." Reggie fishes in his pocket.

"It's all right. I got bus fare."

We walk her to the door. The gathering is thinning, but still loud. ". . . let's face it, the whole notion of prisoner rehabilitation is completely outdated . . ."

". . . culture of narcissism . . ."

". . . old *Saturday Night Live* skit? White crime: guy goes to work, shoots a dozen people, then himself. Black crime: guy runs from a liquor store with a six pack, trips, gets snatched by the cops."

In the doorway, Reggie kisses Natalie's cheek. "We'll figure it all out tomorrow, okay?" A bright Metro stops behind her, its doors sighing open. "Sleep well." She nods.

Then, while Ariyeh and I wait outside, he plays the room one last time, pumping hands, smiling, laughing, patting backs. "He's good," I say.

"Yes." Ariyeh rubs her eyes. "*Too* good. I don't like the looks of this Bowen fellow."

"It's really impressive, the way he moves between worlds. Comfy with the money in there, whereas this afternoon he was getting down with the neighborhood boys."

"He certainly doesn't lack opinions, does he? I'm sorry about that book business. Sorry I ever mentioned—"

I wave it off. I'm about to ask after the vanished schoolchildren when Reggie shows up saying he's ready. An irresistible energy gust. Ariyeh tosses the rest of her wine, and I follow Reggie's Honda down the street.

———

Blind Billy's green wooden walls are lined with black-and-white photos from the thirties, forties, and fifties: KCOH, Houston's only all-black radio station, now defunct. The DJs, King Bee, Daddy Deepthroat, Mister El Toro, in suits and ties behind long boom mikes, grip fresh-pressed 45s—"race records" before they were labeled "rhythm and blues." Emancipation Park, Shady's Playhouse, Club Ebony, and the El Dorado: places from which the station broadcast during Juneteenth celebrations.

The long-gone DJs, encased behind glass, are among the few black faces in the place, and Blind Billy's is a far cry from Club Ebony. The room is vast, with a dance floor, stage, and round plastic tables. Two hundred, three hundred people, young lawyers, investment advisors— well-educated, on-the-make professionals, the kind who pop in and out of the mayor's office. Hart, Shaffner & Marx on his second pint of Guinness flirting with dainty, martini-soaked Talbot's.

Signs for Route 66, Texaco filling stations, hand soaps, and seductive colognes—the signs are carefully tarnished and pleasingly scratched so as to appear old and authentic. The room smells stale and sweaty, but sweetly so, a mix of White Shoulders and organic shampoos.

The band, piano and brass, six lanky black men in gray suits, is tightly in synch: three-chord blues with no rough edges, measured, leveled, buzz-sawed to boring perfection. Between songs, the singer, Quo Vadis in wraparound shades, tries to hype the crowd. "And they say the blues is *dead* in Houston! Lemme tell you, tonight we all the way live!" But his voice is weary, his stage gestures lazy. The audience seems pleased, anyway, clapping, whistling, stomping.

Ariyeh quarrels with Reggie at our corner table. Seems Rufus Bowen will provide Reggie with computers if Natalie will work for him as a gofer/hostess, entertaining his out-of-town clients. "It's not right, and you know it," Ariyeh says, stirring her Tom Collins with a lacquered fingernail. "She's going to school, raising her kids—"

"A job right now won't hurt her. When her year at the Row Houses is up, she'll need someplace to go."

"A *year* from now. Why rush it? I thought the whole idea was to give a young mother a break, some breathing space—anyway, anyway, why Natalie? Who *is* this guy?"

"He's a perfectly legitimate businessman, and one of the few black CEOs in the city. I don't know—when he dropped by the other day, he took a shine to Natalie. Which, I have to tell you, I count as a personal success. She's really turned herself around since coming to us. It's not like he's forcing her to prostitute herself or anything—"

"You're *sure* about that?"

"Of course I am. He just wants her to keep some people company, escort them to restaurants, concerts . . . this could be a good, long-term thing for her, part of her recovery. He sees her potential. And he *asked,* honey. He doesn't need our permission. Natalie's an adult. But he asked. He wouldn't dream of interfering with our program."

"Since when did the Row Houses become a vocational school for computer training? You said the project was about restoring neighborhood pride—"

"Exactly, sugar! And pride begins with education."

Ariyeh shakes her head, sips her drink.

Reggie turns to me. "You gonna lecture me, too? Another *dispatch* from the *mayor?*"

I spread my hands.

"Yeah, but you *thinking* it." He leans over and kisses Ariyeh's cheek. "I gotta go sell myself to these wallets now." He nods at a nearby table, where five or six men from the gallery laugh and pass around pitchers of

Bud. "You may not like cutting deals, baby, but there's honor in it if the goal is noble."

"I know that, Reggie."

"You used to be proud of me."

She strokes his face. "I still am, sweetie. But I worry about Natalie."

"So do I. I won't let anything happen to her. Promise."

"Go schmooze."

"I love you, baby."

"Go, go." She smiles.

I reach over and squeeze her arm, the way I did when we were girls and Bitter had scared us with the Needle Men. We listen to the music, not speaking. She looks tired, and I don't want to trouble her with questions about school or the missing kids. I want her to be able to depend on me, the way I'm counting on her, a self-possessed young woman, a confident, successful black woman who can show me how to *be*.

There again: race. Always, and ever, race. How sick I am of it! Even now, the frat boys at the next table eye me up and down. They don't know what to make of me. Am I *white* enough for you, frat boy? Look close, Charley, do you see a hint of yellow, the shadow of a shadow, a leaf-tip turning in early fall? Do you imagine me naked? What do you think? Do you suppose my nipples look more chocolate than strawberry? Do you think I don't know you, don't despise you, don't want you?

"Hey, honey." Ariyeh pries her hand from mine. "Not so hard."

We order another round of drinks. The band takes a break, and when they return I'm surprised to see big Earl joining them onstage. Tonight he looks completely different from the way he does at Etta's. The purple suit is gone; he's wearing a tux. Hair slicked back. The energy I've seen him put into flirting is channeled now into flattering the crowd. "Y'all doing all right? Sure is good to see y'all." Masking in front of the ofays. Watering it down for the mainstream. Just another imbecile Negro. God*dam*.

"Look. Earl's moonlighting," I say.

Ariyeh laughs.

"Ariyeh, you ever date a white boy?"

"Cuz, there's more than thirty-one flavors. Why would I choose the blandest?" She rubs my arm. "They're not all like . . . what was it, Dwayne? And forget Sister Davis."

Clattery laughter rolls from the bar. Earl launches into a ballad,

"Heads or tails, you lose."

I listen closer. I've heard this before. The other night at Etta's. Bayou Slim. But before that . . .

". . . *lose!*" Earl shouts.

I don't remember. My head spins. I finish my wine, pull a few bills from my purse.

"Party-pooper," Ariyeh says.

I'd like to crawl into bed with her and hold her all night. "I'll call you." I kiss her cheek. "I didn't want to spoil the evening with it, but I think we need a plan, soon, for getting Bitter to a doctor."

"All right, honey. You're right. I been thinking about that, too. We'll work it out. Sleep well." She glances sadly at Reggie. He's several tables away with a group of men, adding figures on a napkin. I wave but he doesn't see me.

I push through the door, past King Bee and Daddy Deepthroat, into the hot, billowy air. I drive with my windows down, humming the blues, trying to picture Slim's face. I've not seen it well through the smoke in Etta's Place. I pass the glass towers of Greenway Plaza, a few gated communities (military security as domestic architecture; money as gris-gris, casting a spell, or an illusion, of safety) then, back on Bissonnet, the CAM, the Museum of Fine Arts, several bistros and wine bars—white folks enjoying late dinners at cozy sidewalk tables—then the new brick homes of gentrified Montrose. I miss the sound of my aquarium at night, bubbling steadily in the dark, the soft purring of my sweet old parrots.

Finally, I'm back in the Quarter: weed lots, broken windows, hip-hop pounding its way out of a Caddy. Somebody has pumped a boarded grocery full of bullet holes. A calling card. A warning. Proving who's king.

BEST I LEAVE *you craving mirrors, child, cold, hard faces giving nothing back to the world but the grim old world itself. Best I leave you with an empty purse so you're forced to fill it with your findings. Your inheritance? Mystery and intransigence. Restlessness, your one and only ID.*

My mama's voice, in a dream. Not the sorts of words she ever used in life, and yet, somehow—on some level I never reached—they feel just like her.

Without vigilance, you're at the mercy of the wind, a handbill torn off an ice house wall, scuttling past street signs none of the neighbors can read, scuffed doors bolted tight against the heat, truck exhaust, dust, cats pawing through broken bottles, used condoms, bloody Kleenex in a field, past the crying of left-alone babies, the chatter of television, which at least has something to say, the silence and stillness and don't-give-a-rat's-ass of everyone else, the cops' empty promises, the morgue's waiting boxes, the empty white-hot of the sidewalks chewed by the earth, the wasted basketball practice of a knock-kneed little boy, the wasted lessons of a gifted girl whose ma can't keep paying for the family's out-of-tune piano, the sludge in the pipes beneath a dead-grass patch, dead pigeons, wood splinters snagging the bill—snatched up by an old man wasted in the middle of the day, a hungry, grinning scarecrow squinting so the words'll keep still, words he can't decipher, words—

LATE MORNING. Neighborhood quiet. And styling up the street toward me, the man from the Beamer. Shades. Overcoat. Heavy winter boots. I rise and head for the door.

"See, Miss Ann, see, your problem is this. You got a gotch-eyed view of players. Look here, don't run away, aight? Just want to chat. I'm safe, see, all on my own 'thout no posse. Ain't even got a burner." He opens his coat to show me nothing's underneath except his slender frame in khaki pants and a T-shirt that reads, "According to the Surgeon General, It's OK to Smoke Your Competition." "Most days, I don't leave home 'thout my .22 Raven"—said gruffly to impress me. And damn it, it *does* impress me in spite of myself. "But I's out looking for you this morning, and I wanted to dress proper for the occasion." He gives me a smarmy grin: Welcome-to-Taco-Bell-may-I-take-your-order-please?

"What do you want?"

"I tol' you, maybe we knock boots or something, eh? Aight." He holds up a ring-studded hand. Creamy white palm. "I'm sorry. I'm moving too fast for you." He looks me up and down. "Damn. You got a boy-thing or some shit going for you, hm? No hips, little tits. But you're cute. Got a sexy move on you."

"Listen, asshole, I'm not some street whore—"

"No, you surely ain't."

"Then stop talking to me like one." I breathe slowly, trying to quell my fear. "I want you to leave me alone."

"Might be I got something you need." He steps closer. "What's your story, Ann? Your connection to the Row Houses?"

"None of your fucking—"

"See now." He lifts his hand as if he might hit me. "I make it my business to know who's who and what's what hereabouts. I see a tourist like yourself starting to settle in, I wonder what's up. I'm the local caretaker, know'm say'n?"

I watch the man's hands, step past him, down the porch and away from the house. I don't want Bitter endangered.

He follows me. "Here's how it goes, see. Kids from the 'burbs come by looking to get high. I stuff a few bread crumbs into a Baggie, pass 'em off as rocks. Sell 'em some oregano, they think they getting weed. So I bring a profit into the 'hood and send the white boys home with health food. No muss, no fuss. They too scared to come back and bitch about it 'cause they know I'll bust their covers with their folks. It's good business. Street smartology. Now tell me. What *your* business here, hm?"

I fold my arms.

"Looking for a man to take care your sweet little ass? Let me introduce myself. Street name Rue Morgue. But you can call me David. See how polite I'm being? Opening up to you and shit. Come on. What's *your* name, cakes, hm?"

"Are you an Edgar Allan Poe fan?"

"Edgar *what?*"

"'Rue Morgue.' It's a Poe story."

He frowns. "Morgue's where the farm gets bought."

"Right. Never mind."

Of course he's got it, beneath all the crap: a genuine charm; the quick wit of my old schoolmate, Troy; Dwayne's physical smoothness; Reggie's certainty. He knows he's got it, too. *A good king.* And he knows I'm responding to him on some basic level. Like soup on low simmer. With me, with men, hell—ever since the shut-in boy—it's always been the *basic* that betrays, even when I know better. A twitch, a grin. A forbidden look across a room.

"Okay, *don't* tell me. Let me show you something." He touches my elbow. I pull away. "I just want to walk you over to the church here. What I'm gonna do to you in church? Two minutes. Don't be skittish."

"In the church?"

"That's right. You want to understand this place, sugar, you need to peek inside. Come on."

I follow him, warily, past a narrow alley. Grasshoppers and ants. Old peaches. Sour milk. A whiff of chicken compost, searing and rotty. A broken bottle of Bacardi 151. A couple of Chicano boys blast by us on bikes. One yells back at the other, "Ain't never gonna catch me, *ese,* no way, *entiendes?*"

The church is a small wooden furnace. A weekday service has begun. We stand in the open doorway peering inside. Beneath low-hanging light fixtures, waxy as milk cartons, people fan themselves with cardboard pictures of Jesus stapled to Popsicle sticks. Sweat and sweet cologne. Coughing. Grunting. A steel guitar player jump-starts a tune. He's joined by drums and a Yamaha organ; together, they whip up a frenzy for the Lord, pumping train-car rhythms beneath soaring gospel melodies and a rap about *the power of Jesus coming down to meet us.* "Sacred steel," Rue whispers, grinning. The guitar sustains a high vibrato: Mother Mary weeping for her murdered son. The worry of every mother here. As at Etta's, no young men. Only a few older guys, eyes closed, nodding to the music next to their wives, who are wearing long print dresses. Rue indicates a line of young women in the front row leaning raptly toward the reverend in his thick purple robe. "This is what I want you to see," he says. "Look at 'em lusting for the preacherman."

"What are you talking about?"

"Watch their faces." Bottle-cap eyes. Twittery smiles. Cornrows thick as coleus plants. "Every one of 'em wants that man 'cause he's the only young fella they ever see, 'sides players like myself, who's worth a shit. All the other dudes, they wasted by noon every day, lollygagging on their porches or down at the happy shop."

"And whose fault is that?"

"Hey, I don't force nobody to sniff, snort, shoot, or swallow. I see a need, I rush in to fill it, that's all."

"Caretaker."

"Word. Who else looking after these poor motherfucking junkies? Me, that's who. I'm the on'iest friend they got. Meantime, all the young ladies here suffering the scarcity of good men."

The women are spruced up in high heels and low-cut blouses. I remember Shirley telling me back in Dallas, "Black women are always having to share their men. After a while it kind of whittles your spirit, you know?"

"God is a good, good god!" the preacher shouts. "He show you the path to Paradise! Ain't no *gas station map* gonna get you there! Ain't no

Triple-A knows the way! *Merciful* Jesus!" The ladies bounce in their seats.

Rue touches my elbow and guides me back outside. "So. You gonna settle in here, Ann, you need a good man to look after you. Too much competition for the preacher."

"But not for you?"

"I keep my ladies in line. One at a time. See? I'm *respecting* you, Ann. Ain't lying to you. *You* the one cowering behind high yella. The one with secrets. Aight, fine. That's your weight. All's I'm saying is, don't go getting high and mighty on me . . . 'cause *which* one of us being honest here and which ain't?"

"Why in *hell* do you think—"

The hand again. Inches from my face. "Fuck the dumb, sister. Even a tourist like you can see what it's like here. I do what I have to, stay in business. And in this outlook, *my* business the only *going concern.* Now some players, they don't give a shit. Make their deals and move on. Me, I look after folks. Some poor asshole jonesing, can't pay right away, I float him a while. I feed hungry kids. *I'm* the man what makes it all work. Last year? Listen up, last year 'bout this time, some bad smack hit the streets, see. Suckers popping left and right—twenty-four hours later, big ol' welts where they stuck the needle in and that's it, sister. Next stop, heart failure. So I start cruising, gathering up all the shit I can find. Take it down to a doc I got an in with at the med center so he can analyze it. Clostridium." He says the word slowly—again to impress me. "Bacteria in dust and soil. Me and my cornerboys put the word out. Public education. Community service. That's what I'm about."

Hosannas from the church.

"Why me?" I say.

"I ain't gonna lie to you, Ann. You got me curious, showing up out the blue like you done. I want to know your story. I can tell—see, I been *watching* you—you're looking to learn. Hoping to find—"

"Not oregano." Jesus, what do I mean? Why am I even talking to him?

He laughs. The sacred steel slithers past quirky, sorrowful blue notes.

"So what can I do for you? What do you need?" Rue asks.

"I need you to leave me alone, thank you."

"Seriously, Ann." He slides his shades down his nose.

"Seriously?"

He licks his lips.

"All right. Seriously. That little boy Michael at the Row Houses? Stop threatening him. Stop trying to deal to him and his mom."

"I thought you might say that. And I'll go you one better. I'll take it on myself to educate the boy. Tutor him."

"No. Just back off, that's all. Please."

"Boy'll need a mentor, he gonna survive. 'Specially with *that* mouth. He lucky I ain't capped him already. For you, Ann, aight? He golden now. Won't nobody touch him. That's a promise."

"Thank you."

"And in return, I 'spect a little respect from you. How 'bout it?"

"We'll see."

He appears to enjoy my defiance. He walks me back toward the house. Quietly, then, the Beamer rolls up beside us from around a corner. Lord. Was his friend waiting for him the whole time? Covering his back? Of course. Rue's a "player." Nothing happens here without a game plan.

"My nukka," Rue says to the driver. "What up?"

"We got us a situation, Morgue. Joneser. Threatening to talk."

He turns to me. "Business, babe. Caretaking. Remember the deal, then. Golden boy. Respect."

"Wait. I didn't make you a deal," I say. "I asked you for a favor, a *humane* act—"

He laughs. "Deals is favors and vicey-versey, Ann. This here's fucking America. I get back wit you soon. Oh—and *Telisha?*" Damn him. "Say hi to your old uncle for me, aight?" He reaches into his left boot, pulls out a small silver pistol, laughs once more, and steps into the car.

———

Ariyeh takes some loss time so we can kidnap Bitter. As I'm waiting for her in front of the school, the custodian I'd seen before yells at a pair of boys who are trying to shimmy up the flagpole. "Boot camp, boys, that's where you're heading! Got no respect . . ."

Ariyeh slides into the car, chuckling. "Old Johnson."

"The janitor?"

"Yeah, he sure gets bent out of shape."

Harshly, he swats at one of the boys with his broom. "Wind up in the pen . . ."

Ariyeh waves at him. "Hi there, Mr. Johnson. Keeping them all in line?"

"Cain't stay on top of it, Miss. No way." He slumps against the pole, hugging the broom like a bride.

Ariyeh waves again, then we head for Bitter's place. We've told him she wants to inspect a house she's thinking of buying; she needs his opinion. "Ain't setting up shop with that bull-head Reggie?" he'd asked her.

"No, no."

As I drive, I distract him with an old Cab Calloway album I found at the CD store. He's sitting in the back seat, humming. Earlier, I'd asked him if he knew Rue Morgue. He shook his head.

"He knows all about you and me," I said.

"Guys like him connected. Don't mess with them."

"No, of course not."

Now Ariyeh's telling me about a meeting she attended last night to discuss the school disappearances. "Nothing but finger pointing. A local church leader said public schools were unsafe. Too democratic. That's not how he put it, but that's what he meant. Naturally, he wants more funding for private religious schools. The fundamentalists and the city council are pushing vouchers—the *marketplace* mantra. The teachers blathered on about unions and higher pay. Parents blamed the schools for all their problems . . . *no one there* mentioned the missing children. It was astonishing."

Six boys have vanished now, she says. A quiet, nearly invisible riot in the streets, more horrible, finally, than Vida Henry's insurrection.

"—too busy trying to impress each other or scapegoat someone else, 'cause it's easier than actually solving anything."

"Were the cops there?" I ask. "Any progress?"

"No. Whatever's—"

"What the hell—" Bitter's stiff now, alert. "A *medical* clinic? You—"

"Take it easy, Uncle."

"What the hell *is* this?"

I park the car and assure him no one's going to cut him open. "It's just so they can check you out."

"You lied to me."

"You lied first, Daddy. Telling me your pains had gone away," Ariyeh says. "Now let's stop whining about it and get it over with, okay? It'll probably turn out to be nothing."

At the receptionist's window in the cramped waiting room she flashes her Blue Cross card. Bitter and I sit in the molded plastic chairs, the kind you see in airports, designed for people about to move on. Muzak and women's magazines. Sulking, Bitter crosses and uncrosses his legs.

Mercifully, a nurse calls us right away, weighs him, takes his blood pressure—frowns—then leads us to a bright room where we're joined by a young blond doctor. He looks like a surfer, tan, slicked-back hair. He hooks Bitter to an EKG machine, asks about his pains. Bitter stares in horror at the little white pads on his chest. I study a poster on the wall behind the doctor, a cartoon cutaway of a man's right lung.

Bitter grabs himself.

"What is it? Are you experiencing angina?"

"Ain't *got* no vagina. Kinda doctor are you?"

In a few minutes he's better. "Well, the good news is, the EKG shows nothing serious," the doctor says. "You haven't had a heart attack. But your blood pressure's high, and these pains you're having suggest to me we should take a closer look. I'd like to order an angiogram—"

"You just said it's nothing serious," Bitter says.

"I said—"

"I heard you. Ain't going no hospital."

The doctor doesn't push it. He's got other patients to see. Or breakers to catch. He wishes us luck.

"These aren't the Needle Men," Ariyeh tells Bitter back in the car.

"Don't be too sure. I once knew a fella back in N'Awlins went to the infirmary, come back with spiders in his veins."

"Daddy—"

"God's honest truth. They can inject you with *anything* in there."

We take him home. While he shuffles through his records in the living room, Ariyeh and I try to hatch another plot. "We could tell him the utility company has overcharged all its customers, and he needs to go downtown for a refund check—"

"He won't trust us now. He'll never get in the car. Short of brute force . . . what's the rest of the week look like for you?"

"I'm driving down to the prison, see this fellow Bitter told me about."

"Well, at least it's not a crisis. I guess there's no rush."

"Try to get some rest, hm? Tell Reggie it's time for some TLC."

She nods wearily.

Uncle's found Satchmo. The cornet grunts and shouts as though it'll lift the house off the ground.

I stand on the porch and wave good-bye to Ariyeh. Bitter slips an arm around my shoulders. "Don't like no dirty tricks," he says. "But I 'ppreciate you worrying 'bout me, Seam."

"No you don't. If you did, you'd go to the hospital and get that test."

He laughs. "I never passed no test in my life. Don't mean *nothing.*"

"You know what I'm saying."

"I just got you back, Seam." He kisses my cheek. "I ain't going nowheres. Promise."

12

KWAKO hammers a railroad spike through a piece of oak the size of his arm. Then he splashes brown paint on a milk jug, jams the jug on the spike—a raccoon's face or a bear's—stands the oak up straight and whittles it with a small axe. I've parked my car on a gravel patch near the sign welcoming visitors to the Multicultural Museum. When I first walked up, he nodded hello but said he needed to finish this detail, so I'm standing to the side by a holly bush, watching him conjure an animal. I haven't seen Barbara.

This whole coastal area, southeast of Houston, remains flooded, slushy and sodden, seething with mosquitoes. I wonder if the city or the county has done any drainage studies here, considered easements for detention ponds . . . a ten-year . . . no, a *fifty*-year . . . storm-event capacity . . .

Mud speckles my Taurus and the bottoms of my shoes. The humidity is as dense as a sheet. Kwako drills holes in the wood then inserts a pair of garden spades. His stiff leather gloves smell like hot rubber. He pulls them off, stands back, almost bowing to his work. Mockingbirds cackle in the willows. "Miss Washington," he says. "How you been?"

"You remembered my name."

"Tell you the truth, not many white—'scuse me—folk like you drop by here. You's easy to recall. What can I do for you? Interested in one of Barbara's quilts?"

I hesitate, wiping my shoes on the slick Bermuda grass. Its blue blades tickle my ankles. Kwako smiles at my awkwardness, steps behind me to a pile of loose wood. He bends, wags his head to bring me over. I squat beside him. "See this here?" He brushes a finger through a groove in the oak, stirring brittle, leaflike fragments. His long arms are like crate slats. "Wing casings," he says. "Formosan termites. I bought these-here rayroad ties, sight unseen, to sculpt with from a fellow over Loosiana way, but most of 'em worthless. Critters munching 'em." He snaps a board across his knee. It crumbles like old bread. "The Formosan is a fearsome thing. Imported sometime in the forties on army cargo ships, friend of mine says. Now they eating up the French Quarter over to N'Awlins, eating their way down the coast. Back in June, during the swarming season, couple we know down the road apiece was serving dinner to a roomful of guests when a cloud of these things come flying out of the dining room walls, dropping into the gravy. Kindly drained the sociability out of the evening."

"Hurricanes, termites, floods . . ."

"Yeah, we up to our butts in plagues." He grins, in love with his life in spite of it all.

A door slams. I peer across a tomato garden to the house. Barbara is touring a small group of visitors around the grounds. One man hands her some money; a woman next to him carries a box. "Bingo," Kwako sighs. "On'y sale this week." The people head to their cars and Barbara returns to the house, emerging a minute later with a bundle of laundry, which she hauls to a tiny shed adorned with horse collars and rusty plow blades. A washer cranks up inside the shed. Barbara comes back out with a pair of shears. A red scarf wraps her head. Brown skirt. Squash-yellow blouse. Kwako calls to her. "'Member Sister Washington?"

She waves the shears, wipes her hands on her skirt, joins us. Sweating, tired. Her hands are blistered. "Miss Telisha. Welcome back." She pats her forehead with her arm.

"If I'm not disturbing you . . . ," I begin.

"No no." She slips the shears into a dress pocket. "Let me make us some tea."

We follow her to the house. It's hotter inside than out. Her kitchen smells of nutmeg and vanilla. Small blue bottles with trumpet lips line her windowsills. They're filled with sunlight. A framed painting of Jesus gazing upward, looking very much like a twenties movie star, Rudy Valentino or somebody, tilts on the dining room wall; a yellowed palm leaf fans out behind it. Kwako and I sit at a table whose Formica top is peeling, patchy like a giraffe's hide. Chunks of lumber and metal lie scattered throughout the house, even in the kitchen, and Barbara has to step around them as she pours water into a kettle and reaches into a cabinet for ribbed glass tumblers.

Kwako watches me, stroking his tangled beard. The house settles and creaks. I can barely breathe in the heat. I undo the top button of my blue cotton blouse, rub the soppy V at the base of my neck. "Elias Woods," I say. "I've received permission to visit him up in Huntsville."

"Well, now," Kwako says. Barbara pulls fresh mint leaves from a sprig.

"I wanted to ask both of you, since you know him, if you'd mind accompanying me."

They look at each other.

"You wouldn't be allowed inside—you'd have to wait for me somewhere while I actually talked with him. But prison . . . it's not a drive I want to make by myself." I'm aware I'm talking quickly, unsure of myself, embarrassed. "I'd ask my uncle, but his health's got me worried and I don't want to strain him right now. My cousin works during the day. So I thought of you."

Barbara dumps ice cubes onto a counter and fills the tumblers. Kwako's still tugging his beard. "He's gonna lead you to your daddy, is he?"

"My uncle says Elias knew him. That's all I know. I just want to put some questions to him. I know you don't know me very well, and this is a lot to ask—"

"Here you go." Barbara sets the tea in front of me.

"—but you made me feel welcome last time I was here. And you know Elias—"

"We didn't traffic with him all that much, you understand," Kwako says. He slurps his tea.

"Well. I'm probably on a wild goose chase, anyway."

Barbara reaches over and pats my hand. Her callused fingers feel like wood grain. Kwako says, "I heard your daddy play once. I's telling Barbara after you left last time. Little club near Baytown for sailors and oil workers. Must have been . . . oh, '65 or so. '66, maybe. Bayou Jim Washington. Hell of a player. Dark and slender, wearing him a fancy new Stetson and slick black boots."

I lean forward, waiting for more, but Kwako shakes his head. "On'y time I ever seen him. Didn't talk to him or nothing. Didn't know Elias knew him. Them days, Elias was spending lots of time in the city with the law students from over at Texas Southern, doing sit-ins at the lunch counters. Real active, he was."

"Did he really kill his wife?"

"Cops say he confessed. They's always at each other's throats, Elias and his woman."

"Why?"

"Like I say, we didn't know him all that well."

Barbara pours us more tea.

"Anyway. I'd be happy to pay for your time, since I'd be taking you away from your business . . ."

"When you going?"

"Thursday."

Kwako glances at Barbara. "Gives me two days to buy new wood and finish my bears."

"Gives *me* time to scrub the linens."

"Yeah?"

"Yeah."

"Well then, looks like you got company," Kwako tells me. "Little vacation might be nice. We hardly never get one."

"I'm very grateful."

We finish our drinks in silence, then Kwako asks if I'd like to see some of Barbara's quilts. I understand he's suggesting I buy one in compensation for the favor they're doing me. We squeeze into a back bedroom. It's also jammed with lumber. Lovely quilts of all colors droop over clothes racks, chests of drawers, chairs, and the bed. Outside, a rose bush scrapes the window screen. The bed's headboard ticks in the room's awful swelter. The air burns my throat. I stumble against a framed poem on the wall. Barbara catches me and it. I apologize; she smiles. I study the words. "These were part of our wedding vows," she tells me. "Goes all the way back to slavery days." She straightens the frame on the wall:

HE: De ocean, it's wide, de sea, it's deep
Yes, in yo arms I begs to sleep
Not for one time, not for three
But long as we'uns can agree

SHE: Please gimme time, suh, to "reponder"
Please gimme time to "gargalize"
Then 'haps I'll tu'n away from out yonder
And answer up 'greeable for a s'prise

Barbara's eyes mist, but I can't tell if it's nostalgia or the heat. "Reminds me of the song my mama used to sing while she did her piecework," I say, fingering a brown and yellow quilt on the bed. The fabric cools my palm. "*Foller the drinking gou'd . . .*"

Barbara grins. "*When the sun come back / When the first quail call / Then the time is come / Foller the drinking gou'd . . .*"

"So it's a famous tune?"

"Oh my, yes. Old slave song, from the Underground Railroad. My grandma taught it to me."

"What's its significance? Do you know?"

"Sure. Grandma said there's a feller name Peg Leg Joe, former sailor, an abolitionist, who'd travel from plantation to plantation, working, and while he's there, he'd teach the slaves this song. Always, the following spring after he'd gone—when the first quail called—a few slaves would disappear, heading north, following the Big Dipper, on the trail he'd scoped out for them." She steps past me and unfolds a huge blue quilt from a chair. "I made this one after patterns Old Granny taught me, designs going back to slavery." She runs her fingers across appliqué and beadwork in the upper right-hand corner. "These represent stars, see, the spring constellations. Plantation women worked from can to can't—sunup till after dark every day—so the stars was there in the morning when they started, just beginning to fade, and they's there when they finished up at night. After supper, the women would all gather on a porch and commence talking and piecing." She asks Kwako to help her spread the quilt on the bed. Vibrant colors—reds and greens across the blue. But I'm embarrassed for her when I see how crooked the lines are: just like Mama's. As if hearing my thoughts, she tells me, "Old West African superstition, says Evil travels in a straight line, so the slave women, they'd sew their lines all cattywompers, block Evil's path."

"On purpose?"

"You bet. To throw off suspicion, too—see, these quilts was signs in the Underground Railroad. The patterns formed a map. When they got word it was safe to travel, the women would hang their quilts out over windowsills or on porch railings, signal folks the running time had come. The masters, they didn't think twice about it. Figgered quilting was just a hobby for Mammy, kept her happy in the evenings, and the sloppier-looking the work, the less attention it drawn to itself. But all the slaves knew what these things meant."

"Road guides."

"That's right. Hidden in plain sight." She pats a square to the left of the stars. "Shoofly."

"My mama used that one."

"Well, Shoofly say it's time to *shoo!*" She points to another square, just below the first. "This here's the Monkey Wrench . . .

" . . . which turns the wagon wheel . . .

" . . . till you come to the crossroads.

"When you see the flying geese . . .

" . . . you stay on the drunkard's path through the woods . . .

" . . . and follow the stars up north."

The "drunkard's path" is another raggedy-ass pattern Mama made. I run my hands across it. "So this is how it's *supposed* to look?"

Barbara nods. "Your mama must have been real proud of her roots, hewing to the old piecing ways."

"She—" I lift the quilt, rub it against my cheek. My eyes sting. "I don't know."

"You like it?" Kwako asks. "Two hundred bucks, even. Real bargain."

She scowls at him.

I clear my throat. "I *do* like it."

"We'll work something out when you pick us up on Thursday, how's that?" Barbara says.

Kwako peers out the window, past the rose bush, picking his teeth with his little finger. "Yessir, business sure slow today."

"No, that's okay," I say. "I'd like the quilt. I'd be honored to have it." I pull the checkbook from my purse.

"Here at the Multicultural Museum, we only prepared to deal in cash," Kwako says.

"Oh. Of course. Well then—"

"Thursday will be fine," Barbara assures me, touching my arm. "Take it. I hope it pleases your mama."

"Actually," I say, "my mama's passed."

Kwako steps over to help me fold the quilt. "Then I guess we'd better find your daddy, eh?"

———

On a dirt road between flooded rice paddies and Houston's southern edge, I stop the car and pull Barbara's quilt across my knees.

In Dale Licht's house, *in that white man's house,* she sang a slave song, stitched a freedom map into her African patterns. My mama, who ran from the niggers, who denied her own family. My mama, who refused me a black heritage (though she *did* name me Telisha, didn't she—why?), weaving for herself a rich, down-low world.

Hidden in plain sight.

What did she value about her own darkness? What part of her wouldn't let go? I bunch the beaded stars in my lap, lift the fabric to my lips, and kiss the flying geese.

The sky is smudged paper, soiled by refinery smoke. Heavy air force planes drone low over the land whose still water glistens among spreading weeds. A chain-link fence, tilted and slack, runs along the road near my Taurus. A rusty sign on it says, AMERICAN INDUSTRIAL SECURITY, INC. Through my rolled-down window I smell the lot's years of neglect. Rotted leaves in the mud, a thousand insect eggs gone to ruin. Dust scuffles. The day's bad breath. Wrecked cars sit in a field up ahead. On broken antennae they snag cottonwood fuzz from the air, strands of wind-ripped spider webs. Foam rubber spills from split seats. Torqued metal. Fine raw material for Kwako. Gather up rubber, plastic, leather, glass. Hammer, sand, plane, and saw. Make me a mama, sir, will you please, sir? A figure I can lift and carry. Pencil mouth. Shoe-heel ears. A bra stuffed with nothing (those cancerous breasts). Top her off with a plume—a shredded get well card, sent a day too late.

I'm staining the quilt with my tears. My hands hurt, gripping its edges so hard. If I could make it through the muck out there I'd comb through the death-cars, the nuts and bolts of abandonment, until I found a radio that would sing to me from far across the years, my mama's voice, the voices of buried slaves, steady, fearful, hushed: *Foller the drinking gou'd / Foller the Risen Lawd.*

———

Bitter stares at the receiver in his hand. "Where's the cord?" he says.

"It's a cell phone," I explain, tossing the wrapping and the box. "I want you to keep this handy on Thursday while I'm gone. If you have the slightest pain, even a twinge, you call Ariyeh at school. I've left the number on the table."

"Ahh—"

"I'm serious, Uncle. Don't mess with this."

He leaves the phone on the counter, next to a jelly-smeared knife, then goes to play a record. I pour myself a glass of water, walk to the porch, stretch my back and arms. Across the street, in the Magnolia Blossom, two paper-pale men stroll among the tombstones. Satchmo purrs "The Potato Head Blues." I stiffen. I don't want to assume, automatically, that any fancy-dressed white man poking through a black neighborhood is the enemy. I'm no conspiracy nut, like Reggie.

"Want a beer, Seam?"

"Thanks." I take a last look. The fact is, I know a developer when I see one.

———

On Thursday, I spin along the swamp roads, pick up Kwako and Barbara. On the radio a newscaster tells us that the "former H. Rap

Brown," now known as Jamil Abdullah Al-Amin, is awaiting trial in Georgia for murdering a sheriff's deputy. "Mr. Al-Amin once helped lay the foundation of the civil rights movement, along with Julian Bond, John Lewis, Huey Newton, and Stokely Carmichael, registering voters, forming the Student Non-Violent Coordinating Committee," the newsman says. "In the ensuing years, the civil rights leaders scattered into various philosophical camps, some distinguishing themselves, others falling into disgrace."

In the back seat, Kwako clucks his tongue. "Hot-headed boogee. Had so much going for him. How he let it all get away from him? It's just like Elias."

I switch the radio off. "Tell me about him," I say.

"Elias? Well, let's see. I 'member the day the Texas Southern students sat at the Weingarten's lunch counter over on Almeda Street, protesting the WHITES ONLY sign. Elias was with them. Till then, Houston papers was proud to say, ever' day, how 'docile' the city's coloreds had been. But one or two lunch counters, and that was *it* in Houston. The moneymen was too damn skittery. Signs came down straightaway."

"And that was the end?"

"Not overnight. The Major Leagues had integrated their teams, so when a guy like Willie Mays come to town, you had to put him up in a nice hotel with all the rest of the players. Baseball what finally broke the color line here. But Elias and them others, they was out front early. Solid and brave."

"So what happened to him?" I ask. All around us, in barbed-wired fields, cows wobble, heat-stunned, near steaming stock tanks. Old barns crumble into kudzu. I roll my window up, punch on the AC.

"Drifted out to West Texas, worked at the Pantex plant, making nukes. Come back here—"

"No, I mean how did *he* let things get out of hand?"

Kwako scratches his beard. "That you'll have to ask him."

"Is there . . . I don't know how to put this."

"Say it."

"Is there something wrong with us? These men were heroes, right? H. Rap Brown? But now he's just another black man with a gun. Another brother in jail . . ."

"Yeah, and his old buddy John Lewis is an important U.S. congressman. Don't go painting with a broad brush."

"You're right, you're right."

"Sometime I think the big shots of history just got lucky to be where they was. Circumstances a hair different, you know, they'd be sinners 'stead of saints. Hotheads, all of 'em—that's why they's out front when history ring its bell. Looka the Alamo—we call those fellas heroes, right? Hell, they's a bunch of rough-and-tumble scalawags. If they'da died in a saloon fight, which was *real possible* in most their cases, we wouldn't be saying their names."

We pass tupelos and sweet gums, a "Live Minnows" shop, old red-clay mule-cart roads winding off among dark pines, past gravestones sinking into weeds.

"Still, there *is* a lot of black men in jail," Kwako mumbles. "That's a fact."

Barbara spots a fruit stand and asks if we can stop. I pull over by a series of pine crates stacked to form tables. Watermelons, apples, and pears. From my purse I grab a wad of bills. "On me," I say. I hand her ten twenties. "And this is for your lovely quilt."

She smiles and tucks the money into her bright yellow skirt. "You like to learn piecework? I'll show you sometime. Then you can be like your mama."

"I'd like that," I say.

She greets the big, hearty man behind the crates. He's filbert-colored, gray-haired, and sweating. Horseflies swarm a row of cantaloupe. The air smells rancid and sweet: moist sugar, overheated auto brakes.

"Hardwoods mostly gone from here," Kwako says, glancing around at the pines. "Steam skidders dragged 'em all away . . ." A wistful bemusement hovers just at the edge of his voice, reminding me of Bitter. It accounts, I'm sure, for my ease with him.

"Did you finish sculpting your bears?"

"Three oak cubs." He grins. "And a brand new zebra made from Coke bottles and a suitcase."

Barbara asks the fruit seller to bag her up half a melon and a pair of Granny Smith apples. She leans close and whispers to him. He leads her to a box of Ziploc pouches next to some peanut sacks. The pouches are filled with fine white grains. Barbara smiles at me, embarrassed.

"That'll be two bucks for the fruit, dollar forty-eight for the kaolin."

It looks like chalk—fertilizer for houseplants or something. Barbara seems shamed by it so I don't ask her, but as she turns from the fruit stand, she opens the pouch, pinches a bit of powder between her fore-finger and thumb, and sucks it into her mouth.

"Dirt," Kwako tells me softly. "Fresh from the Georgia hills. She craves it like some folks crave popcorn or crackers."

Barbara's shy now, but I give her a sympathetic smile. She admits, "I'd eat it for breakfast, lunch, and supper, with a little iced tea, if I could, but it's bad for my system. Stops me up, you know, and leaves me tired."

"Forgive me. I'm curious," I say. "How did you—?"

"When I's a girl, my mama'd give me fifteen cents and say, 'Go get me some kaolin from Miz So-and-So.' She ate it whenever she's preg-nant with my little brothers and sisters. Said it settled her tummy. Sure enough, when I's carrying *my* firstborn and got sick in the mornings, I remembered what she'd said and hunted some down for myself. Been hooked ever since."

"There's a big dirt trade from Georgia and all through the South, over here to the coast, even up to Chi-town, along the Delta," Kwako tells me.

Back in the car, as we're heading through the woods, Barbara says, "You know the way the earth smells after a long dry spell, then a spit of rain hits it, stirring up old pebbles and leaves? That's how kaolin tastes to me." She chews a creamy pinch. "Doctor tells me, 'Girl, this stuff is used in paint, ceramics, fiberglass, it's used to make paper—it ain't to be eaten!' and I know he's right, but Lord, my mama was right too. Calms me like nothing else." I'm glad she trusts me enough to give me a glimpse of her life. Two kids, boys, she says, both grown—I wonder how old she is?—working in the Ship Channel, loading boats. "Hell-raisers, but they made good men. Married now. Responsible daddies. We're right proud of 'em."

Kwako says, "You done good, Mama."

"It's 'cause I had my dirt!"

We pass the remaining miles listening to a Sonny Rollins tape Kwako has brought, foggy sax twisting around mushrooming drum-beats. As we approach Huntsville, I notice blueberry fields on either side of the road and remember passing through here as a girl, in Mama's car, traveling from Houston to Dallas. I recall black men in ghostly white suits picking the berries and realize now they must have been prisoners working for the state. In high school, one of the persistent rumors was that Creole women, just out of jail, hung around "nigger" cemeteries near Huntsville. They'd "do" a boy for a six-pack of beer.

On the town's outskirts, sleek new housing crowds bulldozed fields; the unfinished homes are only about ten feet apart—a developer's strategy to reduce the taxable land. Corporate campuses, white and bland. Condos. Hotels resembling ski lodges, made of hill-country limestone. Billboards say, DO NOT PICK UP HITCHHIKERS. In the town itself, new additions have been tacked to older homes, a sign of prosperous times in the prison industry. Satellite dishes, swimming pools. College boys swerve past us in freshly waxed sports cars; farmers rattle along in flatbeds.

All I know about the Texas prison system, from reports in the mayor's office, is that the state once fed inmates a powdered meat substitute called Vita Pro, whose nutritional value was nil—and there was some question about where the unused meat was going and who profited from its sale. In the early eighties, the prison director was forced from office under suspicion of corruption. But this town is thriving; building cranes, skeletal girders soak up the sun beneath buzzing black police helicopters.

Downtown, in front of tobacco shops and clothing stores, men linger in shadows, wearing blue, short-sleeved shirts, khaki pants, wraparound shades. They light each other's cigarettes, mill about uncertainly, clutching plastic bags, manila folders. Ex-cons, I figure, out on parole, sniffing the outside air, testing to see whether it's poison to them now. Tattoos smear their arms.

Near the vaguely Italian courthouse, narrow cafés serve Diet Cokes and Fritos, All You Can Eat Noon Specials, to men in cheap ties—middle-management types. We spy them through the windows. I spot only a few women on the street, mostly in front of a lumberyard converted into a county museum and on the steps of a Baptist church so large it appears to be swollen.

I have twenty minutes to make my appointment. With Barbara's help, I choose the nicest-looking café in the main square and drop her off with Kwako. "I won't be long," I say. "Are you sure you'll be all right?"

"We're fine, honey." She slips the dirt inside her purse. "Kwako'll read the paper, and I'll do a crossword or two. Take all the time you need."

"It's good to have a break." Kwako pauses on the sidewalk, stretching his arms. He seems frail here, out of context. But the café looks reassuring, full of dark faces.

Once I've seen them comfortably seated, I check my scribbled directions and make my way to a thin, tarry road surrounded by chain-link fences trimmed with barbed-wire. Every fifty feet or so, cinder-block guard towers shade my car. The guards grip cell phones. They look bored. I drive slowly, carefully. A sign in English and Spanish informs me that my presence here means I've automatically consented to a possible search. I come to a large sally port, but then I see a small VISITORS sign shunting me off to the left. I turn and immediately I'm stopped by a uniformed man with a cell phone. "He'p you, ma'am?" I give him my name. He asks me to wait in my "vehicle." Puny trees ring a pale brick admin building just up ahead; it looks like the tidy home of a college president. After ten minutes or so, the man returns—I didn't see where he went—and directs me past the building to a nearly full parking lot. I lock the car and head toward a chain-link gate manned by two other sullen uniforms. They buzz me in and point me toward a boxy structure. Inside, on a warped corkboard nailed to the gray stone wall, handwritten notices announce TDC rules, the Employee of the Month, car and house rentals. A battered water fountain gurgles in the corner. A carrot-haired man smacking gum asks for picture ID, hands me a clipboard, orders me to sign in. In the "Reason for Visit" column I write "Dallas Mayor's Off." He squints at my words. "All righty. Follow me. Oh—you can't take that purse. We'll hold it for you here." I hand it over; he stuffs it in a cabinet with other purses, paper sacks, even two or three Happy Birthday balloons, then leads me through a narrow doorway to an outside path lined with artificial flowers and tall Cyclone fences festooned with concertina wire. From somewhere in the distance a loudspeaker shouts, "Clear on outta the rec room now. All you sweet little bitches get back to your shitters." The officer glances at me, reddening, as though I wasn't supposed to hear that. We come to a squat building, red brick, with barred and meshed windows. He opens the door with a key, steps aside. As I slip past him I smell the spearmint gum he's chewing, a pondlike cologne. The room is dim. Green plaster walls, flaking. A dusty, old-papers smell. A soft drink machine rattles behind a scarred oak table. R.C., Orange Crush. Through yet another doorway we come to a long wooden counter rigged with a Plexiglas divider, about a foot high. Chairs on either side. Three other women are sitting on my side of the counter, speaking in low tones to men opposite them, fellows in orange jumpsuits with blocky black numbers stenciled on their breast pockets. Guards—I overhear one of the inmates call them COs—lurk in each corner of the room, leering openly at the women. I take a seat and cross my arms. The room hums faintly—from what, I can't tell: an air-conditioning unit (though it's hot in here), a generator under the floor.

"Jesus, baby," says one of the inmates, "my lawyer thought DNA was an additive in *food coloring*."

Soon, a CO leads a tall, shaved-headed, middle-aged man to a wobbly chair directly across the counter from me. He's carrying a thick leather book, *Black's Law Dictionary,* hugging it to his chest like a Bible. From time to time his mouth twitches as though he's working an invisible toothpick. His eyes are yellow, his ears flat and fleshy like the leaves of a large, overwatered houseplant. Skin the color of an avocado's woody heart. "So," he says to me, a bass rasp. "Miss High Society come to see the ghost. Who are you, High Society? Can you help me?"

"Thank you for seeing me, first off." My voice trembles.

"Who *are* you? What you want with me?"

"My uncle, a man named Bitter, maybe you knew him as Ledbetter, did some carpentry work for you once. He said—"

He slams his hand on the book. "They *rejected* my last appeal. You know that, right? *That* why you here?"

"No . . ."

"Giving me the needle next month. So what I need to know, Miss High Toes, is can you help me? You got any pull with the Big Juice? Tell me again. What's your lookout?"

"Well I'm—"

"Kind of a bull dagger, ain't you?"

"What do you mean?"

"Traipse in here, cleaner than the Board of Health . . . I'm some sort of freak show for you?"

"I think you knew my daddy."

"Hell, I probably *fucked* your daddy. When was he in?"

"He wasn't. He was—"

"They told me you work for a mayor or something."

"That's right."

"So can you raise me? You must have some pull."

"No. I'm afraid not."

He leans closer to the Plexiglas. "See, the thing is, I should've only did a nickel. But Mr. Charley, he won't listen to *me* no more."

I lean back and sigh. "Did you kill your wife?" I blurt, wondering if I can wrench a single straight answer out of this guy.

He waves his hand. "See, you want to know—that day? Let me tell you. That day I's hanging out at the happy shop 'cause the crumbcrushers at home, five and six year old, they driving me nuts all the time. You know how it is. So I's feeling *good* when I get back. Fry us up a mess of chicken wings. She puts the critters to bed. I'm busting suds in the kitchen, next thing I know she's having at me with the bread knife. The fucking *bread knife.* She's all, 'You drunk, irresponsible . . . leave me with the kids . . . never know . . .' That shit. So of course, I'm gonna do what?"

"Of course," I say.

"Now, your mayor, he can get with that, right? You tell him. I done my nickel. That oughtta be enough."

"Jim Washington," I say. "Did you know him? Can you tell me anything about him?"

"Fuck. You heard of Karla Faye Tucker, right? They send a sweet piece like her down to Hell—Little Miss, just like you, Jerry Falwell, God, and shit in her corner—what shot I got? You wasting my time."

I try to imagine my daddy as someone like him: scared, belligerent, improvising moment to moment just to save his neck. I try to see this man sitting bravely at a lunch counter—a tabletop similar to the one separating us now?—carrying the banner of civil rights. Suddenly, in this sad, stale room, filled with curses and last-minute pleas, the world seems lost, jerry-rigged, hopeless. Does it matter that we "won our rights"? We'll lose them again if we don't keep fighting, and who has the strength to stick? Does it matter what my daddy was like? He's gone. We'll all soon be gone.

"Hunnert and twenty-seven," Elias says.

I shrug.

"Hunnert and twenty-seven."

"What about it?"

"Number of poor willies George W. murdered since moving into the governor's mansion. Regular slaughterhouse. What you gonna do about it? *Can you fucking help me?*"

I rise. The chair scrape echoes dully off the walls. "I'm not going to do anything about it," I say, turn, and nod at a grinning CO to let me out of the room.

On the outside path the red-haired guard and I pass a cluster of cons in blue T-shirts and sweatpants taking their exercise on the other side of the fence. One rushes forward—he looks no more than twenty—asks me, "Are you *anywhere,* know'm say'n? I'm jonesing, babe, swear to God. Anything, anything at all." Another calls, "Hey mink! Hey bitch! I got it for you right here!" He clutches his crotch. "Ain't a thang! Even got us some raincoats!" He pulls a package of condoms from his pants. Behind him, an armed CO yells, "Shaadap, girlie!"

Red-head mumbles, "Ol' Satan's a silent partner in the ownership of some folks, eh?"

As I leave the admin building and head to my car I'm thinking *Straight lines; Evil travels in straight lines.* I'm cold despite the heat. My bones feel soft. I have to turn and go back. I've forgotten to ask for my purse.

————

Off-duty COs crowd the café tables. Sweat rings wilt their cotton shirts. White guards in one part of the room, blacks in the other. A young brother says, "One thing I learned about white dudes. You can hang with 'em long as no ladies around. Soon as poon's on the scene, the whole deal just freezes up."

"—don't *want* to work," an ofay shouts at his buddies. "*You've* seen 'em."

Barbara hands me the sugar jar. I stir my coffee, brush my bottom lip with my pinky. "Dirt," I whisper. She cleans herself. "Thank you," she says.

Kwako sighs. "Hard to figger. Always seemed a reasonable man to me. Lockup must put you through some changes."

"Oh, he changed *before* that," Barbara says. "Or he wouldn't be in lockup to begin with."

"Anyways, I'm sorry you didn't get what you needed."

I nod. "Thanks for coming with me." The coffee fails to steady my nerves. The laughter, the flamboyant gestures of bragging men, the shifting, suspicious eyes in the room . . . we *all* ought to be locked up, protected from our own ugliness. The smell of pickles from Kwako's half-eaten sandwich turns my stomach.

"What's a six-letter word for 'resistant'?" Barbara asks, tapping her pen on the table.

Driving through town, we pass the compound where Elias will receive a lethal injection a month from now: a dark, straight wall topped with razor wire. Behind it, peaked roofs and banks of curtained windows. At the base of the wall, scrappy flowers lie in wet clumps beside torn posterboards, remnants from a march against an earlier execution.

Back on the highway, Barbara and Kwako snooze. I pass the blueberry fields. A white-suited hoe squad chops weeds beneath the brambles, watched closely by armed, sunburned deputies. I doubt the land here has changed much in eighty years—the developers haven't planted flags yet—nor has the treatment of prisoners. I imagine Cletus Hayes, feet shackled, stabbing the ground with a shovel. Behind him—behind *me;* I concentrate hard and on comes the mask; the hypnotic shuffling of chains, steady waves drawing me back, back—behind me, a fat guard in a Stetson brandishes a polished Springfield, just like the ones we use in the army. He yells, "Faster, boy! This rate, won't be enough flavor in that sweet blueberry ice cream I'll be licking later. Meantime, you'll be drinking your piss in the brig!" My spine burns like kindling. Eyes itch. Whenever this asshole says "ice cream," my mouth waters and I think of children eating, skipping, sailing kites—the kids Sarah Morgan has dreamed of with me. I think of her and the seed I've planted in her womb. I ponder generations, the world continuing without me. I can't grasp the enormousness of it all. I look up at the mule-cart road, imagine it paved in the future, a sleek new jitney jingling by, ferrying—who? A light-skinned young woman, perhaps. My great-granddaughter, glancing out at the fields, trying to picture me here, her color—*vanilla, with just a trace of berries if you look real close*—her confusion, her advantages a consequence of my having been in the world, of having been a *man* in the world, for all this country's attempts to tear me down. I lift my shovel—*anh! anh!*—and bust the earth's dirty lip.

13

BITTER SAYS Grady died peacefully in his sleep—though apparently he was sleeping in a vacant lot at the time. Drunk in the middle of the day.

"Doc says liver failure." Bitter rubs his eyes. "Well. It ain't like we didn't see it coming."

Like your heart? I nearly ask.

"I on'y wish he coulda been comfy in the mud-dauber shack. Got word 'bout an hour after you'd left for Huntsville. Tried to call Ariyeh on that fancy new phone you give me, but I couldn't figure out the buttons."

"I'm sorry, Uncle."

"Regulars down at Etta's pitching in to give him a proper burying. Can you take me to the coffin shop?"

The funeral home is on Navigation Boulevard, next to a Mexican restaurant. With its sandy stones of various brown shades and a tall chimney, it looks like a spotted giraffe. A sign by its entrance says the place specializes in shipping deceased immigrants back to Mexico, Europe, and Asia.

Inside, a tape of soft, slow harpsichord music augmented by a recording of water, wind, and birdsong competes with a loud air-conditioner in the front window. Dim lights in cheap tin frames—imitation gaslamps—cast a jaundiced glow from the white walls onto a deep red carpet. By the door, a small window has been covered with Saran Wrap poorly dyed to resemble stained glass.

A thin man in a dark brown suit greets us. His head is as smooth as a jelly bean.

"Are you the undertaker?" Bitter says.

The man blanches. "I'm the funeral director. The memorial counselor. Anthony Crespi. How do you do? You're here on behalf of—?"

"Grady."

"Ah yes. I'm terribly sorry for your loss, sir. But we'll create a beautiful Memory Picture for you. Shall we step into the display room?" He leads us into a spacious, red-carpeted chamber. Through a hidden speaker, a bird chirps over turgid organ chords. The coffins, arrayed in neat rows—wooden, metal, gleaming, dark—look like sleek catamarans ready to cross an ocean.

"Let me introduce you to our Classic Royal," says Mr. Crespi, waving his hand. This guy doesn't waste any time. "Based on contemporary European models, equipped with a fully satin-lined interior, a fine mahogany gloss." He steps to his right. "This is the Classic Regal, very popular, with a wider shape, you'll notice. Wonderful craftsmanship. Very versatile."

Versatile? He won't be drag racing in it. Oh, these vultures! They know how to nail you. Who ever value-shops for the grave? *I can get you a much better deal across town, with power steering, whitewalls, AM/FM radio, tinted windows—in case, you know, God's face is too bright.*

Naturally, most people will choose the more expensive models. Cutting costs might indicate, to family and friends, disrespect for the dead.

"The White Pearl. One of my favorites," says Mr. Crespi, his bald pate dewy with sweat. Waterfalls *shush* through ceiling speakers. "I can also show you the relative advantages of the Valley Forge by Batesville, possibly the most respected casket-maker in the world, or the Keystone by York, another fine establishment."

I flash on coming back here soon, making arrangements for Bitter; flash on Mama's north Dallas grave. My knees wobble. Bile rises in my throat. Bitter touches one of the lids. "What's this for?" he asks, tracing a rubber lip like the lining of a Ziploc bag. His mouth is tight. He's barely holding himself together.

Mr. Crespi smiles. "Protective caskets—"

"Why does a dead man need protection?"

"To prevent, uh . . . alien and foreign objects from—"

"Maggots and things?" Bitter says.

"Well, yes, uh . . . in the past, protective caskets designed to keep out . . . critters . . . used impermeable gaskets as sealing devices. Unfortunately, in an air-tight atmosphere . . ." He clasps his hands behind his back. His eyes plead with Bitter to say he's heard enough.

"Yeah?"

"In an air-tight atmosphere, methane gases tend to build. A by-product of anaerobic bacteria, which, as the pressure builds—"

Bitter laughs, a mean little sound with no pleasure in it. "Are you saying the coffin could explode?"

Mr. Crespi clears his throat. "That wasn't unheard of. But now, happily, we have these permeable rubber linings, which allow caskets to burp, as it were, preventing dangerous buildup."

The wind and water grow louder.

Bitter says, "The whole cost, everything—embalming, the box, the hearse—" Each word appears to injure Crespi. He's wincing. "What are we looking at?"

"Depends."

"Roughly?"

"Insurance?"

"No, hell no. Grady couldn't afford nothing like that."

"All right, well, with a medium-sized casket—"

"One that burps?"

"Right. Say, two thousand. Refrigeration and preparation, another four hundred. Escorting your friend to the religious service I estimate at anywhere from three to five hundred."

"You make out okay, don't you?" Bitter says.

"I'm pleased to provide a valuable community service."

"I'll bet you are. Give us the cheapest, burpingest box you got."

"Very well, sir. This weekend, then—say, by two o'clock Sunday afternoon—your friend Grady will be waiting for you here in the Slumber Room."

———

Etta has laid her hands on some primo barbacoa: ribs, goat's heads, cow's heads ("eighteen-pounders!"), cheek and tongue ("*cachete y lengua*," she calls them), potato salad, lima beans. "Let me sweat you up some meat!" She stands behind the bar doling out unseasoned brisket. "Seasoning kills the true flavor, darling—it's like smothering a kitten in a blanket."

We're all lined up with paper plates. Out back, over a pit filled with tender mesquite, more meat sizzles. Earlier, Etta had passed around a collection bowl for Grady's funeral expenses. She was the biggest contributor—the only person here with a steady business. Her arm shakes. Sauce dribbles from her ladle to the floor.

"Used to fish with some white folks down in Galveston," a friend of Bitter's says. "Sometimes they'd invite me home for supper. You ever dine in a white man's house? Shit. Ever get asked, don't take no chances. Eat *before* you go."

I choose a chair in a corner, by the Coors crates. My back aches. Sleeping on Bitter's hard couch is catching up with me—not just the physical discomfort, but the frustration of watching him do nothing about his frailties. I've had my eye on an apartment building a couple of blocks away that advertises daily and weekly rates. I'm thinking about this when Bitter joins me. "How you doing, Uncle?"

He nods and grins wanly, but his eyes are moist. One of his buddies says, "I'm getting ass-over-tea-kettle *snockered* tonight. For Grady."

I reach for a Hen Dog. The drummer raps a rim-shot. Earl chants, "I've got no home in this world!"

While the band plays I reread a letter that came for me this afternoon at Bitter's house. I didn't have time to study it before and just stuffed it into my pocket. It's been opened—inspected?—and badly resealed: Elias apologizing for his "crud behavior" during my prison visit.

"In here, they want to make you into a monster," he writes. "Sleep in the cold, the dark. In ad seg, you get no education. And there's no respect. The old cons, they just want to do their bids and be left alone. You can *live* with them. But these young lunkheads in here now, they yelling all the time, showing off, like they up on stage. It's like sleeping with seals—seals what puke all the time and go around sticking shanks in other seals."

I sip my drink. Earl closes his eyes, moaning a slow spiritual.

"Anyway, I wanted to say I've lost it all," Elias goes on. "Too many years of busthead, I guess. The truth is, I don't remember your daddy. I don't remember much of anything. A few big dreams when I was young. I remember making bombs in the desert. My coworkers at the nuke plant, they was all Christians. Figured they was helping God's plan. Comes the end of the world, you know, Jesus'd show up in His chariot, they said. I always pictured Him in a low rider, with a little plastic statue of His mama hanging from the rearview on a string of black pearls. I remember a few faces over the years. My poor wife.

"The thing is, whatever made your daddy run, it probably wasn't you. Money. Or booze. Or a woman. Your mama, maybe. But not you. That's all. I hope it helps."

I cram the paper back inside my pocket. Snockered. Damn straight. Here's to Grady. My eyes fill. I brush the water away. For tonight, at least, yesterday can take care of itself.

The scarecrow pats Bitter's shoulder. The next casualty, I think. "*Laplie tombe, wawaron chante,*" Bitter says. The man nods and wanders off. I raise my eyebrows. "'When the rain is coming,'" Uncle sighs, "'the bullfrogs sing.'"

————

The Slumber Room burbles with underwater sounds, squishy, squidlike: some ungodly New Age music tape. Mr. Crespi wears a blue coat that fits him as snugly as a wetsuit. "Lovely to see you again," he says and guides Bitter and me to Grady's coffin. "I hope you have a pleasant visit. If there's anything I can do . . ."

How good is your rouge and your paint? Your plaster of Paris? Can it cover up waste? The bones of grief? "We're fine," I say. "Thank you." He withdraws.

The casket glows, gray, in the light of six candles, each the size of a cereal box. The room smells of roses and also of rust from an old air-conditioner in the window. Three or four unruly hairs stand up on Grady's head. Lifelessness has hardened like mud on his cheeks. Last night I dreamed of Mama in an open hole in the ground, looking natural and calm, as if she were taking a nap.

But there's nothing natural about Grady. If he were a manikin, I'd say he was poorly made. If we propped him up, he'd fall apart. This is a *corpse.* The ugliness of the word is exactly right. Whatever was human here has fled. All that's left is inertia. A rigid and useless container.

Bitter plucks Grady's sleeve. "What did you do to yourself?" he whispers, shaking. A humming in the walls. The wiring. "What in the world did you do?" He starts to sink. Yes, I'll be burying him soon, I think. Like a keepsake; tucking away all that's left of my old life. Just a little rag and bone. My throat tightens. We lean against each other. I help him outside and back into the car.

————

Crespi stands by the funeral home limo, at the Magnolia Blossom's gate. A brackish smell—shrimp and brine—sails on the breeze from the Ship Channel. While the preacher prays over Grady's grave, and mourners fan themselves with programs from the service, I stare across the street at Bitter's yard, remembering muggy afternoons just like this when Ariyeh and I were kids playing "Jail." She was the sheriff, I was the thief. She'd shut me inside a cardboard box. "You're a bad, bad girl and I have to lock you up."

Of course, I thought. Look at me.

"Ashes to ashes, dust to dust . . ."

It was just a game, but each time we played it, I felt indelibly shamed.

They want to make you into a monster.

Near Crespi now, the white men I'd noticed before, strolling among the tombstones. With them is Rufus Bowen. I lower my shades. They watch our party for a moment—did Bowen catch me looking?—then walk half a block to a black and white Volvo.

You're a bad, bad girl, and you'll never know why.

A woman next to the reverend gives him a sultry smile as he drops wet dirt onto the casket.

———

Tonight, when Bayou Slim makes his appearance at Etta's, interrupting Grady's wake, the room gets still. His forehead is creased like a snappy pair of slacks. His fingers shiver. He doesn't even make it through one song. The melody's an agony, the beat a punctured truck tire. He quits abruptly, drops his head, then rouses himself to beg a few coins. Stumbles out the door.

Several Gulf Coast bluesmen adopted "Bayou" as part of their stage names. "Heads or Tails" is a local standard. Echoes of my father? Simple coincidence.

But I get up to follow, glancing to make sure Bitter is okay. He's hugging one of the brandy women, who's wearing a Lady Day gardenia.

I scan the parking lot. Pickups. Sun-blistered vans. Across the street the Flower Man's house is ablaze: Christmas lights, Halloween devil lights, lanterns, candles, flashlights bolted to the wall. They shine randomly into a field snapping with little white bugs. Train wheels clatter somewhere off to the west. *My daddy's gone, my daddy's gone, my daddy's gone.* I pull Elias's letter from my pocket and let it drift away on the breeze.

Then I see him in a tumbleweed snarl. He brushes his pants, tosses a bottle into the field, hoists his guitar case onto his shoulders: piggybacking a clubfooted child. "Slim?" I call. I cross the street.

He squints at me.

I stop a few feet from him. "I just wanted to tell you, sir . . ."

"What's that?"

"I enjoy your music."

We're face to face in the Flower Man's pink and purple light. The glare makes the ground, our clothes, our skin seem rough, made of tarp. Slim's breath is rank; his eyes like Bloody Marys. "Music?" he croaks.

"I think you're a lot like my daddy used to be. No," I say. "No. I think you're *exactly* like him."

"You need a daddy?" The voice is whiskey in a cracked wooden cup. His belly rumbles.

"No. Maybe."

He touches my arm. I start to touch him back, but he coughs, "Got a buck?"

"Sure." I laugh. "Sure I do." But I don't. I've left my purse in the gut bucket.

"Thank you," he says, though I've given him nothing. He weaves away through the weeds.

14

SOME OTHER TIME/ROOMS/DAILY, WEEKLY RATES, says the sign. Six stories. Wood and brick. Peeling tan paint. The rooms are furnished—bed, table, chest of drawers—and they're only fifty dollars a week. I nod hello to the man behind the lobby desk as I carry my case to the stairs. He's wearing a sleeveless T-shirt, eating a plum, watching an old *Star Trek* episode on a portable black-and-white TV. He doesn't offer to help me. The plum leaks on the scarred oak countertop.

The stairs are dark and narrow, littered with Sprite cans, crumpled Camel packs, want ads, broken glass. Sour fried food. I emerge onto the third floor's radish-colored carpet. Loud voices, thumping from behind closed doors. Peanut shells line the baseboards. Earwigs sift among them. I'm beginning to have second thoughts—I'd noticed the squalor before, when I'd checked the place out, but it didn't seem *this* depressing.

My room reassures me. Large. Wide windows. I flop my suitcase onto the creaky spring bed. Torn strips of dark blue wallpaper curl like the petals of an iris. The closet smells of men's suits: sweat, watery cologne. An old rubber doll's head lies on its ear in a corner. A single coat hanger.

An empty Lipitor bottle sits in the medicine cabinet behind the mirror in the bathroom. Someone has painted a twisting vine around the hot water knob in the shower. Part of a Stephen King paperback lies shredded on the toilet tank. Of course the faucet drips.

Cooing sounds next door, through the wall: an elderly man and woman consoling each other. The windows overlook an abandoned freight yard, flatcars loaded with late morning light. A yellowed mattress curls in a field of sunflowers and weeds. Grime sprinkles the windowsill.

For the first time ever I have my own place in Houston. My birth city. My home. I try to imagine living here, driving to work, hanging out with Ariyeh.

Bitter wasn't happy I left his house, though I assured him I was only two blocks away and I'd eat with him every night. He wore three nutmegs tied in a rag around his neck and sipped tea steeped with anise seed and corn shucks: bad blood medicine. "If I'm sick as you say I am, Seam, how can you leave me?"

"I'm not *leaving* . . . so you admit you're sick?"

"Nothing my spells won't cure. I'm talking 'bout *you*. How *you* feel."

"You won't *let* me be a nurse, will you? *Will you?* No. You're determined to end up like Grady."

"That's low, Seam."

"I'm sorry, Uncle, but it's true. You heard what the doctor said. Your symptoms are severe enough to warrant more tests. Yet you sit here doing nothing. It's like my stepdad when Mama was sick, smiling all the time—'Everything's hunky-dory!' Anyway. It's better this way. You'll get your space back, I'll have some privacy, and maybe my spine will loosen up. Keep your cell phone handy. You've got the number of the pay phone over at my place, right?"

"*Mayor's* girl." He sniffed. "Come and go when she please. Too good for my couch, is what it is."

"That's *not* what it is. I've *told* you what it is."

When I pulled away this morning, he was sitting on his porch gazing off into the graveyard trees, singing mournfully,

Mo pas connin queque quichause
Qu appe tourmenter moin la . . .

Now, I sit here feeling homesick. Not for Dallas or my job. I'm sure of that. What, then? My fish and birds? How long can I stay away? What are my plans?

I lock the door and head downstairs, meeting, on his way up, a middle-aged man carrying cabbages. In his slender hands they look like skulls. He asks me how long I'll be around, warns me about several broken steps if I go past the fifth floor. He laughs and says the building is haunted. A soldier is said to appear at night in one or another room, his uniform hard to place, asking, "Are you with us or against us?" He wishes me a pleasant stay.

The desk clerk watches Mr. Spock subdue a rubbery beast. Outside, cottonwood fuzz fills the air. An Arco gas truck grinds its gears past the railroad tracks. The phone booth door won't shut all the way. I punch

Shirley's number and cover my ear with my palm.

A man answers. I ask for my friend.

"Telisha?"

"Yes. Who's this?" Though I know right away who it is. My fingers tingle.

"What's up, sugar?"

Jesus. "How are you, Dwayne?"

"You know. Free-styling, whiling it all away. You? You're—where? Houston?"

"That's right." So she couldn't resist his snake oil. Did he whisk her away to the Strictly Tabu? Pull his *dark side* shit?

"Shirl's in the shower. We've got Rangers tickets. Afternoon game."

"Tell her I called, will you? Checking on my pets."

"Will do. Listen, when you're back to town, T, what say we have us a reunion? Some dancing, a drink or two? I kinda feel we parted on a sour note, and I'd like to make it up to you."

"I smell a dead cat on the line."

He laughs.

"Tell Shirl I'll try her again."

"She may be busy for a while. My girl *do not* play, see."

"Good-bye, Dwayne." The receiver feels hot. I place it in its cradle and slump against the booth.

Back inside the building, the stairs seem nearly insurmountable. My knees are Silly Putty. Food sizzles behind closed doors. Korean or Vietnamese. Heavy garlic. Rice. My bed jiggles when I throw myself on it. Weary, dizzy with heat, I'm out soon, dreaming of buttons, fingers, tongues.

When I wake, I get up, splash water on my face. The faucet-stream is yellow. I undo my blouse and open a window. A roach slithers from under the sill and out through a rip in the screen.

Homesick for Mama. Is that it?

Or is this about sex?

Buck up, T. Stay focused. Remember why you came: searching for the men. Cletus, Daddy. Bullshit. They're far too distant—always *were*—for me to really reach. I've found they answer nothing.

And hell, I don't want to think about sex right now, the smell of gin, the messy wetness, a cold, hard hand on my breast . . . the breath of the heat, the pull of the dark bayou swelter . . . somewhere, the *whoo*-ing of owls . . . the leer of the shut-in boy, Dwayne's cocky assurance that he knew what I wanted, Reggie's charming grin . . . his skin against my neck, arms, wrists . . .

Pillow tight between my legs. Stop this. Think of Ariyeh. Call him an asshole. Go ahead. "You're a fucking asshole, Reggie!" I shout at the walls. "You'd be like all the rest!" But the cottony pillow feels fine against my chest, soft, giving, warm . . . no. Get off this. What else? What else?

Mama's quilts? The patterns Barbara showed me?

Yes, all right. I sit up, set out thread, shirt collars, scraps, and cuffs. Barbara gave them to me once we got back from Huntsville. "A running stitch is simple," she told me. "You work the needle in and out"—*in and out, baby, in and— damn it, girl, concentrate!*—"so each stitch is divided from the next by a little space. The smaller the stitches, the more you'll make what looks like an unbroken line, but that kind of humbuggery ain't important. Nothing wrong with a big ol' stitch — 'Toenail Catchers,' we call 'em. Anyways, to sort of limber up your fingers, hon, maybe it's best you start with a straightforward diagonal."

Seamstress? Well. Let's see about that.

I thread the needle. Soon, linked strips emerge, the color of milk chocolate. "Don't worry 'bout right and wrong," Barbara had cautioned me. "Improvisation is the key to lively work. Taking the familiar and jazzing on it—repetition, revision—losing yourself even as you're discovering what you can do."

As I work, a noisy kiddo scurries down the hall. Did my great-grandmother or my grandma Jean make quilts in the late afternoons in Texas City, while Mama flew through the building with her dolls, lamb stew bubbled on the stoves, and men made their way home from flaming refineries?

I close my eyes. Do I have a feel for the needle, the way Sarah Morgan did? Stitch in, stitch out . . . forward, back . . . now and then . . . *awful pains, labored breath* . . . yes, the building is haunted . . . or *I* am . . . I slip into a rhythmic trance, slip out of myself, a brittle, spinning leaf, blown back through the years . . . oh my Lord, oh my hands, the knuckles ache, my spine's bent, but I tug and tighten the dyed cotton thread the way I have for decades, taking patterns now from the Negroes who've sheltered me in my shame. Bearing a black man's child: my sin, my exit from the garden.

And why did I do it? Passion? Spite? Curiosity? Are the motives any clearer to me than they are to anyone else, or was I merely responding to life, its bawdy surgings, borne in my small, white frame? Wasn't I using my fundamental privilege as an American, the will to freedom, to snatch any identity I wanted—or believed I required? Repetition, revision. Improvisation. White hands toggling, tying, wrapping, winding, pulling forth from dusty castoffs old Negro patterns, liberty maps, the chance to start anew.

But the price, the price is far too steep. *Awful pains.* Cletus, lost now in a nondescript meadow. Me, wasting my last days in exile, in a city that stinks of oil. Jean, the child Cletus gave me, heeds no pattern in *her* life. What freedoms can she choose? Drudge work for others and the forceful attentions of men. Born into *my* exile, *my* limitations, she has only a meager scrap pile from which to piece her way.

A thumping on the stairs down the hall. The little girl, Helen, Jean's child. For her, the garden is just a rumor, a myth of vanished generations; no map, no matter how lovingly stitched, can lead her back to Paradise. I'm patient with her each night after supper, training her to thread the needle, to cut the flour sacks for batting. I show her flying geese and the drunkard's path—*it's all right if it's crooked, child; Evil travels in straight lines.* She does well sometimes. But afternoons, she whips up and down the stairs, desperate for escape. Well. God knows this is no place for a child, especially a girl with skin as fair as hers, who can see, even at this tender age, the cruelties of difference and disparity. Already her future is beyond my poor imagining. What do I hope for her? What did I hope for myself? What can I give her and her children but a legacy of rootless confusion, a fissure between two worlds? Ah, what have I done, what have I done? I open my eyes. I've pricked my thumb with the needle; a fat blood drop wets the cloth.

The hallway is silent now. The couple next door quiet. The garlic smell has lessened. Through my window I hear, from the church down the block, foot stomping, a ratchety organ. I set the cloth aside, with its impure stain. Walk to the window. Cats prowl the freight yard below. Birdshit paints the phone booth. Dazed, still—caught between Sarah's time and my own—I sit on the sill, listening to *Praise Jesus.* Dirt rings the windowframe. Houston's skin. Barbara would lap it up. Thinking of her, I run my finger through the grime, lift it to my lips.

———

Three A.M. I get up to pee. The smudge around my mouth is like the margarita salt I remember feeling with my tongue, the night of my date with Dwayne. Dirt from the windowsill. I'm going nuts. The heat. No sex.

Don't start, T. Besides, I was already restless. I felt this way right after Dwayne, after Mama died, before driving here to Freedmen's Town—as if a lock on a box had been broken and I couldn't keep the lid on any longer, holding myself inside. *Who I was* kept drifting away, like smoke from dry ice, and others kept floating into the space, filling the box with *their* presences. Is this what intimacy is like? Am I simply not used to it? The fear I felt with Dwayne—is that what it means to really give to a man? Mama's sickness and death . . . if you love, you'll grieve. No avoiding it.

I wash my face. As my hands rub my lips, I drift once more, and for a moment I'm a girl again in Bitter's house, bent above a rusty-drained sink. Mama's hands flit behind my ears, across my eyes and nose, dribbling warm water down the bones of my neck and into my filthy shirtfront. "Child, child, you have such gorgeous skin." Through the open bathroom window, trilling frogs. "Why do you want to cover it up with all this nasty bayou dirt?"

The plumbing shudders. I shut off the water. Mama's words were often harsh, admonishing me to straighten up, behave a certain way, be careful . . . but her touch was gentle. Early on, in Houston, she was a lovely, conscientious caretaker. After we moved to Dallas, I don't remember her *ever* touching me: another reason, I realize now, I've longed for the bayou heat. It was inseparable for me from the warmth of Mama's arms, the safety of her nearness.

When *my* turn came, I made a poor caretaker, working late, spending little time in the house (am I doing this again, now, with Bitter?) . . . but in part, it's because Mama *kept* me distant. Dale, so upbeat all the time despite her loss of strength, Mama stoic, silent. She gave herself over to the cancer as easily and completely as she'd surrendered to the 'burbs. I'd drop by after dark, find her asleep on the bed we'd set up in the living room so she could watch TV. Dale would be upstairs, showering, humming to himself. He always left a little supper for me, warming in the oven. A lamb chop. Roast beef. In the television's gray-blue light, Mama's face looked as gaunt as a prisoner of war's. Studying her each night in her final days—when she was more removed from me than ever—I thought of the stories I'd read in history classes about captured soldiers or kidnap victims: how utterly dependent they were on their captors, how the guards were forced to become caretakers. Sometimes, a prisoner would be so overwhelmed by the bitter nature of this relationship, he'd take on his captor's behaviors and beliefs: Patty Hearst robbing banks. One of my books said, *The recognition of complete dependency on an unreliable caretaker is too terrible to bear.*

And what if that caretaker is your neighborhood, your country, everything you see and hear? For the folks here in Freedmen's Town, Houston is an unpredictable benefactor, ready to turn on you any minute. The price of the slightest misstep, the mildest error, is high. So what do you do? Assume your caretaker's skin, if you can. Mama ran to where no one knew her and turned herself over to—turned herself *into*—the enemy.

But those nights in the makeshift bed, in front of the TV talk shows, she showed her true self to me as I gnoshed my lukewarm supper . . . only, till just this moment, I didn't quite put it all together. Her mask fell away, eaten by her illness, and the prisoner emerged, barely breathing . . . the dry husk of a woman who once sewed the old slave patterns, who'd named her girl Telisha. At *some* point, before the trauma of uncertainty split her, she celebrated where she'd come from. This was the mother I never knew, but she was there, somewhere, buried deep inside the plush white suburb that whispered and hissed each night with the sound of automatic sprinklers.

Funny. I remember a recurring dream I had in my teens, as my curtains rustled and the sprinklers sighed at night: I was crawling through Dale's house, among splintered tables and chairs. Whenever I told her about this, Mama just pursed her lips. She wouldn't answer when I asked, "What do you think it means?"

I've never put much stock in dreams, but lately, hearing her voice in my sleep, imagining her fears, I think: naturally, trauma resists neat forms. It defies being packaged as a story. The pain is so huge, we want to lock our splinters away in a box. But sometimes the heat of memory sets off a spark, and the box starts to burst . . .

Mama—without a story from you, how was I supposed to contain my imagination? What else would it clutch at but the crumbles of your mask? With only broken bits and no list for piecing them back together, what could I make of my life?

I stand at the window now, looking out on the Bayou City, listening to the frogs. Why did I come here? Because Mama didn't want me back in Freedmen's Town. She didn't want her trauma passed to me (but, of course, her trauma was all she had to give; every stitch of her energy went into fighting it, denying it, and day in, day out I absorbed her intensity). She didn't want me to find the cause of her splintering. What was it? Lack of money? Shit jobs? My daddy? What tool did he split her with—as if I didn't know? The cocky world of men (*I'm a caretaker, know'm say'n*)? Well, here I am, Mama, right where you didn't want me to be. You want me out? Come and get me, then. You'll have to come and get me.

15

MENTALLY, I check my questions for Ariyeh. Forget my reasons for returning to Houston. What would you do *now,* if you were me? Ignore the impulse to ditch Dallas and settle here now that I've found you and Bitter again? Ignore my "family" ties—and my concerns for Bitter's health—and resume my safe and steady job? Or burn it *all* down, start fresh somewhere else?

We've got to deal with Bitter, and soon. Since Grady's death he's moped around, frailer than ever—and just as stubborn about his gris-gris.

She suggested I meet her at school. She'd only have forty minutes for lunch. When I arrive, children are running through the courtyard, tossing gooey pizza into trash cans. Teachers herd them into the building. Two cops in creaking leather coats stand outside the office speaking softly to a group of women. I find Ariyeh inside in a classroom whose floor tiles have peeled and curled in the heat. The fluorescent light hums like a kazoo. In a corner, a gerbil snuffles among pine shavings in a wire cage; the room smells of its flat, bleachy urine, of Kool-Aid and bologna.

Ariyeh tells me two students, nine-year-old boys, were discovered dead this morning in a Dumpster a block away from school. On an anonymous tip, police arrested a black man seen running from the site just after dawn. "They're saying it's Johnson."

"The janitor?"

Ariyeh nods. "We're hearing rumors that he confessed to murdering the other missing kids. He's leading cops, one by one, to the bodies. I don't believe it."

All the teachers are angry. Johnson's a good man, they say. He wouldn't commit these atrocities. Why would he snuff so much healthy black promise? I remember him at the flagpole, swinging his broom at a little boy's butt. Classes have been canceled, arrangements made to send the children home safely.

I stand out of the way while Ariyeh phones parents, bundles homework into backpacks, soothes a few weeping girls. Near me, two boys, apparently unruffled by the commotion, pore over a thin purple book. "What's that?" one says, tapping the page.

"That's *is,* is what it is."

"Iz-iz?"

"*Is.* 'He *is* happy.'"

"I don't get it."

Finally, Ariyeh says to me, "Let's get out of here."

"Where can I take you?"

"Reggie."

At the Row Houses, things are nearly as hectic. Reggie is sitting in his office, holding Sasha, Natalie's baby girl, on his knees, while surfing the Net on a laptop—compliments of Rufus Bowen. Michael and three other boys are helping Reggie reorganize his files. They've scattered papers and folders all over the floor. Michael looks cool toward Reggie. "Hey, it's the *'bout it 'bout it* chick." He winks at me. Sasha's crying. Natalie's at work, Reggie explains. He starts to tell us about a news site he's found on the Web that claims America's tobacco giants colluded with the old apartheid government of South Africa. "Blood money, blood money, *all of it.* You were right," he says to me—when Ariyeh interrupts him to tell him what's happened. "Oh, sweetie," he says. He hands Sasha to me then pulls Ariyeh into his arms. The child squirms against my chest. I'm reminded again of Sarah Morgan and the baby that changed her life.

"Got a quiet corner?" Ariyeh asks.

Reggie suggests the last Row House on the block. "Go on down," he says. "I'll be there soon's I log off and give these boys their next set of instructions."

She nods and steps out the door. I pace the office, trying to calm the baby. "What's with Michael?" I whisper. Playfully, Sasha pulls my hair.

He sighs. "You heard me the other day, dissing rap. On top of that, now he's upset with me for letting his mom work for Rufus. I guess I'm with him on that one. Turns out, between school and this new job, we hardly ever see her anymore, and when we do, she's beat."

"But you got your computers?"

He clicks the mouse. "Yeah, but she seems so unhappy. And Michael
. . . well, I *used* to be his hero." A pained smile. "Maybe it takes too
many compromises to keep a place like this running."

"You've done much more good than harm." The baby burrows into
my shoulder.

"I don't know. I don't know anymore." He tells the boys to separate
pink and green pages. Michael just sneers. I wonder if Rue Morgue has
been mentoring him. I wonder what "mentoring" means.

Sasha has spent herself and is hovering now near sleep. Holding her,
I follow Reggie to the sharecropper house. It's cool, dim as evening
inside. Ariyeh's sitting on a butter churn. Reggie walks over and slips his
arms around her. They whisper together. He kisses her cheek. My limbs
grow weak, and I tighten my grip on Sasha. "*Shhh, shhh,*" Reggie goes,
his mouth in Ariyeh's hair.

The baby is limp in my arms. Light, moist, the color of angel food
cake. I lean against a saddle on a wall. A kerosene lantern sits on a bar-
rel; across the room, a pair of high-topped leather shoes. I imagine
plucking a rooster in the corner, washing it for supper, calling my children, hearing shouts of alarm in the street . . . *what's that? what are they
saying? a riot in the white part of town?* . . . oh Lord, oh Lord, this can't
be good . . .

Hold me . . . I squeeze Sasha tight . . .

"Oh shit," Reggie says, pulling away from Ariyeh. He checks his
watch. "I have to pick up Natalie. She's got afternoon classes. The buses
have been running late all week, so I promised her—"

"I'll go," I say right away, watching his hands on Ariyeh. "Stay with
her." Hurriedly, I hand Ariyeh the kid. I'm too aware of my skin, my
longing for touch. It'll be a relief to step into the sun. Motion. Distraction. Escape.

Reggie gives me directions. I kiss Ariyeh's cheek, then leave the little
house.

In the car I rub my arms until my skin begins to sting. I don't want
to want. Need. Be. I'd like to wipe myself clean. Sexless. Skinless. Free.
"You're an asshole," I whisper. "Right? I'm not attracted to you. Not in
the least. I'm not attracted to *anyone.*" I slip on my shades.

E-Future Systems is on Kirby Street, in a two-story glass building
near a couple of barbecue chains and a Tex-Mex place advertising

"Heaven-on-Earth Cabrito." The receptionist, behind a glass-and-marble counter, tells me to take a seat in the red-tiled lobby. The chairs resemble mousetraps ready to spring. The backs are low; my legs ride high. A fake fern spills from a pot beneath granite stairs. The receptionist speaks into a phone stem attached to her head. It looks like a carrot just out of her reach. She's a pretty honey color.

Rufus Bowen enters the room, laughing into a cell phone. "Dude, what's your burn rate?" He's wearing a sleek gray Armani suit, the kind most of the Dallas mayor's boys wear. He punches off the phone, leans over the counter and exchanges a few words with stem-lady. Then he turns to me. "Miss Washington. Good to see you again. Natalie will be ready in a few minutes. She's with one of our clients right now."

I picture her straddling a guy in a big leather chair. I have no idea what her job is.

"Would you like some coffee or tea?"

"No, thanks." Crazy: I feel the baby's warmth, again, in my arms.

He spreads his hands. A casual gesture of power, the kind Rue Morgue might make. "What do you think of our little operation here?"

"Very impressive. I'm not sure what you do, exactly."

"You've heard of the Nielsons? The TV ratings system?"

"Yes."

"We provide a similar service for Internet users. We rank the most popular sites, keeping tabs on them so investors can judge where to put their money. It's been quite lucrative. Just last month, we made our first public stock offering."

"Congratulations."

He sits next to me and actually manages to look *comfortable* in one of these chairs. "I hoped we'd get another chance to talk sometime. I was fascinated by what you said that night in the gallery. 'Human scale,' was it?"

"Right."

"Does our building qualify?"

"Well, two stories, no problem," I say. "Anything over four is getting out of hand."

He laughs. His breath is warm and smells of chocolate.

"I'm serious." I watch him. He seems to *want* a serious answer. "Bedrooms, kitchens—the rooms we actually inhabit, for our private comfort—are built to human specifications. What makes us think public buildings—community spaces—should be any different?"

"Yes, but the population is so large"—is he humoring me? flirt-ing?—"we need to accommodate—"

"Size isn't the answer." I've made this point time and again in plan-ning sessions—usually to no avail. "We build multilane superhighways to ease traffic congestion, right? But they entice even more people to abandon mass transit, so the new highways become glutted. Local cir-cumstances. Hand, foot, eye. Always the best measure."

"So you'd tear down all the skyscrapers?"

Now it's my turn to laugh. I lean away from him. "Why not? They're made to intimidate the individual, aren't they? Make him feel small in the great institutional shadow."

"My my. You're certainly the innovator."

"I don't know whether you're flattering or insulting me."

"No 'or.' Pure flattery." He smiles. "Actually, I'm looking for an innovator to work with us. Someone who knows the ins and outs of public relations, who's comfortable in that gray zone between business, politics, citizens . . ."

"City planning is hardly PR."

"Still, it's a public service. Clearly, you understand the value of image, of selling ideas."

"And what ideas do you need to sell?"

"*Myself.* The idea that a company run by a black man can be integral to the city's health." He sits forward. "You know what it's like, right? I'm one of the few black CEOs in this town. That means I've got to be twice as prepared as my white counterparts. I've got to be smoother, better-dressed, better-behaved. Hell, I've had to learn to play *golf!*" He laughs. "Control my temper—slightest irritation, I'll get tagged as the 'angry black man,' and that's the end of my business."

"I imagine a lot of folks are extra careful around you, too."

"Oh, absolutely! You *do* understand! Some of these fellows, man, they get so self-conscious . . . I never figured politeness would make me *cringe.*" He folds his hands on his knee. "I founded this company, gave it direction . . . when I started, my friends assured me, 'Green is the only color business looks at.' But when it came to raising the scratch, I learned early to send *white* representatives to our potential investors. You're with that, right?"

"I am."

"So."

"Is this a job interview?"

"When can you get me your résumé?"

I laugh, but he's not kidding.

"I trust my instincts," he says. "Move quickly, lock my key personnel into place. That's why E-Future has grown so fast."

"Can I ask you . . . what were you doing in the cemetery the other day?"

He smiles and smoothes his tie. "We need some tax shelters. We're thinking of acquiring land, developing new sites."

"Disturbing those graves?"

"We were just looking."

"For the sake of argument. If I came to work for you, that's the first thing I'd try to talk you out of. It's a historic neighborhood. It needs to be left alone."

"It's crime-ridden and poor. It's going to be developed sooner or later. That's inevitable. Isn't it better if a black man has an interest in it?"

"Is it?"

"I'd like a chance to convince you."

"If you're serious about this," I say, slow, measured, "you need to know . . ."

"Yes?"

"Things are up in the air for me right now."

He nods. "I hope you don't mind. I've talked to Reggie. I know a little about your situation. I *was* going to call you."

I feel my face go hot.

"Your uncle, your ties to this place . . . it got me thinking. I figured you might be interested in a position in town."

"I don't know."

His earring catches the sun. "What do you want? *Humanly?*"

Our eyes meet, then Natalie appears in a doorway behind the receptionist's desk, wearing a long red dress.

"Think about it," he tells me, rising. "We're a solid, honest, black-owned company, still on the ground floor but growing. And I'm committed to investing in our local community."

Another caretaker. These men. Goddam.

Natalie tells Rufus good-bye. He smiles at us both, hands me a card with his fax number on it and the scribbled instruction, "Résumé."

"You can just drop me off at home, and I'll walk to class from there,"

Natalie says. For several blocks we sit stiffly in the car. It's hard for me to concentrate on anything but Bowen's offer. I ask, "How's Michael these days?"

"Hanging."

"And you? The job's working out?" I brake too hard, jostling us.

"Takes a lot of time away from my kids—and half my pay goes for child-care. I'll probably have to quit school soon."

"Oh, I hope not. That would be a shame."

"The hardest part would be telling Reggie. Hell, school's not gonna bring me anything better'n this."

"Anyway. I'm glad things are nice for you," I say. *Nice?*

She snorts. "A year ago I was nearly dead on the street. *Anything's* nicer than that." She points to a shack on the edge of Freedmen's Town, next to a burnt store and an abandoned car. Someone has spray-painted on a cinder-block fence, "Five-dollar whores in two-dollar gowns at the funeral of Hope and Love."

"Old freak room in there," Natalie says. "We'd cook the rocks, I'd smoke that sweet stuff and, man, I didn't care how many fellas asked me to give 'em brains. I'd suck 'em all night, long's they kept the goods coming. Living high in the Rock Resort! I have to say, I miss it sometimes."

"Well. I hope you find a way to stay in school." She's too tired to listen. Maybe it's just as well. Join a sorority? Look at Goya? Where would *that* get her?

She steps out by the Row Houses, thanks me again. Behind her, Michael sails through the air with a ball. Angry. Innocent? Golden.

————

Editorials appear in the *Chronicle* decrying America's "declining values" and the "pathology" of African American communities. The child-murder suspect—the paper doesn't name him; *is* it Johnson?—was "apparently delusional": a blurry bio of a blurry existence on the edge of booming Houston. No word yet on whether all the bodies have been found.

Reggie has been exceedingly attentive to Ariyeh; I've seen little of them both. He's commissioned a new sculpture from Kwako for the Row Houses, and she's been helping them clear a space next to one of the porches.

Bitter is still wearing nutmegs, feeling chest pains. "You're sleep-walking right into trouble," I told him last night.

"You know what they say, Seam. Never wake a sleepwalker. Let him go where he wants, 'cause he just might head for hidden treasure."

He no longer seemed mad at me for leaving his house; resigned, maybe. *She's her mama's child, all right.* He asked about my "accommodations" and the possibility of my fixing him some okra one night. "Of course," I said.

"This come for you." He handed me a letter. A second apology from Elias Woods: "I just want everything to be *right* before I go. Please forgive me."

When I left, Bitter was sitting on his porch singing,

Papa, li couri la riviere,
Maman, li couri peche crab.
Fe dodo, mo fils, crab dans calalou.

————

Coming home, Lord, coming home. Wade in the water, children, wade in the water. Wade in the water, children. God's a-gonna trouble the waves. Walk together, children. Don't you get weary. Don't you get weary, there's a great meeting in the Promised Land. Ya-a-as, Lord, I'm trying to make Heaven my home.

Ariyeh weeps softly beside me. The dead kids' parents huddle in the front pew. Crespi stands by the door, clasping his hands. Photos of the children, enlarged to the size of standard house windows, have been affixed to posterboards and mounted on thin wooden easels behind the altar.

A gap-toothed grin. Merry eyes.

The choir sings, *I'll lie in the grave and stretch out my arms, lay this body down. Lord, I'm-a coming on home.*

Reggie holds Ariyeh's hand. Before the service, he told me he didn't trust the cops' version of the murders (apparently, few of the victims' bodies have been retrieved). Johnson is in custody. No public details. No talk of a trial. No *story*, Reggie insists: "They're setting this one up to just go away." He has pals who work for the city; they've heard that Johnson thought it was better to kill black boys than to let them be raised in a blighted environment, where they were bound to go bad. In his foul logic, he was doing them, and the community, a favor. "Doesn't wash," Reggie said. "Crazy shit. I don't like the smell of it."

In the meantime, the victims' parents wanted to go ahead and commemorate their children, as a healing gesture.

The missing boys' smiles, caught by the camera, remind me of curved boats rocking in a current, drifting me back to my own Bayou City childhood, which has also vanished; to sitting in church with Mama, who's gone missing too. *Soon I'll be done with the troubles of the world. Going home to live with God.*

Flowers and wreaths spice the room with an earthy sweetness, reminiscent of Dale Licht's aftershave (he always overdid it). I imagine him at Mama's memorial service, weeping for a woman he probably knew better than I did. For a moment I miss him, his genuine love for Mama, his exasperated tolerance of me. I miss the love of others. Do I have the love of others? My not-family, Bitter, Ariyeh?

Coming home, Lord, coming home.

A man drops to his knees in front of the altar, asking God's mercy. It sounds like a curse. Ariyeh wilts; I slip my arm around her.

Don't know why I want to stay. This ol' world ain't been no friend to me.

16

I'M SITTING on the stoop when the Beamer appears at the curb. I'm not surprised he's found me. He's "connected." "My crew is in effect elsewhere. Get in."

Righting the balance, I think. Apparently, Rufus Bowen has offered me an opportunity. Rue Morgue can point me in other directions—pull me into the *dark side,* and not some yuppie version of it, either. It's taken me over a dozen years to catch up with myself. Seems I'm faced with the choices, now, I would have stumbled across if Mama had left me where I was. Naturally, I can't nab back lost time . . . but missed identities?

Of course Rue Morgue has found me. I cleared the trail for him.

As I get into the car, fear touches my spine, the way someone taps your shoulder to get your attention. But I'm not as afraid as I thought I would be. Things were different for Mama—she had no options, no outs. When she met my daddy, it hadn't yet occurred to her that high yellow was a ticket to the Thicket and beyond; every encounter was good and real and rippled outward into every other part of her life. She was at the neighborhood's heat-blasted mercy.

Not me. I can always return to my mayor (thanks to the lift Mama gave me). I can slip back inside the great white world. This is just a game. And no matter how tough this fast-talking do-rag is, I'm in charge. After all, *he's* panting after *me.*

He's wearing winter boots, a Kangor cap, and an L.A. Raiders jersey. "Looking fine this evening, Ann."

"Thank you. You, too."

He grins. "I'ma show you my 'hood."

"All right."

"Get you home, safe as milk. 'S all about respect, see."

No, Player, it's about what *you* can do for *me.* Take my mind off

Reggie, for one thing. Distraction. A substitute. A rough confirmation: I must be no damn good to dream of my cousin's man. You can show me exactly how low I am. How low was my poor, desperate mama? Was it just like this with her and Daddy? Prove to me, Rue, that the world's as bad as I think it is.

We cruise past flat, moldy-green shacks nearly hidden beneath willow limbs. A bizarre parody of an upbeat city tour. "Kick-ass form of smack—brand-name 'President'—X-ed three of my favorite junkies here back in '94. I used to give 'em lessons how not to OD, but . . . over here, in that alley, see, I saved a strawberry from a wack headhunter one muddy night, liked to cut on folks . . ."

He seems to need the outside world's approval, wants to show me a player with street cred works as hard as a mayor's girl. A man of his people, like Reggie.

Past a soup kitchen serving slumped men in Levi's beneath a white neon cross. "Little boy, Raymond Evers, beaten by his parents there. Couple of real juicers. Got me some base cars over here . . ."

I remember running through these streets as a girl. Some of my friends were so poor they ate laundry starch for supper; their lips glowed white beneath the flickering streetlamps. In the fall, we'd sell candy and raffle tickets over in the white neighborhoods to raise money for our school. After sunset, we'd come back here and hide in a vacant lot, eating most of the candy ourselves. My friends laughed about the ofays. "They look like cartoon pigs in storybooks!" I laughed too, but uneasily, knowing how much lighter I was than my pals.

"Hey, baby, I be hella good to you!" a young man yells at a pair of strolling women. They ignore him, and he shouts, "Say, bitch, wasn't for your chunky *boo*-tay, you'd have no shape a'tall!"

Rue laughs. That's it, put them in their place, eh, Player? After all, it's the women who hold down the jobs, who are raising the kids, who are *participating* in the world, while you poor boys are locked out of the action. Right? It's *our* fault. Fact is, sugar, you punked out on us on the plantation, way back when, when you should have gone to war for your kids and us, and you've never forgiven yourself, have you? Or at least you think that's what *we* think. Bitter's generation blamed whites. You blame black women—*all* women, who won their rights at your sorry expense. Isn't that the story? Well, stick with me, baby. I know all about being no damn good.

While we're sitting at a stop sign, I notice a couple of Mixtec girls, their hair in braids, tied by leather shoestrings, sitting on a curb, spooning orange Benadryl into their babies' mouths and cooing, "*Shh, shh.*" Rue looks the girls over, without comment. He's probably figuring angles: how can I corner the Benadryl market?

We pass a candy store, its windows barred, and I'm back in the lot again, eating toffee with my friends. We were poor, but I was part of something then. In the 'burbs, where Mama meant to "better" me, shit, I became more aware than ever of my freaky *lack-of-fit* . . .

"Fuck-up folks," Rue says, pointing at a crowd in front of a darkened happy shop. "Sketching away the hours. Say y'all," he yells out the window, slowing, stopping. "Need some Sudafed? Efidac? Got some Ephedrine from Mexico."

A kid—he can't be more than twelve—sucks vapor from an emptied air-freshener tube. I glimpse embers glowing inside it. Others pull on hand-rolled cigarettes, spilling chalky grains on their shirts. No one answers Rue, and he peels around the corner.

We stop at a low-slung building behind a boarded-up Circle K. The plywood walls are held together by rusty nails driven through Pepsi bottle caps. When Rue gets out I don't know whether to sit or follow. Finally, I unlatch my seatbelt. "Delivery," he says at the door. It opens a crack; a thin man in dreads, wearing jeans but no shirt, squints out at us. Cans of Night Train clutter his wooden floor. Behind him, an alcohol rehab certificate is taped to the wall next to a "Free Mumia" poster. A Virgin of Guadalupe candle. A Land O' Lakes tub filled with soggy cereal. Above a small TV, black bananas curl on a hook. The place smells strangely sweet, like the wax lips I bought as a kid for Halloween. A noisy swamp cooler hustles in a busted corner window. Rue holds out a rolled-up Baggie. The man pulls three bills from his pocket. No words. Hand-bump. Then we're back on the street.

From a cooler in his trunk Rue has pulled two malt liquor cans. I take a sip. Everything will be all right, I think, if I play along with him. He'll think *he's* setting the rules. Rap grinds from his speakers, all about bitches and hos. I remember the days of Otis, Aretha. Try a little tenderness. Respect.

Rue tells me he's begun supplying Strychly Speed to local cockers— "a new line of business I lucked-up into." It's a strychnine-laced drug designed to quicken the reflexes and ward off shock. Just as I'm trying to imagine the *outré* sex practices he means, we stop outside a corrugated steel warehouse. He leads me to a small wooden door beneath a cracked bulb; a series of coded knocks, soft and rapid, then we're inside on a sawdust-covered floor reeking of dog shit and bug spray. Bloody feathers float through yellow light. "Ten on the red hat!" someone shouts. Another counters, "Thirty on the gray shirt!" A third man yells, "Ready, pit!" and men surge forward toward a wide dirt ring. Intense, blurry scrabbling. Rue nudges me ahead of him, closer to the action. Past T-shirted bellies and John Deere caps I glimpse a pair of roosters—green and white, yellow beaks. Steel strapped to their spurs. Their hackles stiffen. One bird rolls beneath the other, leaps up and spears his opponent's lung with a razored foot. The injured rooster hunkers and refuses to budge, coughing up blood, wheezing—a sound like a broken door hinge. Tens and twenties circle the room.

Rue retreats into a dusty corner with a short man restraining two pit bulls on leashes. A leather bag, more bills. I loiter near a plywood booth where a Mexican man—red, roughened, fresh from the fields—sells cracked corn, maple peas, atole. He offers to polish the cockers' gaffs on an electric whetstone. Two men pass me on their way to what one calls the drag pit, a small chalked area where another pair of birds prepares to battle. "Is he farm-walked?" one guy asks the other. "Yep. Real good game. Won six last month, back to back, over in Sunset." They spit snuff into small plastic containers. One wears a rooster-spur earring.

A few women stand by a dented beer keg, chatting freely but eyeing each other suspiciously: after the roosters are done, these girls will be in a different kind of competition for the men's attention. What was it Shirley once said to me?—"Black women raise their daughters, but they love their sons. It's ingrained in us—even when we're moms—to view younger women as a threat."

I move close. ". . . he dogged her and dogged her, and she just gave it up."

"Man's gonna hit, he'll *hit*, no matter how you play him. Then he'll head on out."

"That's right. Have dick, will travel."

They laugh.

"When you cut your hair, girl? Look like you just lathered up and took a straight razor to your sweet ol' skull."

"Got tired of fooling with those damn relaxers, you know?"

To my eye, they're all too dark for the red and purple dresses they're wearing. "Boy-thing" or no, I've got them all beat, I think. No wonder Rue came to me: only a fool would choose ground beef over filet mignon. I laugh at my own boldness, stand a little straighter. Move it or lose it, T. They look my way and frown.

Everyone at the drag pit—birds and men—looks beaten to a frazzle. Someone shouts, "Pit!" and the roosters go after one another, legs flailing, feathers drifting wildly like snow. The birds seem stuck together. Two handlers step in to separate them. "Roundhead's hurt," a man mutters. The birds are placed behind the score lines again; they glare and scratch the dirt. Released, they collide midair, then tumble to the ground. I can't tell who has the advantage, but blood blackens the ring. The spectators press forward. They're no longer yelling. Suddenly, we're witnessing a funeral. One of the roosters droops and quivers in a puff of dust. His handler picks him up, blows on his beak, then sets him back down—a final sacrifice. The other bird slashes. Rue tugs my arm. "It's over," he says. "Let's go."

"Is that bird dead?"

"If he ain't, he will be once they pull his head off."

———

In the stairwell in my building, I continue to play along. To play the player. This is no one-way deal, no matter what he thinks. He kisses my neck. I let him take my hand.

Through an open door we hear a TV talking head insisting on ousting Saddam Hussein and making the world a safer place to live. "Zat so?" someone says to the screen. "Let me tell you, Mr. Pun-*dit,* white folks' problems ain't nothing but white folks' problems. Ain't *our* lookout."

We pass a twenty-something girl on the second landing. She's wearing a halter top and a short yellow skirt. In her right hand she holds a dead white moth, in her left, a compact mirror. She crushes the moth, grinds its wings between her fingers and, watching herself in the mirror, spreads the dust on her eyelids. "Beautiful, baby," Rue tells her. "You gonna go far." I tug his hand.

As we stand at my door, and I flick through the keys on my ring, he grins like he's about to spring a trap. Poor, deluded boy. He's in as much need of healing, education, and understanding as I am. I see this; he doesn't. Things are so fucked up between black men and women—*have* been for so long—it's hard to see *anything* clearly.

Inside, I kick the doll's head over to a corner, out of the way. I remember Ariyeh as a girl changing her dolls, taking black Marks-A-Lot to their cheeks, trying to make them look like her. "They already look like *you*," she used to tell me. Rue watches me now, and I see he's thinking something similar. He thinks he can do whatever he wants to me, the nice, polite dime piece. He doesn't believe I have it in me to throw a niggerbitchfit and bring the whole building running. I don't know if I have it in me, either, but I tell myself, You're in charge. You're in charge. Look at how he looks at you. The shut-in boy, all grown up. And he's yours now. Yours.

He pulls me to him, more gently than I expected, and I imagine myself in Reggie's embrace. That's it, Player. Fill my fantasy then drain it. Take it all out of me. Whatever you say, whatever you want. I won't think about the dangers. Or the pleasure. Absolution's what I'm after.

As his mouth finds mine, I feel a familiar drift, the dropping of a mask . . . truth is, I never feel so white as when a black man wants me. It's my difference he desires; he wants to tear me down, but this impulse feeds his passion. The fact that he can't really reach me fuels it even more. That's it, Player, that's it. It's all just a game and I've won it in advance—look how lost you are, grabbing, tugging, gasping . . .

He carries me to bed. For a moment he looks at me as if he's asking forgiveness, not for what he's about to do or for the street life that's killing him, but as if he were every missing father in the neighborhood, as if we were every sad night ever spent by a man and a woman who want to please each other but never learned tenderness.

He holds me to the mattress. Lips brush my nipples. Considerate, slow. Skillful. That's it, Player. I'm too self-conscious to come, but don't you stop, all right, don't let up. Slip me all your pain. Let me kiss it. Make it better. Show me what Mama felt the night she met my daddy. Mama, see, your story's not over. You're not really gone . . . you've got to come save me now, save me, see, my soul's in trouble here . . .

I rise and rise, in spite of myself: spasms of joy. Rue collapses, his wet bald head on my chest. After awhile he strokes my hair. "You taste salty," he says, smiling. I watch his face. The face all the boys wear. Spiteful. Proud. But just a bit uncertain. Pleading, even. Another mask, and not too good a fit.

Then he's up, pulling on his pants—lest he or I mistake all this for intimacy. "Okay, then," he says. Just another deal, more business, my part of the bargain. Right, Player. I see your hands trembling.

He clears his throat. "Welcome to the 'hood. You official now."

"Part of the life here?"

"Part of what I *say* you part of, aight?" But his gruffness is unconvincing now.

It costs me nothing to play to the end. I ask what he expects me to ask. "When will I see you again?"

"I be back for more. When I feel like it."

"I just wait for the word?" Fat chance, Player.

"That's the way, baby." He leans over and kisses me softly. "That's the way. Check you later, hm? You be saving your sweet ass for Rue."

The door whispers shut.

Silence settles so abruptly in the room, I lose my breath—I realize I've been close to holding it for an hour. This is who we are, I think, watching Rue from my window. This is how we act in our neighborhood. This is all you can know.

I lie down again, rub my eyes until they're wild with sparks, Juneteenth rockets in the air . . . through the bursting, spinning hues I float up, down, around . . . stroll through the door, see myself as Rue did, a woman stripped of all her masks, spread across the sheet. Her skin's a pale no-color in the light reflected from outside. I'm a soldier, fighting it out on the streets, cockers and junkies my comrades, under fire, most of them badly wounded . . . and this lady from her privileged world, who wants a taste of the *real* . . . she's smart enough to know there's a battle on, and she doesn't want to be shielded . . . hell, I'll give her what she wants . . . whatever she thinks she's missing . . . pump her till her fucking eyes sting . . . living and losing, *that's war, baby, who's the good, good king . . .*

But that's not the way it happened. If it were, I could tell myself I wasn't responsible, but right from the start tonight, I set the rules we played by.

Did I get what I wanted? I'm not sure.

I get up, pull on my panties and a shirt, fluff my quilt on the windowsill, and watch the freight yard below. Steel tracks shoot like arteries in every direction. Boys spray-paint empty train cars, seizing the moment even as the moment moves on, the paint fading a bit as it dries.

The kids wear do-rags and denims, orange jumpsuits like the ones I saw in lockup. Fireflies lift toward the stars.

A dark shape wings past the trees. Once, when I was little, Bitter told me, "In childhood, if you hold a dying bird, your hands'll tremble all the rest of your life." I think of the drag pit cockers. When did they first hold a dying creature in their hands?

I think of Rue tonight.

"A child weaned when the birds migrate, well, she'll always be restless."

Right now, Bitter's hoodoo makes an odd kind of sense to me. Or it makes as much sense as anything else. Who's to say everything's not connected? A painstaking pattern of omens and spells. Who's to say my little dance with Rue—part of a loose chain from the shut-in boy to Troy to Dwayne, these beautiful young bastards—didn't begin in this neighborhood some twenty years ago, when the birds headed south?

And I was taken north.

My eyes fill, wetting the quilt. Living and losing.

That's the way, baby. That's the way.

———

I try to sleep. The room is dark but for patches here and there touched by refracted blue moonlight. A hot breeze razors through the freight cars below. In my stepdaddy's house I used to lie awake, nights, wondering what to do with who I am—except in north Dallas, breezes rustled overwatered oak trees, TV antennae. I can hear Dale's voice barreling through the rooms, "Front door locked? Check. Windows latched? Affirmative," like the soldier he'd once hoped to be (flat feet and poor eyesight kept him safe, but bitterly restless, at home). I know what he'd say to me now. "So you had to defy your poor mama, before she's even settled in her grave, and go back to that hellish place she saved you from. And what have you found there? The usual assortment of wastrels. Does any of this *surprise* you? Does it *aid* you in any way? *Strengthen* you?"

I don't doubt he'd speak out of love for me. Genuine concern. He took pride in his wedding photos, his annual Christmas cards with our strained family portraits, his wife's driver's license with its predictably bad picture, but one that—washed-out, blue—revealed none of the *Houston* in her.

Whiteness as a bureaucratic norm, the default mode, while I'm stuck in my own Middle Passage.

I remember the night I sat at the kitchen table, my senior year in high school, filling out Affirmative Action forms for college. Dale made his evening check of the house. "Front door? Roger." Then he paused above me and said, "You know, race is always the least interesting thing about a person." He knew how vexed this subject was for me. Mama, who'd been helping me negotiate the paperwork, looked up at him, and said, "Yes, hon, but it's not negligible, either."

Oh, to have that moment back! To grab her by the shoulders, as I failed to do—shyness? shock? embarrassment?—and shout, "Tell me more! What has your experience been? What am I hearing? Regret for the choices you've made? What *about* those quilts of yours, Mama? Those slave patterns you stitch? Just what do you think you're doing? *Just what in hell do you think you're doing?*"

I'm not sure she could have told me, or herself, even if I'd known enough to ask.

My own piecework lies on the windowsill now, a rough brown square softened by the moon. Sirens in the distance. I wonder if Bitter is sleeping, if Reggie and Ariyeh are making love, if Rue is out caretaking. For nearly an hour, I sit and listen to the city I've carried so many years inside me. Moths tap the torn screen.

17

I DON'T KNOW all of Montrose, though this is the neighborhood Ariyeh lives in. As I check the rough map I made based on Bowen's directions over the phone, I think, wryly, how similar this process is to following Mama's guidance—*left here, honey, no right*—when she was so addled by anger, denial, hurt, God knows what else, she couldn't see two feet in front of her. No, not fair. She left you your name, didn't she? Her quilts? She wasn't like the mayor, who can erase whole subdivisions, canceling their tax bases with one mighty slash of a pen or by ordering his speechwriters to delete a phrase or two. Mama left a few things behind. The *Crisis*. C's letter to Sarah Morgan. Maybe she wanted me to return here, after all. More likely, it occurs to me, she knew I'd come back, anyway, and she didn't want to be entirely silent when I did.

I make a left at a corner showing growth pangs—a brand-new multistory bank on one side of the street; on the other, a dilapidated house with a bail bondsman's sign out front, in English and Spanish. A young Mixteca stands on the bail bondsman's lawn, glancing frantically up and down the block. She yells a couple of names.

On a call-in show on my radio, an angry right-winger blames poverty in America on unwed black mothers. Wonderful. Don't these guys ever change? My bathtub is smarter than they are. I punch buttons until I find Me'Shell NdegeOcello singing "Soul on Ice." The song adds to my cheer. I've surprised myself: I'm riding pretty high today. No nasty side effects from my one-on-one with Rue. I matched him move for move—because I was determined to—and the sucker probably knows it. As a purely practical matter, the sex has relaxed me a little, as I hoped it would.

Another left, and I'm at the wine bar Bowen suggested, the Resplendent Grape. He's sitting at a shaded table on the walk out front, his suit coat off, collar and thin red tie loosened just a notch. A wrinkle-free cream shirt. He stands and pulls out a wrought-iron chair for me. I lock my car. "The house merlot here is fabulous," he tells me. "I took the liberty of ordering you one." He hands me a tall, wide glass.

"Thank you," I say, and sit. Sunlight sparkles through the trees, dappling the tabletop, Bowen's biscuit-colored arms and rolled-up sleeves.

"I'm really glad you called," he tells me. "I've been sitting by the fax machine. So. Do you have a résumé for me?"

"Before you pitch me again . . . I saw the sign."

"What sign?"

"In the cemetery across from my uncle's house. Future Home of Such-and-Such . . . what is it? Apartments? Condos?"

He smiles. "I explained before—"

"I don't know all of Houston's ins and outs, but I know, Mr. Bowen, just from looking at the site, that you'll probably have to secure a density modification before you can make a move, and you'll need to hold a public hearing, which means official notification of the neighborhood, which I know for a fact the neighborhood hasn't received yet."

He eyes me appreciatively.

"It's an old trick, right? Slap the sign up, make it look like a done deal, take the wind out of the neighbors' sails before they even know what's happening, before they realize there's still time to stop it . . . especially if you're dealing with a poor, uninformed populace. But I *know* the trick, all right? And I'm watching."

Still smiling, he says, "I'm sorry to disappoint you, but through our friends at City Hall, we got an expedited process."

I glare at him.

"It's all legal and aboveboard, I assure you. Now. Résumé?"

I clutch my purse to my belly.

He sighs, leans across the table. "Nothing's etched in stone, Telisha. May I call you Telisha? The sign represents the wishes of some of my partners, but we're still exploring options. One of the scenarios I'm floating, and there's some interest in it as a PR move, is to renovate not just the graveyard but some of the surrounding houses. Okay?"

I don't believe him, but want to keep my own options kicking. I reach into my purse and produce my résumé. He takes it from me as gingerly as a man fingering a satin bra. While he looks it over, I glance around: yuppies and buppies from Vinson & Elkins. Brooks Brothers breaking brie with Goldman Sachs. These folks run whatever show they're part of, or they couldn't afford to sit here of a late afternoon.

I overhear an elegant black man telling a wavy blonde—a fairy-tale Rapunzel—"White culture is dying in America, baby. Elvis has left the building."

"Is your planning office in Dallas pro-business?" Bowen says. "No-growthers? Which way do they lean?"

"A healthy mix of both. Slow and measured growth is our mantra, though reality has outrun our plans."

"Dallas is a mess."

"I agree."

He sets aside my pages, sips his wine, studies me. "Are you used to working with white liberals? Because that's an animal you'll encounter often in our circle. 'Economic conservative, social liberal'—that's how they like to present themselves, at least to me."

"Sure."

"In my experience, white liberals are geniuses at telling us what we need but morons at actually listening to what we want."

"Like black leadership."

He laughs. "Exactly. I have a couple of old buddies—warriors from the civil rights days, you know, afros, 'Free Angela' buttons, the whole bit—their fire got hot again when Farrakhan organized the Million Man March. They begged me to go with them. I tried to tell them, I said, 'Ben's Chili Bowl, the Florida Avenue Grill—how many other black-owned businesses in D.C. can you name? There's not *nearly* enough places to feed and bed all these guys, so you're going to head up there, without women, to crow about yourself as men—and all the while you'll line the white men's pockets? Where's the sense in that?'"

"So Farrakhan—"

"He's just a failed old Calypso singer who still craves the spotlight."

"And Governor Bush?"

"Hey, he lets the dogs run free in the business world, and that's all right by me. I'll support him if he decides he wants the White House." He orders us both more wine.

"What's your story, Mr. Bowen? How'd you come up, and where? I mean, since you know so much about *me* . . ."

"Rufus. Please. Right here. Texas Southern, U of H."

"Let me guess. You benefited from Affirmative Action, but now you oppose it on principle."

"I admit the contradiction. In certain individual cases, like mine, probably yours, the program did some good. But yes, on balance I think it's harmed us, stolen our motivation, made us dependent on social handouts—"

"Easy to say *now* from your high perch."

"Listen, every day I sit in meetings where my opinion is the last one solicited—and I run the damn company! As far as I'm concerned, there's no perch high enough—"

"I'm sorry," I say. "I'm not trying to pick a fight, I'm—"

"My father owned a car repair shop over in Freedmen's Town, and all my life I couldn't wait to get out of there. When guys my age moved into the middle class we were 'turning traitor.' Now some of my friends sit around their gated yards and complain about the 'other Negroes'— people like your uncle and your cousin, like Reggie. That's not me, see. I still have loyalties to the old neighborhood. But I don't apologize for wanting to lead a more comfortable life. Or for wanting to *improve* the old stomping grounds."

"For being 'economically conservative'?" He laughs. Of course he's right, I think. This is what being with a man is *supposed* to be like, nice surroundings, pleasant wine, intelligent conversation. "It *was* a good thing you did for Reggie, arranging for that computer."

"I was happy to help him out. He's doing great work."

"But I've got to ask you—" I sit forward. "Can I be really candid with you?"

"Please."

"Natalie. Me. I mean—"

"What?"

"If I didn't know better—"

"Ah," he says. "You mean, am I just a predator in disguise?"

"Well, no. No, I'm—"

"Seizing whatever I fancy and nailing up my signs?"

"I'm sorry I implied that."

"Natalie's having a tough adjustment, with the child-care and all, but I've given her a wonderful opportunity."

"I realize that."

"One-two-three: Reggie introduced me to her; she was in need; I saw we could help each other. Purely pragmatic. And she's going to be fine. I really believe that. Let me turn the tables on you, Telisha. Are you playacting some silly 'Roots' deal, or are you serious about becoming part of the life here again?"

I lock on his big brown eyes.

"All right," he says, settling more loosely in his chair. "Have we faced our demons enough here today?"

"*If—*," I say, raising a finger. "If you really want me to come work for you, I have to say, PR's not my thing. The tax shelters, real estate— future plans?"

"Sure, we're always looking to diversify our investments."

"That's what I can help you with. Land-use planning."

He scoots his chair next to mine. "And when you don't agree with the board's decisions, Telisha—if, say, we go condos instead of historic preservation—you're cool with that?"

"No. But I'm an adult. And a professional. And believe me, as a city planner, I'm used to losing. As you say, Dallas is a mess."

"I'm glad we could talk." He touches my shoulder lightly. "I'll get the wine. And how about dinner Thursday? I'd like to hear more. You know, how you'd define the job."

The man knows how to smile. And how to wear his shirts. "Thursday's good," I say.

———

We meet at the River Café, and before I know it we've emptied a bottle of pinot gris. He hasn't officially offered me a job, and I have no clue whether he's really interested in my ideas. I tell him I'd like a chance, with the help of a corporate benefactor, perhaps, to explore the marshlands near Kwako's place, see if the city's running sewer lines out there, and if not, if it might. I'd like to study the possibility of mild grading and leveling, to facilitate sheet-drainage . . .

"What's in it for E-Future?"

We kick around investment alternatives: housing projects, shopping parks . . .

He worries that we're getting too far afield from the company's Internet core. Abruptly, he switches subjects, lightens the mood. He tells me about an avant-garde play he saw once in Dallas. He lusted for the white actress. "She was droning on and on in a deliberate mono-tone, but I didn't care. 'God, she's beautiful,' I thought, 'I could watch her all night.' But, in fact, after twenty grating minutes, I thought, 'God, how long will it take her to die?'"

I fear I've lost my shot at the job—before I've even decided if I want it—but from time to time he circles back to my suggestions. I'm convinced, finally, that he *is* taking me seriously and is simply trying to balance business with amiability.

After the plates are cleared, and we're sipping amaretto, he says, "So. Is it a stretch for you to trust a black conservative?"

"Still being candid? I don't have a lot of experience with people like you."

"You really want to live in Freedmen's Town?"

"I don't know. It's where I grew up. After my mama died . . . I just . . . I needed to see it again."

"Doesn't Ariyeh work at the school there, where all those kids went missing? The janitor or some crazy—"

"Yes." The drink tickles my throat, a pleasing burn. "They're saying he once tried to talk the city into opening separate schools for black boys. Ariyeh told me this. He felt they were straying, all of them, a whole generation—they needed tough love, hard work. A boot camp kind of deal was the only way to save them. When his proposals were rejected, something in him snapped—"

"Ah, the famous snap."

"—and he went around like the Axeman, 'eradicating'—his word—the community's 'evil.'" Surprised at myself, I pull a Kleenex from my purse. Dab my eyes.

"Telisha?"

"I'm sorry. Those missing kids just . . ."

He takes my hand.

"Shut me up." I try to laugh.

"No, it's all right."

"How could he hate his own people so much . . . despise those poor kids . . . I don't want to believe my mother felt even a smidgen of that kind of hatred—of Houston, of me, but maybe, on some level, she did . . ."

"How does it go? 'Love is a struggle . . . no, love is a battle, love is a war, love is a growing up. No one in the world knows love more than the American Negro.'"

I blow my nose. "James Baldwin," I say.

"One of my favorites."

"Truly." I push my empty glass away. "*No* experience with a man like you. A CEO quoting James Baldwin?"

"Would you like to come work for me?"

"Am I really needed?"

"You're really needed."

"Too far afield? On the fringes of your mission?"

"As I say, I trust my intuition. I know I can use your skills."

I feel my face flush. Another benefit of the tumble with Rue: I actually feel attractive now. And someone has noticed.

"I'll get you home now," Rufus says and picks up the tab.

Outside Some Other Time, with the parked car purring, he leans over to kiss my cheek. I touch his earring, the half-moon slope of his ear. "Business and pleasure," I say. "I don't think—"

He moves away. "You're right."

"Not yet, anyway. Okay?"

He smiles.

"I have a lot to think about. But thank you."

"Two weeks? Can you let me know by then?"

"Two weeks."

"Good."

"Rufus?"

"Yes?"

"Are you married?"

A long belly laugh. "No."

"Just checking all the parameters."

"As a solid professional should. It's been a pleasure, Telisha. See you soon, I hope."

"Good night."

Once he's gone, I stand for a while listening to crickets, watching the moon rise; its milky light, through low, ropy willow limbs, casts braided patterns on the sidewalks. On the stairs, inside, I'm startled by a young soldier. No. He's no ghost. Just a kid dropping dexies, wearing a faded old army shirt—the kind you can get in a secondhand store.

Stuck with duct tape to my door, a torn piece of notebook paper, "Rue" scrawled in runny blue ink. That's all. I suppose I'm to understand he's mad at me for not sitting and pining for him. I crumple the paper, stuff it into my pocket.

Blouse, pants, hose—I take them off and lay them all on the bed, wash my face and arms and chest. A baby cries down the hall, then drops into a hurt-dog whimper. Three or four others take up the call. I weave to the window, a little drunk, watch nothing move in the moonlight.

A knock at the door. Jesus. Rue? "Who is it?" I throw on some clothes.

"The night manager, ma'am. Sorry to disturb you."

I slip back the chain. A skinny kid, identical to the afternoon *Star Trek* freak. "You just got a phone message." He hands me a Post-it note:

Ariyeh . . .
Bitter—Med Center—Emergency

My face goes numb. So. It's finally happened. "I see." A drop of saliva slides from my lip to my chin; I'm too slow to catch it. "Thank you."

"No problem. You have a good evening, now." As he ambles down the hall, he snaps his fingers to a tune in his head.

I turn back inside. The room is just as I left it, which somehow surprises me. Dirty, almost empty; except for my suitcase and a few scattered clothes, no sign that anyone sleeps here. I wipe my mouth, grab my keys, and head for the hospital.

18

THE DOCTOR smells the wine on my breath. He frowns, turns away. Ariyeh watches me closely. Behind a closed pink curtain we sit in a lemon-colored cubicle just off the emergency room. Bitter's propped on a gurney, on blocky blue pillows. His shirt is open, tossed to the sides like discarded wrapping paper. Rubber pads, the size of clam shells, cover his chest. Wires connect them to an EKG machine. The doctor, who resembles a chubby Humphrey Bogart, has fed Bitter a couple of nitroglycerin pills. The chest pains have eased, Uncle says, but now he complains of a headache.

"You say he refused an angiogram once before?" the doctor asks Ariyeh, writing on a fat yellow notepad.

She nods.

"Well, this time we're doing one. I want to admit him to the hospital tonight and schedule the test for tomorrow, just as soon as we can."

"Did he have a heart attack?"

"Only a mild one, if that. These mimic his earlier EKG results. But the recurring pains . . . an angio's the only way we'll know what's going on."

While Ariyeh phones Reggie to tell him she'll be staying with her father tonight, I sit by the gurney holding Bitter's hand. "What happened?" I ask.

"I always told you my grave's waiting for me, there in a leafy corner of the Magnolia Blossom."

"What happened, Uncle?"

"Creepy ol' Crespi grinning in the shadows—"

"Uncle!"

"Got so bad this time I nearly threw up. Called Ariyeh on your gadget."

"I'm glad."

"Don't let 'em stick no wires up inside me."

"Uncle, they need to see what the trouble is."

"Inside should *stay* inside. Good Lord packed it that way."

"And what happens when it gets fouled up? These people can help you."

"Had a friend once in N'Awlins, he went to a back alley boneshop for his heart pain. Doctor fed him a baked potato with some red sprinkles on it. Turns out, them sprinkles was ground-up juju, and next thing my man knows, scorpions is pinching his guts from the inside, spitting their poison into his veins."

"Uncle, the state of Texas doesn't recognize voodoo as standard medical procedure. And you don't have any enemies, right?"

He closes his eyes. "What I'm *really* feared of?"

"Yes?"

"I'm feared *none* of it works, Seam. Not the hoodoo, not the fancy machines."

I pat his shoulder.

"I tried so hard to kill Grady's demon. Put fish bile in his whiskey once, shook it all up . . ."

"You've got a *good* heart, Uncle." I kiss his cheek. "That's what's going to work here."

"Reggie says hi," Ariyeh says.

Bitter snorts.

"Looks like *you* had quite a night."

"Big city living," I tell her. "You know."

She narrows her eyes but doesn't say any more.

———

The orderlies move Bitter to a small room on an upper floor. Another patient shares the space, an old white man who has apparently damaged his liver with drink. He's watching Mussolini give a speech at high volume on the History Channel.

Bitter remains attached to the heart monitor. The nurses want to keep him flat, so it's hard for him to pee. He has to lie on his side and use a plastic bottle. His roommate rises and pisses every ten minutes or so, only partially shutting the bathroom door. We hear every drop. A horse drilling a grassy field. When he comes back to bed, he turns the fascists up.

Just past dawn, a big orderly who looks like Frederick Douglass wheels Uncle down a chilly hall to the angio room. Bitter's half-asleep, a blessing. He mutters but doesn't fight. Buhler, the cardiac specialist, a gruff, no-nonsense German Texan who smells of bagels and coffee, lets Ariyeh and me stay in the room. Swiftly, as casually as you'd scan a morning paper, he runs a tube through an artery in Uncle's groin, worming it all the way into his chest. On a nearby monitor we see the grid in Bitter's heart. It's like a city planner's map. Arteries branching this way and that. Buhler points to a pinched spot—a feeder road next to the larger byways. "See there? About eighty percent blockage in the left main. There's some obstruction in a smaller one, too. He's lucky you brought him in when you did."

As the orderly sails Bitter back to his room, Buhler stops us in the hallway. "Usually, a case like this, I'll stick shunts in those arteries, open them up while I'm in there doing the angiogram, but the location was tricky. Normally, a man his age—" He rubs his neck. "I recommend against surgery and try to treat the problem with medication. I worry about an elderly man's stamina, fear the possibility of stroke. But his blockage is well-advanced, and he seems fairly sturdy."

"I don't want him *maintained*," Ariyeh says. "I want him *fixed*. He's always had a lot of energy. It would pain him to be impaired, and if there's a chance you could solve the problem outright—"

Buhler adds, "Sometimes, too, in older patients, we see memory loss after they've been on a heart-lung machine. You should be aware of that risk, all right?"

"All right . . ."

"Inadequate oxygen, fat like little eggshells—"

"Best-case scenario?" Ariyeh interrupts.

"Best-case, he's completely back to normal, feeling younger than he has in years."

"Then that's the case we're going to go with."

———

She has a good cry after lunch, in the hospital cafeteria. Amid the clatter of plastic trays and Frito bags, she leans her forehead on my shoulder. "What did it get him? *What?*"

"Tell me, honey."

"All his politeness. His goddam obeisance. Yessir this, yessir that. Don't want no trouble. Nosir, not me, sir. Now look. Shit, T, he's going to die. And what did he ever *ask* from life?"

"He's not going to die."

"We don't know that."

"Precisely."

"He just sat there on that rotting old porch and *took* it. Day after day."

I shove aside my cottage cheese. "My mama . . ." But my throat catches, and I have to swallow to go on. "She didn't just sit. She went out and tried to snatch whatever she thought she deserved . . . and I don't think she died happy, Ariyeh. I really don't. I don't think, finally, she felt any more satisfied than Bitter does. Maybe even *less* so."

"So none of it matters? Nothing we do?"

"I'm not saying that. I don't know what I'm saying. Just that maybe—"

"Don't. Really. Thanks for trying, but—"

"I know. I know. I'm just . . . I'm someone who's asked a lot of life, right? Scrambled all over, and now, maybe because I'm tired, I feel I'm just me, you know? Just me. Like . . . what the hell was *that* all about? But not in a bad way."

"You're not making much sense."

"No. I guess not. I'm sorry. Let's go see how he's doing, okay?"

———

Hitler screams at a crowd. "Jesus," Ariyeh says. She turns to Bitter's roommate. "Do you think you could turn that down?"

The old man, toothless, grins. "Feller's a kick in the pants, ain't he?" He stabs the remote.

Ariyeh asks, "How are you, Daddy?"

"Scorpions ain't biting yet."

"*Huh?*"

He looks at me. His heart monitor beeps. It's like a toy truck running in circles. "I mean I'm fine. I want to go home."

"They're going to fix you up, Daddy."

"*Know* they are. That's why I want to go."

His roommate gets up to piss.

"Niagara Falls," Ariyeh mutters.

"Lord, if my peter shot an arrow like that," Bitter says, "I'd water the city till all the sewers bloomed."

Later, Ariyeh naps in a corner chair. Herr Horse-Piddle snores into his pillow. Bitter calls me to his bedside. "Got a hoo-raw for you, Seam. Sit down."

I help him sip water through a pink plastic straw.

"'Member I told you your daddy run off 'bout the time my wife did?"

"Yes. What about it?"

"Well. What I didn't say is, they snuck off together."

"Uncle!"

"Didn't know that at first. But a month or so pass, Cass writes me from Oklahoma City asking for money, lets on she's with Jim. He's up there trying to scratch out a living loading furniture, roaming the southside clubs at night. Didn't make no sense to me 'cause she never could abide him—or so I thought. Said he's just a bum. Guess there's more passion in her hatred than she ever felt for me, and maybe it flipped one day into something like love. Hell if I know. Anyways, never saw either of them again. Heard, about five years later, Cass had died in Kilgore—she'd hooked up with some oil man there. Drank herself to death. Jim, I'm not sure. Far's I know, he vanished up near Tulsa somewheres."

"Heading for the Territory."

He looks at me, puzzled.

"Why didn't you tell me this before?"

"Wasn't trying to keep nothing from you, Seam. It's just hard for me to recount. Cass weren't worth much, I guess. But I miss her, still."

"Uncle . . ."

"Anyways, *you* didn't 'member her, so I figgered the details didn't matter to you. However you look at it, your daddy's gone and I don't know where. I honestly thought Elias could give you more of a picture of him than I could."

"It doesn't matter anymore."

"*Hell* it don't."

"No," I say. "What matters is, I've got *you* back."

He laughs ruefully, wheezing.

"I mean it. You're going to be fine. Remember when Ariyeh and I were kids—we brought horned toads to you in a shoebox, and you said you absorbed their spirits through your skin? Do that now, okay? Soak up all the energy you can. Mine. Ariyeh's. This old poot-butt beside you . . ."

"Careful. You sound like a hoodoo queen."

"Queen Seam."

"Queen of My Dreams."

"I love you, Uncle.

"Love *you*, Seam. I think I'ma sleep now, okay?"

"Good."

"Is that all right?"

"It's good.

"Don't let the Nazis get me."

"Abracadabra. They're gone."

I'M *gonna tell God all my troubles*
when I get home . . .
I'm gonna tell Him the road was rocky
when I get home . . .

I ain't got long to stay here . . .

Wade in the water, children.
Wade in the water.
Wade in the water, children.
God's a gonna trouble the waves.

LONG NIGHT, no sleep. Restless mind . . . drifting, spinning, falling . . . one perspective to another . . .

A prison basement, cracks whorling through its dark green walls. A white-sheeted table with leather straps. Tubes, purring machines. I hover near the ceiling next to a bare, guttering bulb, my senses out-of-kilter, out-of-focus, out-of-body.

I gaze at myself lying prone. Splayed arms, still feet. Study the needles in my soft inner elbows. A man in an off-white coat leans close to inspect me, lifting my eyelids, resting his fingers on my jaw. "Mr. Woods," he says. He repeats my name. Then he calls, "Time!" Pity washes through me. Not for me—for him. He has a tough job. Another man, one in shadows, who I can't see clearly, states flatly, "Elias Woods was pronounced dead at 12:05 A.M., Monday, August—"

Cold. Getting colder. Mud. Dead grass. Steaming earth. I'm still floating, awaiting another execution. *Andale! Andale!* "Get those niggers covered up and let's get the hell out of here!" Drifting, drifting . . . but now I'm outside somewhere, twisting through a misty, leaning oak. My neck burns—*but I have no neck*—and I'm weeping, in the highest limbs, over my lifeless body. Always, I've taken pride in my cleanliness, polishing my buttons and boots. But I must have pissed myself when the rope broke my windpipe, and now a scrawny Mexican boy pitches dirt onto my coffin. If I had arms I'd break the lid and snatch the goddam shovel out of his hands. "Move!" I shout at myself from above. "Cletus, get up! Smooth your uniform!" But my body lies still in a pine box, in soft, red clay. Already I feel it stiffen, grow more distant from me, elemental. Now I'm rising, a final breath through flittering leaves—

Cold. Colder. "Okay. Stop the heart."

My eyes are closed. The room is warm. But this morning, as Frederick Douglass rolled Bitter away on a gurney, Doctor Buhler walked

Ariyeh and me through each step of a double bypass. So now, while Ariyeh paces and chews her nails, and I sit in the waiting room, I see it all unfold. Mentally, I place myself in the cold OR, hovering in an unlighted corner. I give myself a clear perspective.

Today's the day they do Elias down in Huntsville. I tell myself I don't care. Still, I hold his last letter in my purse; punishments scissor my thoughts. Cletus. Elias. The Axeman's blade. But I steady myself and witness the heart's stopping—this killing of the man to save his life.

Cold. Getting colder.

————

"They gonna resurreck me?" Bitter had said this morning while the nurses shaved and prepped him.

"That's right, Daddy," Ariyeh had whispered, wiping her eyes.

"I be like the rabbit bounding out of the briarpatch?"

"Exactly."

"I be Jack the Bear."

————

"Pump on?" Buhler says.

"Yes sir."

Bitter's chest yawns like a trunk in an attic, full of mysteries. Pliable, shiny trinkets. A stiff, steel frame pins back his ribs. Stark, curving bones, like African drumsticks. Glistening tissue. A bag, ripped apart, full of roots and leaves and animal tails: mighty gris-gris. His heart, the size of two fists, a dense no-color—a shade without a name—pitches and rolls until the pump kicks in. Then it twitches. Once, twice, the ear of an agitated cat.

Quits.

An assisting surgeon steps forward, pours a pitcher of ice water into the chest cavity. Cold. Getting colder. Around the stilled, bubbling heart, steam gushes, morning mist.

"T core?"

"30.6."

Buhler cradles Bitter's heart in his yellow-gloved palm. He lifts it out of the chest. Near the top, he snips a tiny hole in an artery. A vein, harvested from Bitter's leg, has been lying on a sheet like a piece of pasta scraped from the bottom of a bowl. Buhler takes the vein, inserts it into the artery, sews them together. A flat line streaks across the monitor. Suction. Ice water.

"Okay. Calcium."
"T core?"
"34.5. 35.7 . . ."
A faint scribble on the EKG machine.
"Ventricular fib."
"Paddles!"
"Okay. Stand clear. Good. Good . . ."
"Got him?"
"He's back."
And the rabbit bounds up and away, across the field.

————

Bitter lies in ICU, tubes taped to his mouth, IV lines snaking from his arms, and a long yellow hose winding from his belly just below his ribs. A machine breathes for him, sighing steadily—the surgeons collapsed his lungs to get a better shot at his heart—and he waggles in and out of consciousness.

I've been with him for three hours while Ariyeh was at school. Now she and Reggie arrive to spell me. "How is he?" she asks. Reggie holds her hand. The room smells stale.

"Resting well."

"Go get some shut-eye."

"Thanks, Telisha," Reggie whispers and kisses my cheek.

I hug them both. Machines burble and beep. My night with Rue is wearing off: Reggie's touch makes me tingle.

In a bathroom, I wash my face with cold water. In the mirror I see the same dragged-down look I noticed on Dale Licht's face the last few days of Mama's life, despite his constant smile, his pretense that everything was going to be fine. The man really did love her, I think. Does he miss me now?

On my way to find a couch, I pass a row of pay phones. Still thinking of Dale, I hesitate, then dig through my purse for his number. I find Rufus's business card, make a mental note to call him again in the next few days.

Five rings, six. Then a windy voice.

Words catch in my throat, as awkward as the tubes in Bitter's mouth.

"Hello?" Dale repeats. The voice of the 'burbs, the law firm, the plush white living room carpet—a world I luxuriated in while disdaining it. A world I never belonged to—but which shaped me profoundly, just the same.

"Hello?"

A young mother drags a boy and a girl past me on her way to the bathroom. The kids wail. They smell of bubble gum and poop.

"*Hello?*"

A world I don't know how to reenter.

A world that ends with a *click*.

———

I dream of snuggling into Mama's lap, reading a book. She points at a colorful picture: a kitten in a ballet dress. "Listen," she says, "and the book will talk to you." She begins to read, and though the words emerge in her voice, they *aren't* her words, they're the words of the page. It's sounding through her to me.

A talking book.

Mama pulls a quilt up over my legs. Wagon wheels. Flying geese.

The whole world is speaking to you. Listen.

Did Mama say that or did I? Or was it the book? The quilt? I burrow into her lap, close my eyes. When I open them, I'm scrunched into a hospital chair, and the overhead light is bright.

———

Bitter has been moved to a yellow room overlooking spindly elms. They stand in high grass, among patches of partridge peas and marigolds, and look like rolled-up maps. I sit by the double-paned window, reading a paper. It's a week old, so nothing on Elias—but there *is* a list of last suppers requested by Texas's death row inmates:

Ronald O'Brien (executed 3/3/84): T-bone steak
(medium to well-done), French fries and catsup,
Boston cream pie, and rolls.

Ruben Cantu (executed 8/24/93): Barbecued chicken,
refried beans, brown rice, sweet tea, and
bubble gum (gum prohibited by Texas
Department of Criminal Justice policy).

David Allen Castillo (executed 9/23/98):
Twenty-four soft tacos, six enchiladas, one
chocolate shake, and one quart of milk.

Jonathan Nobles (executed 10/7/98):
Eucharist, sacrament.

Well. When you get there, say hello to my daddy, Elias. And to the laughing old Axeman.

Bitter stirs but doesn't wake. I watch the gentle pumping of the breathing machine. Above the bed, a steady green pulse zigs across a monitor.

Ariyeh slips into the room carrying two Styrofoam cups of coffee. She hands me one, tells me Reggie had to return to the Row Houses to help Kwako install his new sculpture. It's a six-foot pair of hands, carved in black oak, she says, pressed together as if praying or applauding. *Faith and Celebration*, Kwako calls it.

We sip our coffee, listening to the hungry-bird cheep of the heart machine. Exhaustion pools in Ariyeh's eyes.

"I kind of miss Mussolini," I say.

She laughs.

"Maybe you should take a nap."

"I'm fine. Beat, but I don't think I can sleep." She taps her cup. "Last night?"

"Yeah?"

"Reggie asked me to marry him."

"Ariyeh!" I try to keep my voice down.

She smiles. "I think Daddy's ordeal prompted him some. What's important. You know."

"I'm thrilled for you." Really, I think. Really I am. "He's a good man."

"We haven't set a date. But when we do . . . I'd like you to be my maid of honor."

I cross the room and kiss her cheek. She smells of sugar and cream. "Of course."

"How's that going to work with your job? I mean, what are your plans?"

"I'm not sure."

"E-Future?"

I scan her face. "What do you know?"

"Bowen's been asking Reggie about you. Thought you might be looking for options."

"Maybe. I was wary of him at first, you know. But after talking to him . . . he seems okay." My cheeks burn.

"And the other night? You looked like yesterday's leftovers."

I pluck at Bitter's sheet, start to say something, then shake my head. I'll need a drink or two before I can dish on Rufus and Rue. "I'll talk to you about it sometime. No, I will. Promise. Anyway, before I decide anything for sure, I'll have to go back, take care of my business—"

"I've missed you, T. It's been lovely having you home."

"For me, too. But—"

She anticipates me. "The old neighborhood . . . it's changing for everyone, Telisha. We're all just making things up as we go." She leans close. "You belong here."

A car backfires in the parking lot below. Bitter's eyes flutter. Ariyeh and I move to either side of his bed. She holds one of his hands; I squeeze the other. He looks at us, eyes steady and firm, as if we were kids again and he's the adult in charge, urging us to settle down, now, settle down here in my lap—are you comfy, girls?—let me spin you out a hoo-raw, a tale of Old and New . . .

———

Early evening. Ariyeh has gone to meet Reggie at the Ragin' Cajun. I've just finished some cold macaroni from the cafeteria downstairs, and I'm sitting by Uncle's bed. Buhler has finally removed the tubes from Bitter's mouth. He's breathing on his own now. Pill vials clutter the room like bottles in the Flower Man's tree, warding off ghosts—or the soda containers buried with Cletus and the others, filled with their names.

I'm flipping through television channels with the sound off. I'm shocked to see my boss on a local community affairs show. He looks tired, obviously at the end of a junket. I inch the volume up. He appears to be debating an activist here in Houston, a black man I don't recognize. "The breakdown in our society relates to morality," the mayor says—an old saw of his. "Kids stealing possessional sorts of things. Now, in recent polls in *my* city, only four percent said race is a real concern—"

"Be that as it may, Mr. Mayor, when you have thirty percent dropping out of your schools—"

"It's not thirty percent. That's absurd. It's twenty-three percent."

"Facts are facts."

"Your facts are incorrect. It's twenty-three percent."

"Well, I mean, I think, listen—"

"And among those twenty-three percent, Latinos make up eighteen percent of that twenty-three percent—"

"—make a point here—"

"—and if you count as not dropping out those students who stay in school at least six years, then the dropout rate is only twenty-one percent."

Hasn't lost a step. I wish Reggie could have a go at him. Ariyeh's Reggie. He'd put the mayor in his place. *Breaking ranks? Abandoning ship? That's war, Mr. Mayor.*

"All I'm saying is, life is not lived behind a closed door. All right? That's all I'm saying."

"The point is, we're missing the point—"

Bitter stirs. "Seam?"

"Uncle." I click the remote and pick up his hand. "Uncle, you made it," I say.

He coughs. "Spared for now, but next time and tomorrow—"

"Easy. Easy."

"You ain't going nowhere, are you? Seam?"

"No." I smile. "I'm staying right here."

"Take me home soon?"

"Yes."

"Stay with me?"

"Yes."

"Seam?"

"Yes, Uncle, what is it?"

But he only nods and closes his eyes.

21

IN FREEDMEN'S Town's pharmacies, steel bars block the windows. Cigarette and malt liquor ads plaster the walls—cute young black couples, laughing, smoking, drinking on lovely beaches. I know damn well these pristine resorts are still informally "Whites Only" in the world beyond the posters.

So far this afternoon I've tried three places; none carries the Lipitor Uncle needs. In fact, their drug supplies seem maddeningly depleted. Finally, one clerk admits to me, "Truth is, we don't stock many meds in this neighborhood. The people who really need them can't afford them, you know, and we're afraid gangbangers'll break in here and steal the crap." He shrugs. "It ain't no profit in us carrying pharmaceuticals. Sorry."

I consider asking Rue if he can scare me up some heart pills on the street. In the end, I get the stuff at a Kroger's on Montrose, where wasted queens line up to refill their AZT.

The man in front of me reads an old book as he waits for the pharmacist. A colorful cartoon on the cover. I'm guessing it's a book he's owned since he was a boy. The spine's ancient glue flakes as he turns the pages, and he has trouble holding the volume together.

I step up and order the magic we hope will keep Bitter alive.

I swing by the Row Houses where Kwako, Barbara, and Reggie are dedicating the new sculpture. Its wooden fingers are as tall as I am, brown as bayou water. They point at Heaven as well as the street: supplication to God, a gentle prodding of the locals. The base is a graceful collage of basketball netting, sneakers, television consoles. I recall a Ralph Ellison phrase: *A junkman I know, a man of vision . . .*

Reggie hands me an overnight bag with a change of clothes for Ariyeh. She had called and asked him to prepare a care package for her, for me to take back to the hospital. I kiss his cheek. "I'm so happy for you."

He grins. "You're going to be with us, right? The flower girl—"

"The *maid of honor.*"

"It means a lot to Ariyeh."

"Me too."

Barbara hugs me. She's got a chaw of dirt in her mouth. "How's your piecework coming?"

"Slow."

"Ain't no hurry."

"I've got to return to Dallas for a while, but I'll be back for Reggie's wedding. Maybe then I'll stop by and get some more pointers from you?"

"Anytime."

Kwako is wearing overalls and loafers, a straw hat, sleek new shades. He looks like one of his objects: enthusiasm spot-welded to exhaustion, age nailed to a lingering, youthful zest. He barely follows our small talk. He gazes at the hands he has made, judging their perspective in relation to the buildings behind them. Prayer, peeling walls. Poverty and redemption. How do they fit? Through his eyes I begin to see the neighborhood as a sculptural challenge. It *matters* how we piece it all together.

I take Ariyeh's bag and tell them I'll see them soon. Reggie nods. Barbara squeezes my hand. "You was *made* for this outlook, girl. Get your ass back quick."

"You think?"

"Absolutely."

"Thank you." I reach to hug Kwako's neck. "Thank you both."

The stairway at Some Other Time smells of asparagus and garlic. I pack a few fresh toiletries, change into a sleeveless yellow blouse. A baby wails down the hall. My quilt huddles in a corner.

Outside, at the pay phone, I leave a message on Rufus's answering machine saying I'd be delighted to work with him. I don't know when I decided this. Maybe right away. Maybe just this minute. But it's settled. That feels certain.

I wait on the front steps. Sure enough, in about half an hour, the Beamer turns the corner. The windows slide down: a mosquito whine.

Michael slouches in the passenger seat. The protégé, the new young gangsta. Already he's got a practiced sneer and an arrogant sway in his shoulders. Lost or saved?

"Say, cakes," Rue says. He gets out of the car. "You been scarcer'n Lady Justice."

I stand.

"None of Rue's fillies just ups and disappears, know'm say'n?"

"I didn't have a beeper number for you. My uncle's in the hospital."

"That so?"

"You didn't know? You mean something slipped by you?"

He grins. "You a real little bitch, ain't you?"

You don't know the half of it, Player. "He's just out of ICU. I'm on my way back there now."

"Want a lift?"

"I've got my car, thanks."

He approaches me, rubs my hips. "I missed you."

Michael's leering: learning the moves, living out his rap tunes.

"You're a teacher now," I say. "How's it coming?"

"Shit. It's like these kids got minds of their own."

I laugh. I *do* like his hands on my body.

"He ain't so bad. Might have a chance to make it to thirty, thirty-five, he listens what I say."

"And his mama?"

"Moving on up."

"Are you leaving her alone?"

"I'm watching out for her boy. That's what I promised you."

"Thank you." I step away from him. "I'd better go now. My uncle's expecting me."

"I be looking for you. Don't go drifting away on me, Ann." He slips a hand behind my neck, pulls me to him, and slides his tongue into my mouth. "Aight?"

Michael cheers.

"Bye," is all I say. Thanks for the ride, Player. Good luck. You'll need it.

"Later, cakes, hm?" Something in his voice—a catch, a low plea—makes me think he knows the game is over. He squeezes my butt and returns to his car.

On the sidewalk, young sparrows, the color of old dishwater, squab-

ble over spiky weeds shooting up between cracks in the cement. I pull
Rufus's card from my purse and run my fingers over the embossed word
Future.

———

Bitter's house feels crackly and dry. I pack a couple of paperbacks
into my overnight case, then pull Mama's quilt from the closet. The
hospital provides plenty of blankets, but the quilt will make a cozier
cover. Its patterns flow into one another like geologic layers. Slavery.
The Underground Railroad. Executions.

I touch Mama's skill.

Now Bitter's been stitched together, too.

From the bathroom, I snatch some toothpaste and a couple bars of
soap (Bitter doesn't like the hospital's antiseptic brand). I pass the easy
chair where Ariyeh and I used to snuggle into his lap. *Tell us, tell us
again! Say about the magic!*

The floor settles, creaking.

I step outside and lock the house.

Sunset is a fierce pencil line on the horizon. Beyond the cemetery,
the front porch of an old home has collapsed a foot or two. Fireflies, as
bright, I imagine, as the buttons of a Confederate soldier's coat, glim-
mer in and out of honeysuckle vines.

Rap from a passing Passat swamps a faint blues wafting from an
open window. I hear, but don't see, a basketball swishing a net. A silver
jet streaks the sky, like the tip of a key scratching a new blue car.

After folding Mama's quilt into my trunk, I start to switch on the
radio, then remember Elias. I don't want to encounter a glib pundit edi-
torializing about his death.

Around the corner, three yellow bulldozers knock down several former slave quarters. A new sign—this doesn't appear to be Rufus's outfit;
the competition is swift and fierce—says a four-story luxury condo is
coming soon. Reserve Your Space Now!

Rest in peace, y'all.

In a weedy field, another 'dozer bashes the roof of a brown and white
Toyota. The operator, a young bearded man with no expression on his
face, pulls the levers. Methodical, pointless. The shovel comes down.
The car lurches. The windshield webs. Another blow scatters it. The
front doors pop off like bread ejected from a toaster. The tires deflate.
This is the energy that builds cities and also tears them down. I think of

Troy and Dwayne. Reggie, Rufus, Rue. Cletus. Elias. Daddy. All who've fallen.

The sun is gone now, leaving Houston in shadow. KFC sacks blow through empty lots. "Gris-gris," I whisper, as if I actually had the power to save anything.

"But! My uncle's going to live!" I shout. "Resurrection! Hallelujah! Praised-be! *Stop* in the *name* of love . . . !" I like the sound of my voice. "He dom-diddly-doo-wop *did* it!" My uncle who's not really my uncle: my tie to the most important life I never lived.

How's that for perspective?

In my rearview, Freedmen's Town looks tilled-under and dark, as though no one had ever set foot there. One by one, across the frog-buzzing bayou, windows start to glow downtown. Yellow, white, blue—coloring the heavy, magnolia-scented air. Oh what the hell, I think. I reach for my radio and find some evening jazz.

Midland, Texas, native **TRACY DAUGHERTY** studied with Donald Barthelme at the University of Houston. He is the author of three previous novels, *Desire Provoked*, *What Falls Away*, and *The Boy Orator* (SMU, 1999). He has also published two story collections, *The Woman in the Oil Field* (SMU, 1996) and *It Takes a Worried Man* (SMU, 2002), as well as a volume of personal essays, *Five Shades of Shadow*. His work has appeared in *The New Yorker*, *The Georgia Review*, *The Southern Review*, *Chelsea*, *The Gettysburg Review*, *The Ontario Review*, *The Southwest Review*, and in many other literary venues. His short fiction has been honored with the Texas Institute of Letters Brazos Bookstore Award for Best Short Story and with the A.B. Guthrie Jr. Award. In 1998 he received a Fellowship from the National Endowment for the Arts. He directs the M.F.A. Program in Creative Writing at Oregon State University and is a member of the M.F.A. faculty at Warren Wilson College.